"Thought you  **signal."**

Dani's voice was b

"If I waited any longer, I'd be drawing social security."

"Ha-ha," she said slowly, so Jack understood exactly how funny she thought him, and, contrarily, wouldn't suspect that she really did find him amusing.

No more flirting.

He tipped his hat. "Never thought I'd hear you laugh."

"You didn't. Tanya!" she called again, turning away from the man who kept snagging too much of her attention. "Stopped by for that visit!" She waved Jack back, hoping he'd return to the porch, but he waltzed right by...technically trespassing.

Then again, bad boys didn't ask for permission. Follow rules. Both of which should be huge caution signs...

Dear Reader,

Remember when Mary Poppins stepped into a sidewalk drawing and vanished into another world? Opening a new book has always had the same effect on me. In a flash, I'm transported to different times and places, each stop another stamp on my virtual passport.

In this novel, you'll travel with me to the fictitious Mountain Sky Ranch, a dude ranch in Denver's Front Range in the southern Rocky Mountains. Back in the late 1800s, this area teemed with copper-mining companies supplied by the Central, the first railroad corporation in Colorado. Cowboys, speculators, lawmen and outlaws flocked to this rugged outpost to roll the dice and make their fortunes. Likewise, wranglers, bounty hunters and bandits inhabit the pages of my novel, standing for those timeless principles that define the West to this day: justice and order...courage and conviction.

If you like *A Cowboy to Keep*, keep an eye out for my next book, where we meet the rest of Jackson's family at Cade Ranch. These Rocky Mountain cowboys are proud, loyal and independent men who work hard, play harder and love forever. Visit me at karenrock.com to learn more about my releases or to let me know what you think of my books. I'd love to hear from you!

Happy reading!

Karen Rock

PS: Don't forget to check out Heartwarming's author blog at heartwarmingauthors.blogspot.com.

HEARTWARMING

A Cowboy to Keep

——

Karen Rock

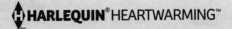

Recycling programs
for this product may
not exist in your area.

ISBN-13: 978-0-373-36823-5

A Cowboy to Keep

Copyright © 2017 by Karen Rock

Printed in U.S.A.

Karen Rock is an award-winning young adult and adult contemporary author. She holds a master's degree in English and worked as an ELA instructor before becoming a full-time author. Most recently, her Harlequin Heartwarming novels have won the 2015 National Excellence in Romance Fiction Award and the 2015 Booksellers' Best Award. When she's not writing, Karen loves scouring estate sales, cooking and hiking. She lives in the Adirondack Mountain region with her husband, daughter and Cavalier King Charles spaniels. Visit her at karenrock.com.

Books by Karen Rock

Harlequin Heartwarming

Wish Me Tomorrow
His Hometown Girl
Someone Like You
A League of Her Own
Raising the Stakes
Winter Wedding Bells
"The Kiss"
His Kind of Cowgirl
Under an Adirondack Sky

To wise and wonderful Tara Randel for reading this book while she managed her family's business and penned her own mysteries and Heartwarming romances. You don't have to say "I'm here for you" because you prove it every day. Thank you, my friend!

CHAPTER ONE

"LET GO OF ME, FREAK."

Jackson Cade's answer was to shove his knee harder into the wanted man's back, clap on handcuffs, then stand. "On your feet, Butch." The ponderosa pines surrounding the small white trailer at the foot of Denver's Front Range rustled overhead.

"Go to hell."

"Someday," he responded drily, prodding a shackled Butch toward his truck, his three-week chase over. He squinted when the midafternoon sun reflected off his side mirror and shot him straight in his good eye.

"Don't you have to read me my rights?" jeered the fugitive as he struggled and yanked against Jack's grip.

"Bounty hunters don't have to do anything they don't want to."

Jack opened the rear cab door. His scar tightened at his grim smile. Some people belonged in cages; he'd learned that firsthand. He made sure they got there. "And right now, the only thing I'm wanting to do is bring you in."

The door closed on his slumped captive and Jack ambled to the driver's side. A pulse of satisfaction beat through him, chasing the shadows that'd consumed him these last two years, though the respite wouldn't last long. No matter how many criminals he caught, it'd never make up for what he'd done, or failed to do.

You promised, he heard his mother's cry again as he slid behind the wheel. *You promised to keep your brother safe.*

His fingers tightened on the gearshift and he revved the engine, as though he could outrun his past, as if his slashed left cheek wasn't a constant reminder of his crime, as though bringing in another lowlife somehow settled his unpayable debt.

He peered in his rearview mirror, studied the scowling crook behind him and nodded. It helped some. He couldn't bring back his brother, and hadn't crossed paths with Jesse's killer yet, but he'd never stop looking.

He cranked up a Waylon Jennings song and tuned out his cussing passenger as his pickup ate up the miles back to fugitive recovery in Denver. He pulled his hat brim low against the late-May sun, dropping in the west over the range.

Purple haze thickened in the timbered notches he passed. Gray foothills, round and billowy, rolled down from the higher country. They were smooth, sweeping, with long velvety slopes and isolated patches of aspens that glowed with newly minted leaves. Mount Evans, scarred by avalanche, towered above the valley, sheltering it from the north.

Nice looking country, he mused as he turned onto Interstate 25, though it wasn't home. He stomped down the marrow-deep ache that sprang up when he pictured Carbondale. His family's cattle ranch in western Colorado, in the center of the Rockies. No sense wishing for something he'd never get back. Or wouldn't go back to. Not when he was reminded of his younger brother everywhere he looked and his guilt hung from his neck, a heavy yoke that made it hard to hold his head up. To stand tall.

Thirty minutes later, he pulled up in front of the one-story bond office and cut the engine beside a black Denver Sheriff Department SUV—Lance's. He'd called ahead, since Butch's warrant stipulated that he'd enter into custody. A department member had told him an officer would meet him. Could be his cousin had come to do the honors.

Butch spewed another stream of expletives when Jack jerked open the door and hauled him out. When he pressed the door buzzer, Lance opened it with a relaxed air that belied his serious intent, his badge glinting. The creases in his blue uniform were as sharp as knives. He wore that smug, got-you look Jack recognized from their boyhood days. He still had the same freckles and left-sided cowlick.

"Sheriff Covington."

"Nice work," drawled Lance, cocking a dark eyebrow at Jack before stepping close to the criminal. "I'll take it from here. Butch, let's walk."

Jack hooked his thumbs in his belt buckle and watched them march to the SUV, satisfied. Justice served. The repeat offender wouldn't be burglarizing homes in the area for a long while.

He took off his sunglasses and headed inside for his bounty. Considering money from his share of the family ranch revenues was dumped into his account every quarter, he wasn't in a hurry for a payout. He did look forward to getting his next assignment, though…

and returning to his trailer for the baseball game and TV dinner that waited on him.

"Jackson Cade for…"

"I know who you are," interrupted the secretary. He'd clearly made quite the impression, since he'd only been to this bond office once before, when he'd taken this case. She averted her eyes behind large-framed glasses that covered most of her pinched features. Short little thing, scrawny, shoulders curled in. Fidgety fingers, twisting at her skirt. She snatched up her phone, spoke into it, then pointed down the hall without looking back up at him.

"Kind of you, ma'am," he muttered, conscious of the office staff's gazes fluttering his way. The paused conversations. The whispered comments that rose like a chorus when he passed. His jaw clenched. He should be used to this, yet somehow he wasn't. He seldom ventured out in public anymore, and much preferred being on his own or hunting runaways—the one job where looking this scary worked to his advantage.

"Hey, Jack," boomed the bond agent, Randall Cook. The gray-haired man smiled and stood, revealing a row of crooked teeth. His line-free face told of years spent indoors crunching numbers, and a touch of pink around his nose hinted at evenings afterward. "Can I get you a drink?"

When Jack shook his head, the talkative man continued, "Was almost ready to call it with Butch. Three other bounty hunters couldn't nab him. Glad the sheriff recommended you."

He shifted in his boots, uncomfortable with praise or anything else that called attention to him. "Glad to help."

"I've got another one for you." Randall shoved a folder across the cluttered table in front of Jack as Jack grabbed a seat. "Bill 'Smiley' Reno. Alias Ned Terrill."

Words jumped out at Jack as he scanned the warrant.

Wanted for drug possession and dealing.

Fifty-thousand-dollar bond.

Known to carry a .45.

Considered armed and extremely dangerous.

A rap sheet that included assault with a deadly weapon, gun possession and armed robbery. Just as bad as he liked them. And he'd been caught with heroin—the same drug that'd ensnared Jack's younger brother after he'd gotten hooked on oxycodone following surgery.

He shoved the folder under his arm and

stood, determination firing through him. "A real sweetheart. I'll get him."

Randall pushed to his feet and extended a hand. "I believe you will. There's more to his story, but I'll let Sheriff Covington fill you in."

Curious, he pumped Randall's hand and strode outside where Lance leaned against his SUV, Butch slumped in the backseat.

"So. Smiley." Lance nodded at the folder. His mouth flattened at Jack's nod and he stepped closer. Dropped his voice. "An informant fingered him in the Remy Phillips case."

The name sounded familiar. It rolled in his mind, then fell into place. He whistled. "The double homicide last month. A home invasion, right? Big society couple."

Lance's brow lowered. "Remy Phillips owns the largest investment firm in Denver and it looks like a professional hit. Since our snitch is unreliable and motivated to exchange information for a reduced sentence, I didn't give it too much credit, especially when Smiley agreed right off to come down to the office to answer questions. Problem is, he never showed. I'd planned on chatting with him the following day at his court date."

Understanding dawned and Jack's eyes narrowed. "Then he jumped his bond."

A frustrated breath escaped Lance's clenched teeth. "Looks suspicious. He's still just a person of interest, but let's just say, I'm real interested. Bring him in, Jack."

"I will." And he would. Forget the ball game. He had much better plans with Smiley's family, the last known address for the runaway and alleged killer. It'd been his mission, since Jesse's murder, to get opiate dealers like this off the streets and make sure no one else died like his brother had.

"Got something else to tell you."

He turned back to his cousin.

"This is between us. Ballistics and crime scene evidence suggest we're after two men. A .45 and a 9mm were used at the scene. Plus, the Phillips' safe was broken into, but the family can't identify what's missing. Whoever wanted it hired two pros for the job, so it must be important. I'm hoping that where there's one…"

"Got it." Jack nodded. Grim. This case looked better by the minute. He'd always liked two-for-one deals. Technically, he couldn't bring in the other wanted man, but he'd hold him. "I'll be on the lookout."

Lance squinted at the sky. Spoke to the sun. "Keep me in the loop, okay? And, uh, heard the family reunion is at your ranch this year. Want to be my plus one?"

Jack's gut clenched and he was glad his sunglasses hid his expression. "You're not my type."

Lance clocked him on the shoulder. "Come on, Jack. How long before you go home? You know they miss you. Especially your mama. And no one blames you for...for..."

"I blame myself." Jack swung into his truck and slammed the door. Engine revved, he peeled out of the parking lot and headed toward Smiley's address. No sense dwelling on family and loss. Action was what he needed.

And retribution.

He glanced down at his forearm. Black ink sketched out a belt buckle with an intricate pattern, the scripted letters *aJc* in the center. It was an image of the buckle Jesse had won in a junior bull-riding championship the year before he got hooked on painkillers and then heroin. Every time Jack looked at it, he was reminded of happier times...of what his brother could have been...how Jack wanted to remember him.

When Jack left the ranch to become a

bounty hunter, he'd vowed that with enough persistence, he'd someday catch the two low-lifes who'd ambushed him and later killed his brother on a back road. Sooner or later their paths would cross and he'd make them pay.

His pickup bounced up a rutted, dirt drive that ended at a listing two-story farmhouse. A tan-and-white pit bull lunged on its chain, snapping and growling, as he strode past and clomped up the steps. With the sun gone now, he needed to secure this house before Smiley slipped away into the night.

The door swung open before he raised his hand to knock. A sour-faced woman peered at him through the ripped screen door. Her worn-out appearance matched her sagging porch. The color leached out of her face when her flat pale blue eyes rose to meet his. They were a little too wide, not enough blinks. She backed up a step and looked down at the Glock holstered on his hip. Something unpleasant worked on her top lip.

"Wha-what do you want? We don't want no trouble."

"I'm looking for Smiley. He here?" The smell of old grease and mold streamed from inside. The pit bull continued barking madly.

She licked her lips. Rubbed her palms together. "Haven't seen him." She raised her voice. "Shut it, Tank." The dog whined and quieted.

He leaned an arm on the soft wood doorjamb. Casual. Just a hint of menace. "Since when? Yesterday?"

Her glance flew to his then dropped. "Can't remember."

"Let's see if I can jog your memory. Mind if I look around?"

"You got a warrant?"

He held it up. "Come in," she said wearily, and lumbered inside, her large ankles ballooning over her slippers, the hem of her housecoat swinging around her calves.

She let him in right quick, Jack mused. Seemed unlikely his quarry lurked here, then. Still, he checked the place top to bottom before he returned to her kitchen, where she stirred something brown and lumpy in a kettle. Goulash by the smell of it.

"So, where's Smiley headed?"

Her wooden spoon stopped and she spoke without looking up. "I told you. I haven't seen him."

He held his impatience in check. Play this game long enough, you learned the rules. Crossing his arms over his chest, he settled his hip against the crowded counter. "You ready to stake fifty thousand on that? What's this house worth? Maybe they'll take that, instead, since you cosigned his bond."

Her mouth dropped open. Worked. She shoved her lank, gray locks off her fleshy face and sighed. "Maybe I did hear something."

"Tell me."

"He and some fella stopped by the other night wanting money. Asked for a ride."

He pressed his lips together and strove to hear his own thoughts over the sudden drumming of his heart. "Who was Smiley with?"

Her brow furrowed. "Ain't seen him before. Evan somethin' or another."

"Evan, or Everett?"

She shrugged. "Could be either, though now that you say it, I think Everett sounds right. Tried not to pay him no mind. A dangerous-looking man. Cold. Real cold."

In a flash, the room receded, the walls, the floors, the roof, as he peered backward to the night his brother lost his life. He saw the two men who'd concealed their appearance with hoodies and scarves on that cold winter night. Pictured the names of the strangers listed on a local hotel registry that night. One in particular, Everett Ridland, had been a suspect in connection with another murder. The name, an alias, turned out to be another dead end.

"Where'd you bring them?"

"Shawnee."

"What's there?"

"Smiley works at Mountain Sky Dude Ranch sometimes. Could be he intended on asking them for money…" Her voice trailed off like the last air from a deflated balloon.

Jack straightened. He'd gotten everything out of her he needed…and more. The chances he'd finally locked onto his brother's killers rose. "Thank you kindly, ma'am." He handed her his card. "You call me if he turns up, now."

Her hands shook as she snatched the card from him and backed away. "I told him. I said, 'Smiley, I don't want no part of any of your shenanigans. Leave me out of it.' So you're saying I'm going to lose my house?"

Jack shook his head. "Not if I get him first."

"Good luck," she called after him, then she shut the door fast, before he'd even stepped off the porch.

A couple of hours later, he drove through a darkened Shawnee and kept on going until his headlights illuminated the stone pillars holding up an arch that read Mountain Sky Dude Ranch. He glanced at his dash. Midnight. A good time to scout the property. The season wouldn't have started yet, so no one should be up and about. He didn't want to explain his presence to anyone in case Smiley or Everett—if it was Everett—got tipped off. His phone call to the owners had gone straight to voice mail.

Leaving his truck, he vaulted over the gate and slipped through the trees. A crescent moon hung low in the star-studded sky. Moving quickly but stealthily, he skirted a pasture of horses, careful not to get too close and spook any. When a number of them lifted their heads and neighed, he froze. Could Smiley and his partner hear that?

After a moment, he glided through shadows and headed for a hay barn. When he grabbed the latch, the unmistakable metallic slide and click of a bullet being chambered behind him sounded.

Reacting on instinct, he ducked, whirled and pointed his gun directly between the prettiest hazel eyes he'd ever seen.

CHAPTER TWO

DANI CRAWFORD NEARLY dropped her rifle when the lethal-looking prowler turned. Their eyes met, a dark promise in the depths of his, and her heartbeat thudded in her ears at his intent, hard-bitten expression. A scar snaked from the top of his left eyebrow, reappeared below his lower lid, slashed his high cheekbone and dipped to his full mouth.

A deadly badge of dishonor, by the look of it.

Some vicious fight he'd survived.

What'd the other guy look like?

Probably rotting in a grave.

A shiver slithered down her back at her fanciful imagination. Strands of hair blew in her face as the wind whistled across the hilly land and coyotes yipped in the distance.

"Hands up!" she ordered, sounding as tough as a gal could while standing barefoot in a tank and sleep shorts. Hopefully her rifle was doing the intimidating.

To her relief, her intruder placed his pistol in the grass and slowly straightened to a goliath height. His muscular, tattooed arms, revealed by a fitted black T-shirt, pointed at the new moon. His predator eyes never left hers and bumps rose on her exposed skin.

She should have grabbed a robe and sneakers. Searched out one of the ranch's rare cell phone signals since she didn't have a landline.

The moment she'd heard the horses and spotted someone moving on her employer's property, she'd grabbed her gun and pursued, her cell phone shoved in her pocket. She would not—could not—let anything jeopardize the ranch that'd become a second home to her, a haven from her troubled past.

And now she stood alone with the most dangerous-looking man she'd ever seen. Her employers were hundreds of miles away, buying a new horse for the stable she managed. Her staff didn't arrive for the new season until tomorrow. Would he know that? Was that why he'd come? She should have listened to her friend Ray's admonishments to stay in town when she'd stopped at his bar earlier. Her tongue darted out and licked her dry lips. His gaze dropped to her mouth, lingered, then rose again.

"Didn't mean to disturb you, ma'am." His husky baritone seemed to move right through her skin, wrap around her chest and squeeze the air out of her like a python's embrace.

"What's your business here?" she asked, her heartbeat and her breath running wild.

He shrugged broad shoulders, something in the deceptively casual move making her even more fearful. His long, denim-clad legs suggested speed and agility; his flat abdomen, wide chest and lean waist screamed strength. Still. She had the gun. Was in charge of the situation. Yet his calm, relaxed demeanor raised doubts about who was really in control.

He acted like having a gun pulled on him happened every day.

Maybe it did. She studied the hard planes of his face.

"Just passing through."

"You should have called if you wanted a tour," she said evenly. Her pulse throbbed at the base of her throat.

The right side of his mouth curled, the easy expression putting her on the defensive just as much as his gun had. Maybe even more. "Prefer doing things on my own."

"That right," she drawled, weighing her options, fear making her bones shake.

Calling 911 wasn't an option, even if she could get a signal. She'd avoided law enforcement since running from her Oklahoma-issued arrest warrant six years ago. Officers asked too many questions. Might connect her to the worst mistake of her past. Were within their rights to extradite her... She tamped down the horrible, nightmare thought.

He gazed at her steadily. "So. Are you shooting me? My arms are getting tired." He rolled first one, then the other shoulder. Didn't look bothered a bit.

And that bothered her a lot. Time to throw this fish back in the stream, much as she'd like to get to the bottom of his visit. Since an access road to the Pike National Forest crossed the property, sometimes disoriented stragglers turned up. It'd be naive of her to think a man like him would get lost, though. An armed man...

Keep him talking or get rid of him? Seeing as she was alone, she'd go with the latter.

"Where's your vehicle?"

"Outside the gate."

"Let's go." She nodded toward the entrance, down one of the dirt paths crisscrossing the property. It passed the two-story main lodge and the corral where they brought saddled horses for daily expeditions.

"I need my gun."

Her eyes widened. "Not on my property."

"I need my gun." His tone sounded easy as ever, yet steel had entered it. An implacable quality that suggested a man used to getting what he wanted.

"Then you shouldn't have dropped it."

He lowered his head and peered at her from beneath his brows. "I'm not leaving without it."

"If we agree that leaving on a stretcher is an option, then go for it." She didn't even try keeping the sass out of that one. In the oddest way, she enjoyed the tightrope feel of this conversation. Recognized it from the days she'd run with the wrong crowd until that fascination had come back to bite her. Hard.

But she wasn't the kind of woman who enjoyed that sort of thrill anymore... Resentment rose at the glimpse of her old self. She'd worked too hard to start over, to become a better person, to ever go back to the way she'd been.

He rolled his eyes skyward and his chest rose and fell. "Ma'am. I have no quarrel with you. Let me have my gun and I'll be on my way."

She blew out a breath. "Kick it over here." He did, and the Glock skidded to a stop at her feet. "Don't move unless you want your head blown off." At his nod, she snatched it up and straightened, her rifle still trained on the trespasser. "I could shoot you. It's the law."

"But you won't." He lowered his arms and crossed them.

There was a breathtaking silence as that sank in. Her mind raced wild along its trail. "How do you know?"

"You ever shoot a man?"

Heat crept up her neck. She willed herself not to turn red like she always had, growing up, when caught out. "Have you?" she challenged, and lifted her chin. Tried looking tough. Lord, she hoped she looked tough.

He gazed at her steadily, and she clamped her teeth together. Swallowed hard.

He sauntered closer and she stared, mesmerized, the way a hare does when cornered by a western rattler. With a small push, he nudged her rifle barrel down. She breathed in the pure male scent of him. Not so much unwashed as worked hard. It made her nostrils flare. Her palms began to sweat. He wasn't a man to tangle with.

"I want my gun."

His words snapped her out of her trance and she backed up a few steps. Her mind turned in circles. She was fooling herself to think she had the upper hand here. Time to level the playing field. She tucked her rifle under her arm, pulled back the Glock's slide to remove the chambered round, yanked out its magazine and tossed the empty gun back.

He caught it neatly with one hand. "Thank you, ma'am. I'll see myself out."

"I'll be right behind you."

His eyes gleamed. "And here I was, thinking you didn't like me," he said, and there was the corner of a grin there, bitten back as he holstered his gun.

Arrogant bastard. "I like your back. Intend to watch it as you go."

His low chuckle made her flush again and then he strode away without a backward glance. Pebbles grazed the bottoms of her feet as she hurried after him, slightly dizzy. Off-balance. Bats called, up in the dark air. A clump of aspens leaned in the wind, intent, watchful. The rush and whisper of them roared in her ears.

At last they reached the gate and her fingers trembled on the keypad.

"No need." He scaled the fence and dropped neatly on the other side. The moonlight glinted on his white teeth as he smiled. "Thanks for the tour."

He tipped his hat and she watched him go. Studied the shadows long after they'd lost sight of him, too. She gripped the gate's metal bar when her knees turned wobbly.

What had he wanted? Not to harm her, it seemed.

Would he come back?

Given her past, she wasn't in any position to be spending time with dangerous men. But, suddenly, she wanted to know more about the scarred man who both frightened and fascinated her.

She gave herself a mental kick and headed back to her room behind the stables.

Bad boys.

She'd more than had her fill of them and wouldn't let another occupy her thoughts. Not when the last one nearly destroyed her life. Not when, with her recent promotion to stable manager, she'd finally achieved the security that'd let her put her past behind for good.

The stranger's striking face returned to her

as she slipped under the covers. She punched her pillow. Hopefully she'd never see him again.

She wasn't so sure her resolve would be up to the test.

JACK'S CELL BUZZED beside his plate of hotcakes the next morning. He nodded to the Shawnee Diner waitress holding a coffeepot, slid his mug to the edge of the table and brought the phone to his ear. It was a three-cup morning. He'd been up since four hanging flyers for his bail jumper, adrenaline jittering through him at the thought that he might be on the trail of his brother's killers—and the redemption he desperately needed.

"Jack."

"Mr. Cade, this is Diane May, owner of Mountain Sky Dude Ranch. I'm sorry we didn't return your call last night. My husband forgot the charger and..." At a gruff throat clearing, she switched gears. "Anyways, how can we help you?"

Out of the corner of his eye, he spied the approaching server. She crept forward, her expression wary. She looked ready to bolt at any sudden movement. He held still. Funny how that pretty gal last night hadn't seemed the least afraid of him. He smiled inwardly as he recalled her sass, her humor, her bravado. "I'm a bounty hunter looking for a fugitive who's worked for you."

A gasp sounded, followed by, "A criminal? One of our workers? Who?"

Murmuring rose on the other end and Jack kept his face averted out of habit when his waitress poured the coffee then scuttled behind the counter. The cash register dinged as the joint's only other customer checked out. A banjo and fiddle mingled in a broadcasted bluegrass tune.

The small restaurant must have been retrofitted from one of the old train cars that ran through this area once, he mused, waiting for someone to come back on the line. Its old-time booths rose high and pressed against small windows. Scuffed wood floors ran the length of the narrow space. An antique mirror reflected the space from behind the polished counter.

"Mr. Cade, this is Larry May," came a man's voice. "What's going on?"

He glanced down the length of the empty restaurant. At the opposite end, the waitress leaned on the through-window and gossiped with the cook. No one to overhear.

"I've got a Failure to Appear warrant for

Bill 'Smiley' Reno. He's accused of drug possession and is a person of interest in a murder case." Steam curled from his black coffee. Using the side of his fork, he cut through his short stack.

"Smiley? I think there's some kind of mix-up. One of our groundskeepers goes by that nickname, but his name's Ned Terrill. He'd never do anything like that."

Butter and syrup melted on his tongue as he finished chewing and lowered his fork. "Ned Terrill's an alias." A phone shrilled on the counter and the waitress picked it up. Outside, a passing pickup honked at a couple of teenagers smoking beside the sidewalk's geranium-filled planters.

"Can't be. He showed us a driver's license. Social Security card, too."

"Fake." The bitter black coffee stung the inside of his cheeks as he gulped.

He waited for the man's sputtering to fade and ate more of his breakfast as he eyed the blue sky that domed over the small city. A good tracking day; he needed to get back on that ranch fast. A picture of the dainty woman who'd confronted him last night came to mind. She'd bristled like she stood ten feet tall; the image made him grin. It was a damn unfamiliar feeling.

"Who can we contact to verify your information? I don't mean to be rude, but this is a bit of a shock. We've known Smiley for years. Our employees are like family."

"Don't mind at all." He supplied Mr. May with contact info for Randall Cook and Lance, hung up and went back to eating. Sympathy for the couple rose. Most folks didn't have much experience with the seedier side of life. They took people at their word. Saw the good since they hadn't experienced much of the bad. His gaze drifted to his cell, willing a fast callback. It was eleven o'clock. Half the day gone and he didn't want to waste more.

He crunched on a bacon slice and recalled how he'd been held at gunpoint by their caretaker last night. Impressive for a civilian... Not that her bold move would deter him from returning and catching his man—or men.

The woman had grit, and she'd piqued his interest nearly as much as this case had. Still, he wasn't about to chase after romance as well as outlaws. He needed to focus on this case, not get sidetracked. His mission was about justice and putting bad guys away—not about finding personal happiness he didn't deserve. Until he caught his brother's killers, his own life would take a backseat. It didn't begin to pay the debt he owed, but it was a start.

Plus, a face like his induced nightmares, not dreams… Strange how she'd stared right at him and hadn't seemed put off. In fact, she'd gotten in his face, challenged him and he'd liked it. No denying that.

His cell vibrated.

"Mr. May."

"Yes. I, uh, talked to Sheriff Covington, who spoke highly of you. I reckon what you're saying about Smiley is true, although you left out the part about there being two people wanted on that murder."

"It wasn't my news to share. Do you know anyone who goes by the name Everett Ridland?"

A pause, then, "Nope. Doesn't ring a bell. You think that could be the other fellow?"

"It's possible." He didn't say the unspoken…that if Smiley had a job at Mountain Sky Dude Ranch using an alias, so might Everett. But what would tie them to the property? "Is it all right with you if I look around the place for the two men? His family says they dropped nearby a couple of days ago."

"My stable manager's up there alone, Jack." Larry's voice grew muffled and he heard him tell his wife to start packing.

"I believe I met her last night. Thought a late-night look-see might be a good idea until she pulled a rifle on me."

A chuckle rumbled through the phone. "Sounds like Dani."

"Dani…" Jack prompted, absurdly curious for her full name. The way she'd been filling his thoughts all morning was aggravating, his anticipation to see her again undeniable.

"Dani Crawford. A Texas gal. Used to be a competitive show jumper. We met her through our son, Ben, who was on the same tour. Sure wish he was here. I'd like his opinion on this, but he's away on business in some rain forest and we can't reach him. Maybe you've heard of his company? Therm Tel? They work with alternative energy."

Jack shook his head and said, "Sounds like an interesting line of work." Diplomatic. Then, "So, would it be all right if I stop by the ranch again?"

"Well. There's one more thing. See, Smiley's girlfriend works there and she'll be arriving sometime today. Smiley and she live together in one of our staff houses."

Silence descended. The bell above the door jingled when a family of four burst inside, a gust of humid air and the smell of exhaust hot on their heels. Jack's mind turned over the unexpected information. "I stopped in a few local businesses this morning to inquire if anyone had seen Smiley around town. The owner of Timberland Outfitters said he sold Smiley some camping gear and supplies recently. Is Smiley's girlfriend the type to help him hide out?"

"Tanya? Nah."

Jack swallowed his last bite and lowered his fork. Seconds passed as he waited for Mr. May to rethink that answer.

"Well," the man said at last. "Course, I wouldn't have suspected Smiley, either. There's lots of places to hide out around there. Most of the old copper mines are blocked, but not all. Got the Pike National Forest next to us, too, plus the Continental Divide. Some ravines are so steep you'd never find them 'less you fell in."

"Sounds like I've got my work cut out for me. I'll need Tanya's address to request a search warrant."

"Technically, she's living in employee housing and her residence agreement gives consent for searches, but better be safe than sorry. Though I urge you to use your discretion, Jack, and find another way to sniff around without raising suspicions. Same for the cabins. Our first guests arrive day after tomorrow and I don't want them scared off."

"By Smiley and his friend, or me?" Jack asked after jotting down the information.

"Both. No offense. But folks will get spooked if they think a wanted man's around."

"If I don't find him before they arrive, I'll blend in. You can say I'm one of your new hires. A wrangler. That'll give me an excuse to ride around."

"You know anything about horses?"

Jack pictured a Christmas photo taken of him and his four brothers and sister, Jewel, lined up on horseback. He'd been ten, his youngest brother, Jesse, one. He swallowed hard. "Enough."

"Good. Staff arrives today and tomorrow, so no one will think anything of a new wrangler joining the crew. I suppose I'll need to hire a new groundskeeper," the owner mused, as if speaking to himself. "And a new cook, if I let Tanya go."

"No." Jack beckoned the waitress for the bill and fished his wallet from his back pocket.

"She might lead me straight to him and his partner. Got the best chance of doing that if no one knows why I'm there."

"Except Dani," Larry cut in. "She's our manager and needs to know what's going on."

A paper receipt fluttered to the tabletop. Jack didn't bother looking at it, his mind full of the gutsy woman who'd looked all too comfortable with a rifle.

"She saw me on the property last night. Looks like she's already in the loop, though I would have preferred otherwise."

"Diane took Dani under her wing when she lost her mother while on tour. She turned to us for a job when she quit show jumping. We trust her and so can you. And she'll be a help."

A long breath escaped him. He wasn't exactly the trusting type. Despite the Mays' assurances, he'd keep his eye on Dani. "I prefer working on my own, but thanks. I'll stay until I've either found Smiley and his partner, or learned they've left the area."

"Sounds like you're the man for the job. Guess you're hired."

Jack pocketed an uneaten apple, dropped a twenty on the table and didn't bother torturing the skittish server for change. A few steps had him out the door and heading to his parked pickup.

"Just don't forget my Christmas bonus," he said wryly, then hung up, his mind intent on catching his man.

Though that didn't explain all of the energy jittering through him. He looked forward to seeing Ms. Dani Crawford again—a lot more than he was comfortable admitting.

CHAPTER THREE

A BOUNTY HUNTER.

Dani leaned her elbows on the main pasture fence and steadied her breath, slowly inhaling the familiar scents of horses, dung and oats as she completed her morning assessment of the herd. Her head refused to wrap itself around the story her employers had called her with minutes ago.

Her midnight cowboy was a bail agent who sought, of all people, their mild-mannered groundskeeper, Smiley, for jumping bail on a drug possession charge. Worse, he and another unknown suspect were persons of interest in a double homicide. Impossible. She'd never so much as seen Smiley pick up a gun. He was easygoing, friendly and the first to lend a hand. He and his girlfriend, Tanya, one of their cooks, always led the line dancing and square dance groups.

But you can't judge a book by its cover... The light stung her gritty eyes as she assessed the ranch's fifty quarter horses, her thoughts whirling. Everyone had believed her to be a hardworking Texas girl with a bit of a rebellious streak. More mischief than outright trouble. When her mother died ten years ago, around her twenty-first birthday, however, she'd become someone else: a person numb to the drop-kick realization her mom was gone.

Living from thrill to thrill had kept her grief at bay, especially after her beloved horse, Dolly, broke her leg during a competition four years later and had to be put down. Not only had she lost a companion she'd loved with all her heart, she'd lost her dream of winning enough competition prize money to pay for college.

Out of prospects and unwilling to go home a failure, what little common sense she'd had leached right out of her and she'd taken acting out to the next level. When her actions nearly landed her in jail shortly after Dolly's accident, she'd come to her senses fast and started over.

Much as she'd labored all these years since to right the out-of-control tilt her life had taken, she never could relax. Deep down, she feared her checkered past wouldn't stay in Oklahoma where she'd left it.

What if the bounty hunter—Jackson Cade—uncovered everything? Discovered the warrant for her arrest? Her stomach rolled. He'd be working here, undercover, as a horse wrangler. Law enforcement on her doorstep. A bounty hunter, and her a wanted woman.

Her head dropped. Bright sun splashed on the grazing herd, and the soft gold air moved up the back of her neck. The group looked healthy and in good shape as they meandered in the space, tails swishing away flies. Some touched noses. Others gazed out across the vast property, absently munching hay from pasture feeders.

If only she felt as peaceful as they did.

Her damp palms pressed on the soft-wood rail as the clear sky hovered above her like an accusation. Jackson Cade threatened everything. She'd love to chase him off, but couldn't go against her employers' wishes.

No. She'd just have to help him find Smiley to clear up this confusion and get him to leave as soon as possible—and not only because of her fear, but because of her unsettling interest in him.

One by one the horses lifted their heads to study a black pickup as it barreled through the front gate. Her pulse slammed. Jackson? While the kitchen, groundskeepers and housekeeping staff had arrived this morning and gotten straight to work on the twenty cabins dotting the five-hundred-acre property, most of the wranglers wouldn't show until tomorrow.

The tall man emerged, wearing a fitted white T-shirt, an unbuttoned plaid shirt rolled up over his forearms and faded jeans, moving with the careless grace of a rider. His lightning-bolt scar flickered across his cheek. It added to his menace, but also made him look vulnerable somehow. An enigma. A puzzle she wanted no part of figuring out.

"Miss me?" he drawled when he reached her. He stood, broad shouldered and slim hipped, his back as straight as a pine tree. Thick-lashed, brown eyes peered down at her, the gleam in them hard to decipher. Other than his scar, his features were regular, his lean face strong and bronzed, but adding to this was a steadiness of expression, a restraint that, despite his sarcasm, seemed to hide sadness.

She turned and propped her boot heel on the fence, trying to rein in her galloping heart. "I missed your back. Wouldn't mind seeing it again soon."

"Well. That makes two of us." He lifted his wide-brimmed hat to catch the small puff of wind that stirred the rising heat. His wavy brown hair lay flat against his skull. A bit of it flipped upward at the tops of his ears where his hat must end. "Till then, I guess I'm your new wrangler. Name's Jack and you're Dani." His voice was as deep as she remembered, but sort of warm in the middle. She nodded. "You've spoken with Larry and Diane?"

"Yes."

She moved around him, restless, and noticed that he turned with her. Had she aroused his suspicions already? It seemed unlikely, but his need to keep her in sight jangled her nerves. "They asked me to give you a tour of the place."

He resettled his hat. "I'm fine on my own. Would appreciate a mount, though."

She tried on the tempting idea of avoiding him for size, then rejected it. "I can't go against their wishes. Let's saddle up. Any preferences?"

She flicked her eyes sideways as he stepped closer and studied the herd. He had a strong brow, straight nose and square jaw—a rugged profile that seemed carved right out of the jagged-topped Rockies. And why was she staring at him?

"That white mare."

Following his point, she spotted his choice. Regret settled in her gut as she eyed the large horse who stood alone on the far side of the pasture, grazing. "She's a bucker, dangerous to approach and not pasture sound. When the Mays return with her replacement, she might have to be euthanized."

He crossed his arms over his chest. "Doesn't look skittish."

"No. Milly used to be one of our best horses until some idiot rode her through a storm. Scared her. Now she won't let anyone on her or near her." Not even Dani, to her profound grief, though she'd tried and tried and tried.

She blamed herself for what'd happened to Milly. She'd allowed an inexperienced kid to take her out, trusting Milly's experience and temperament. And it brought back every bit of guilt she still felt over Dolly's injury and death. She loved horses with a passion, and when she failed them, it cut to the bone.

"I wouldn't let anyone near again, either." He rubbed the back of his neck. She tried meeting his eye but something about its steely sheen unsettled her. It was almost like he looked right through her. Inside her. "You pick, then."

Guessing it was a rhetorical question, she asked, anyway. "How much riding experience do you have?"

"I was on a horse before I could walk."

Of course he was. She kept her eye roll in check and pointed at a buff-colored gelding with a black forelock and mane. His head drooped over the side of the fence and he stared at the distant hills. "Pokey will do."

"Pokey?" One thick eyebrow rose, a skeptical light in his eyes. "Hope I can handle him."

"Guess we'll see." She felt a grin come on and caught it. Getting friendly with a bounty hunter was not on her bucket list. Not even close. "But we can't ride them until we catch them."

"Which is yours?" he asked when they returned from the barn, halters and leads in hand.

She unlatched the gate and slid inside, careful not to make any fast moves. "Storm. The gray mare with the white stockings."

"She's a beauty," he murmured in her ear, and a jolt of awareness rocketed through her. Before reaching Pokey, he stopped near Milly.

Her nostrils flared as she blew, backing up a couple of steps, her ears flattening.

Poor, sweet girl. She'd been born and raised on this ranch. Deserved a better fate than what awaited her. From her own experiences, Dani knew how just one incident could be enough to derail your entire life. She hadn't stopped praying for divine intervention to get Milly back on track and save her, since Dani hadn't been able to do it herself.

To her surprise, Jack extended a hand, an apple in his palm. Milly's head rose and she eyed the fruit down the length of her muzzle. After a long minute, where Dani held her breath and Milly stood still, Jack dropped the treat on the ground and headed for his mount. Milly watched him leave before she edged closer, snatched up the fruit and retreated to the corner of the pasture she preferred.

Phew.

That could have gone very badly. Horribly, considering the thrashing she'd once seen Milly give an overconfident groundskeeper who'd ignored the signs of her agitation until he found himself on the wrong side of her hooves.

What inspired Jack's daring, unexpected act of kindness?

She puzzled over it while they finished tacking their horses, mounted, then headed out of the corral.

"This is the main house where our guests eat. There's also a rec room and the second floor has rooms, too." They passed a large, two-story log-cabin-style building with a wraparound deck that expanded on the side to a thirty-by-fifty-foot space. "We hold our barbecues, line dancing and bingo nights out here."

A riding lawn mower, driven by a red-faced man, hummed by on the field separating the main lodge from the pasture. It kicked up the smell of fresh-cut grass and gasoline with each passing sweep. Pokey jerked his head and stepped sideways. Whatever Jack's reply might have been evaporated as he worked to control the spirited animal.

At last the machine droned farther downfield. "Pokey, huh?" His narrowed gaze flicked her way.

"Not having trouble with him, are you?" Innocence oozed from every syllable.

"No. Enjoying the ride, thanks," he insisted through gritted teeth, his words sounding a bit winded as he settled the horse.

"We aim to please."

"So…Pokey…"

"It suits him, don't you think?"

A quick laugh escaped Jack, a low, husky sound that set off a fluttery feeling in her stomach. "He's a little hot, but nothing I can't handle." His knowing look got her flustered.

With the horses in hand, they continued past the hay barn, Pokey and Storm brushing noses. She lifted a hand to one of the grounds crew, Todd. His eyes went wide when they landed on Jack. Openmouthed, he returned her wave and wiped his wet brow with a rag before he went back to planting bright petunias around their flagpole.

"How many staff members work here?" Jack asked, as the horses stepped slowly on the packed dirt roadway.

"I've got seven wranglers, and they stay there, at the old railroad station—" she pointed at a converted, single-story structure "—with the kitchen crew, which is another three."

"That doesn't include Tanya, right?" He shot her a sharp, assessing look and pulled in a fidgeting Pokey. The belt buckle tattoo she'd spied earlier caught her eye.

"Right." Her throat dried as she imagined what he thought—or conjectured, given Tanya's relationship with Smiley. "She pays rent to stay in her own cabin. Over that hill."

He turned his head and squinted at the distant building on the edge of the Pike National Forest.

"A couple of the groundskeepers lodge with the wranglers, as well, but a couple commute," she hurried on, not wanting him to dwell on kindhearted Tanya, her best friend on the ranch. "As for the cleaning staff, they mostly live off site except Nan, who's been with the Mays forever as a kitchen and housekeeping supervisor. I believe she's mostly retired, though don't tell her that. If you're lucky, she'll make her green chili stew while you're here."

"Till I catch Smiley."

"He's not guilty." Her hand tightened on the reins when Jack didn't respond. "He's not that type." A defensive note entered her voice.

It irked her when people got labeled for something they didn't do. The sooner he found Smiley and cleared up this mess, the better. She needed Jack off this property ASAP.

"So these are all guest cabins?" Jack asked, smoothly changing the subject. The horses' hooves splashed through a puddle left over from an early morning rainstorm. A woman with a mop and bucket emerged from a large stone structure. Behind her rose Mount Logan, its pine-covered incline cut through with a brown switchback trail.

"Some. They're scattered on the property. That one's Stonehenge. It's our biggest. The one farther down with the balcony is the Homestead. We can have up to fifty guests a week when we're full, and most of the season's booked solid."

Pride filled her, temporarily washing away her angst over Jack and the very real danger he represented. As the newly promoted stable manager, she'd worked hard over the winter to ensure their usual bookings returned and to attract new customers with her updated website.

This season was supposed to be perfect—a corner turned from her troubled past—and then the bounty hunter appeared. "You'll stay with the wranglers."

"I'll find my own spot."

At her surprised intake of breath, Storm's ears flicked backward and her gait picked up as they entered the orientation trail used on day one of the guests' arrival. "And where's that?"

"Don't know yet. I'll be on the lookout."

"All my wranglers bunk down together."

He tugged at his shirt collar, creases appearing in the corners of his eyes. The strengthening sun beat down from the vast arc of blue overhead and a trickle of wet pooled at the base of her neck. "I'm not part of your crew."

"You are while you're undercover. Guess that makes me your boss." She enjoyed the extra white that appeared around his dark eyes a little too much. "Do you mind having a lady in charge?"

"Got a problem with anyone telling me what to do. Look, *boss*, we need to get one thing straight. I only take orders from one person—myself." He held the reins loosely in his left hand, his body swaying along with Pokey, his ease in the saddle evident.

She opened her mouth to mention he'd have to hide his tattoo as part of the dress code but decided to put off that argument for another day. Hopefully he'd locate Smiley quickly and leave before their first guests arrived. She'd do everything she could to facilitate those events, though strangely, another part of her felt let down at the thought.

Her mama had always said she attracted trouble like a fiddler attracted square dancing. And her mother had never been wrong. A long sigh escaped her.

There was the time she'd lost a school year's worth of playground privileges for taking Frankie Joe's dare to walk on top of the monkey bars. Another was when the church youth group leader had personally brought her home after Dani brawled with an older boy who'd called her "chicken legs" the first time her mother had gotten her to wear a dress.

She'd been a ponytail-wearing, makeup-avoiding, bruise-and-scrape-covered, bone-breaking horse fanatic who'd surprised everyone by cleaning up good once in a blue moon...and those only happened every other year.

How her mama had despaired of her. If only she could see Dani now. She still wore her hair back and didn't so much as own a tube of mascara, but she'd walked straight since her huge mistake years ago. Would this brush with the law yank her back to that time? Undo all of her hard work to steady her life?

They rode along the sloping path, following a trail that came up the back of a bluff, through a clump of aspens with white trunks and green fluttering leaves, and led across a level patch of lush grass and wildflowers to the rocky edge.

She dismounted. Storm, used to being petted, rubbed her sleek, silver head against Dani's arm then dropped her head to graze. "If you're not leading groups out on horseback, taking them down the Arkansas rapids, fly fishing, zip-lining—"

"Zip-lining?" he interrupted, his tone incredulous, as he eased off Pokey and joined her at the ledge.

"Oh, you'll love it." Her voice rose as she warmed to the thought of the Goliath dangling from a line and speeding over treetops. "Nothing but you, a harness and pine trees. We have the longest and fastest zip lines in Colorado. Six in total, from 850 to 1,900 feet. Right out there." She pointed to the high peaks rising across the valley that comprised this section of the Continental Divide.

He stared at the steep inclines then back down to the flat, muddy water of the South Platt River below. "Thanks for the invite. I'll pass."

"If you don't fit in with the rest, they'll question it. You don't want to alert anyone, do you?"

A hawk wheeled overhead in lazy circles. "I don't think there's much chance of me fitting in, is there?"

"Why not?" she insisted. When she turned to look at him, he was disturbingly close, her senses alive to the brush of his shoulder against hers.

He gazed out at the valley. "You know what I look like."

It wasn't a question—just a statement of fact with a hint of resignation at the edges. It made her soften toward him.

"Lots of people have, uh, scars," she floundered, trying to find a polite way to describe the deep ridge that looked bad enough to have gone bone deep. "It adds character. Makes you interesting. The guests will want to know about you."

A humorless laugh escaped him. "A character? Interesting? Well. That's something. Consider me your newest attraction." He grabbed Pokey's reins and mounted in a move so agile it aroused her deep, feminine appreciation. There was something about a man who rode well.

She watched as he and Pokey disappeared around a bend.

Her next attraction indeed...

CHAPTER FOUR

JACK RODE ALONG the trail, alert for signs of Smiley and possibly a partner passing through. Another horse trotted up behind him and he found himself smiling. Dani Crawford.

He had to give it to her, she didn't intimidate easy and he liked that. Too much. Although he shouldn't make a lot out of the way she dismissed his scar. She hadn't looked him square in the eye since he arrived. Clearly he made her skittish, no matter what tune she sang. He pulled his hat brim down against the low sun and nudged Pokey up a steep incline.

As for his following her rules, that wasn't happening.

"Where's that lead?" He pointed at a yellow-painted wooden arrow that marked a new trailhead on their right.

"Coyote Ridge."

He looked over his shoulder and glimpsed the pretty picture she made in her white tank top tucked into worn jeans, her braided red-gold hair grabbing every bit of light leaking through the forest canopy. The stubborn tilt to her chin caught his eye, as did her unabashed gaze. *Cute* was too small a word to describe a fierce woman like Dani, though it came to mind. Then again, he had no business deciding which word suited her best.

He slowed Pokey as they neared the opening. The trail sloped upward into denser forest then turned out of view.

She and the gray quarter horse pulled up on his left side and he angled his head to see her. Her big eyes swerved out from under his. Why the guilty flash in them? His instinct not to trust her the way the Mays did returned.

"It also goes to one of the old mine shafts," she added offhandedly, her tone a little too casual for his taste. "They used to dig for copper here, and the railroad stopped on our property for it up until a hundred years ago."

His shoulders tensed, his senses alert to every sound. His target could be hiding nearby, and he wouldn't be caught unawares, especially with a woman present who could end up in the cross fire. Of course, Dani seemed more than able to defend herself, though he'd be sure never to put her in that position. "Let's check it out."

He'd already guided Pokey up the path when he heard her say, "But you need to know the orientation trail. It's where we take guests on their first day."

"I'll study the map. Go ahead without me." Pressing on, he guided his horse around a steep turn, hoping to leave his jabbering "boss" behind. He'd have no chance of surprising anyone if she was along chitchatting. More important, he wouldn't risk putting her in danger.

An old mine shaft would make a good hideout, though its proximity to the trail made it doubtful Smiley would use it, unless he was dumb. And overconfident. And Jack liked dumb and overconfident. He liked that combination a lot. It made his job easier.

Hooves sounded behind him and Pokey looked backward and blew. Jack held in a sigh. Dani was turning out to be his hardest tail to shake. Resigned, he asked, "Does Smiley carry a .45?"

The path emerged into a grassy patch and she brought Storm up beside him. The heat waved the air around them. "I've never seen him touch a gun. He's a nice guy. Responsible. Since he didn't let me know he wasn't working this season, I believe he'll show up."

"Let's hope he does." Jack pressed his knees into Pokey's sides when the horse dropped his head to graze. The tall grass bent with each stride, leaving a trampled track in their wake.

"So, what? You're just going to take him in…no questions asked?" Her expression was indignant.

He shrugged. "I'm not a detective or a judge."

"You carry a gun." She pointed at his plaid shirt, as though she could see the shoulder holster under it that held his Glock.

"Goes with the job."

Her eyes traveled over him, making his pulse pick up. They passed out of the sunny spot and continued upward on the rocky track.

"But are you a good guy or a bad guy?"

"Let me know when you've figured it out. Been wondering that myself."

He caught her head shake out of the corner of his good eye. "Irritating. You've got that part down."

His lips twitched. "Was thinking the same about you."

A huff escaped her and he flat-out grinned, enjoying this exchange too much.

"Tell me about Tanya."

"Why do you ask?" Her voice rose, defensive. Was she protecting Tanya? Had Dani helped Smiley when he'd shown up at the ranch? He couldn't rule out she just might be shielding them both.

"Her association with Smiley. How long has Tanya worked here?"

"Five years."

"And Smiley?" He ducked under a low-hanging branch and breathed in the earthy smells of the spring forest.

"He was here before I started."

"Did they meet here?"

Dani rode through a bright strip of sunshine and her hair turned to fire. "I believe so. Am I being interrogated?" Again, a defensive note sharpened her tone.

"Gathering information, is all." He clenched his thighs, urging Pokey up another incline.

"So, are you from around here?" she asked, turning the tables. Rocks rolled beneath the climbing horses' hooves.

"Carbondale."

"Does your family live there?"

"Yes."

"Who? Mother, father, siblings?"

His throat closed around his answer and his eyes watered slightly as he squinted up at the sun. "My brothers, sister and mother," he said when he was sure of his voice. "My father died a few years back."

"Sorry about that. My mother died ten years ago."

He peered at her for a moment, absorbing her stoic expression, impressed by her quiet strength. "My condolences, as well."

"She had breast cancer but didn't tell anyone until the very end. My sister called me while I was touring with a show-jumping group and told me to hurry home. I arrived at the hospital half an hour after she passed." Her voice sank lower and lower before dropping away completely.

They rode for a few minutes in silence as he thought of her loss. It'd been two years since his brother died, but the pain felt as fresh as a newly dug grave. "That's tough."

"You don't realize how quickly everything can fall apart until it does," she murmured, and her eyelashes swept her cheeks. "It makes you never want anything good ever again."

He looked at her sharply, hearing his own thoughts come straight out of her mouth. It unsettled him, this connection he suddenly felt to her.

Time to return to easier topics. "Where are you from?"

"Texas. My father owns a bull ranch there. He's been fighting to keep it after he had a stroke last year."

"It's hard giving up land." He pulled up when a wild turkey darted across the path. Three more followed, necks outstretched, legs and feet a blur. With deep-throated cackles, they disappeared again in the rustling brush.

"I know." She blew out her cheeks. "The doctor says Dad's got to slow down and my sister, Claire, and her fiancé, Tanner, are there helping out. He quit bull riding to help save the ranch and they're getting married in a few months."

"Good man."

"It's not as simple as that." She shooed away the swarming gnat cloud they'd entered.

"Nothing ever is."

"Do you ever string more than five words together?"

"Yes." He bit back a grin at her eye roll when he didn't elaborate. Then he spotted a boarded-up entrance over a rocky outcropping. "Hey. There's the mine."

They pulled up, dismounted and tied up the horses. Wooden slats crisscrossed the space, but a couple had fallen off at the bottom. Could a man crawl in through there? Only one way to find out.

"What are you doing?" she hissed when he dropped to the ground and pressed his good eye against the opening. Light filtered through the cracks and pierced some of the gloom. Nothing inside stirred. It appeared empty.

"Looking for Smiley. You?"

"I told you. He's not here."

"No?" He straightened and studied the remains of a campfire. "Someone stayed here. Only one set of tracks. Whoever it was didn't stick around, though."

If Smiley was on his own, did that mean he and the other guy, maybe Everett Ridland, had split up? If so, an explanation could be that Smiley's partner worked on the ranch and would be able to hide in plain sight as long as he used an alias.

She blinked rapidly. "Could be a camper. We adjoin the Pike National Forest. Sometimes people get confused and pass through."

He poked at the cinders with a twig, his gaze sweeping the bare dirt patch. "That's a nice theory."

"You don't know him."

"I hope to know him, soon." He pointed at

a set of fresh tracks leading away from the campfire onto a small footpath. "Where does that trail lead?"

Her large eyes traveled from the foot impressions to the small trail. "The ranch."

"Where, specifically?"

"Excuse me?"

"Where does it come out?"

"Behind Tanya's cabin."

"Huh."

A deep rumble sounded above them and he instinctively dove for Dani. He swept her into his arms and covered her just before the first rocks of the avalanche rolled down the bluff and smashed into his shoulder, head and back, the dirt rising up around them in a blinding cloud.

The horses neighed as the stone shower continued on and on, his mouth, his nose, his lungs filling with gritty, bitter earth. As for his heart, it bumped hard in his chest. Drummed in his ears. Then, suddenly, all was still and quiet.

Dani's clutch on his shoulders eased and he felt her stand. He shoved to his feet but couldn't see anything, his eyes now burning.

"Good girl, Storm. Pokey. Luckily the horses were just out of reach."

He nodded, unseeing.

The crunch of Dani's boots on the stone-filled area grew louder as she approached. "What's wrong?"

"Nothing." He rubbed his eye, clearing away the grit.

"Can you see?"

"Not at the moment, exactly." A couple more swipes and Dani's outline swam into focus. Her brow furrowed as she stared directly at him, her gaze questioning.

"You didn't wipe your left eye," she observed.

He jerked, realizing his mistake, and brushed dirt off his eyelashes and lid, the damaged nerves there making it less sensitive, according to the doctor who'd treated him.

"Can I ask you a personal question?"

His hands stilled then dropped to his sides. "Can I stop you?"

"Probably not."

"Okay. Shoot," he answered, guessing what she wanted to know…information she might figure out sooner or later.

"Are you blind in your left eye?"

Tension coiled between his shoulder blades as he braced for the pity his brothers had given him after the injury. "Legally blind, but I can see some," he muttered through clenched teeth. "Still want me as a wrangler?"

His jaw worked at the memory of his brothers making unconscious allowances for him, how that'd made him feel less than he'd already felt after letting the family down in the worst way a man could. His chest burned. At last his good eye cleared and her features popped into sharp focus. Instead of looking sympathetic, a line appeared between her lowered brows.

"I never wanted you to begin with. With that scowl, you resemble an extra in a Coen brothers' movie—one that doesn't end well. And you clearly have an issue with authority, but your skills…" She trailed off and looked upward at the cliff. "You know how to handle a crisis. Thanks for saving my skin."

A strange sensation swelled in his chest. "I like Coen brothers' movies."

She headed for the horses, glanced at him over her shoulder and grinned. "Why am I not surprised? We'd better go. I need to tell grounds keeping about this."

He nodded, studying the outcropping. It looked stable enough. What had set off the avalanche? "How often do those happen?"

"It's the first one I've seen since I started here. Why?"

"Just thinking."

"Do you believe someone started it?"

"I don't know, but I'll find out," he said grimly. He gestured toward the horses. "After you."

He needed to get Dani out of the area if his target lurked nearby. Once he spoke to Tanya, he'd explore the foot path and see if he couldn't flush out his quarry.

He swung his leg over Pokey, settled in the saddle and followed Dani. If an armed, reckless Smiley skulked this close to the ranch, Jack's job here had just changed. He wasn't just hunting on the property anymore, he thought, eyeing the graceful sway of Dani's back as she rode ahead. He was now protecting it, and the woman who both irritated and fascinated him, too.

CHAPTER FIVE

DANI KNOCKED ON Tanya's door an hour later, Jack by her side. The cowboy's proximity made her senses fire to life and become acutely aware of the hard brush of his biceps against her shoulder, his looming height and rugged good looks. She inhaled the scent of him—a slight hint of woodsy pine, horses, leather and bar soap, a cowboy's version of fancy aftershave that worked on her.

Not that she had any business noticing a man who looked like the kind of trouble she avoided. The old Dani would have flirted up a storm with this dangerous man, but her new, wiser self knew better than to trust her attraction.

The aroma of fresh-baked corn bread seeped through a window screen, breaking her from her thoughts, and Smiley came to mind. He usually ate at least one pan himself and declared the dish his favorite. Had Tanya baked it for her runaway boyfriend?

She sealed off the traitorous thought. Tanya was good people. Smiley, too. If he'd been caught with drugs, there had to be an explanation. Maybe he'd been wearing someone else's coat or driving their car. Whatever the reason, this must be a mistake. Still, she'd promised to introduce Jack and ask Tanya for the information he needed.

Was she betraying her friend? Yes.

Did that make her a hypocrite? Yes…considering her own past.

The door swung open and Tanya appeared in the frame. Her quick smile faded when she glimpsed Jack. She tucked her dark hair behind her ears, slid her tank top strap up her thin arm and fidgeted with one of her leather bracelets.

"My first visitor. It sure is good to see you. How've you been, girl?" Despite her friendly tone, her eyes kept darting to Jack. Knowing him, he read everything into her uneasy expression. Yet Dani knew Tanya. Her friend was the worst liar, one of the reasons Smiley never let her play poker with them on weekends. Her twitchy right eye always gave her away, as did her tendency to repeat herself when she was nervous.

No.

Tanya was trustworthy, as was Smiley. But

he might be hiding out because he didn't want to be charged with a crime he didn't commit.

Hadn't she done the same when she'd fled to Colorado to reboot her off-the-rails life and avoid bringing trouble, aka her incarcerated ex and the pending charges against her, to her family's doorstep?

The news item that'd shown the composite sketch of her face with her misspelled name flashed before her eyes. And she could still hear her former boyfriend vowing to find her when he got released.

But the police didn't have her correct name and she hadn't talked much about her family back then, so Kevin never knew exactly where in Texas they lived.

She squashed her sudden spike of fear. She'd left that world. Stood on her own two feet now. Nothing would knock her off them again.

Please don't let Jack turn that sharp investigative eye on me...

"I'm good. I like your hair. Did you get a perm?"

Tanya shot her a tic-smile and thrust her hands in the pockets of her jeans skirt. "I'm still getting used to it."

"It's great. I, uh, wanted to introduce you to one of our new wranglers. Jack, this is Tanya. Tanya—Jack."

"Howdy," Tanya blurted, but she didn't step onto the porch to extend a hand. In fact, she hadn't even hugged Dani, which was unlike her. Did Jack's appearance scare her? He really needed to stop scowling around people.

"Ma'am." Jack dipped his head. He stared steadily at Tanya, his eyes dark, his expression unreadable.

"Smells like you made some corn bread," Dani observed when an awkward silence descended. Tanya should have invited them in by now. Strangely, her friend stepped onto the porch and closed the door behind her.

"Yes. I'm hoping Smiley might stop by. He hasn't shown up yet, has he?"

Her shoulder muscles relaxed; Tanya didn't know anything about Smiley.

"No. In fact, I thought I might run into both of you here."

"I haven't seen him." Tanya bent down to adjust a loose strap on her sandal and her hair slid forward, obscuring her face. "I haven't seen him at all."

Unease curled in her gut at Tanya's repetition. "When's the last time you spoke to him? I thought he would have shown up today with the rest of the groundskeepers."

Her gaze flicked sideways at Jack, who peered through the window beside the front door. Tanya brought her hand up to her mouth and nibbled on her nail. "Didn't you hear? We broke up months ago, though I'm hoping to get back together."

Dani shifted her weight onto her other foot. It bugged her that she felt more suspicious than sympathetic. Jack's doing. She could trust her own judgment now.

"I'm sorry, sweetie." When she wrapped her arms around Tanya, she inhaled a familiar whiff of cherry. What did she associate that scent with? "How about I stop by later for a chat?"

Tanya gave her a big, crinkly smile. "That'd be nice."

"Good to meet you," Jack said, as he followed Dani down the porch stairs and onto the path that swept by parked Gator vehicles, used for off-road carting, in front of a two-car garage.

"See. I told you Tanya wouldn't know anything." She waved to Nan, who rocked on the front porch of the May's house. Like Dani and the Mays, she lived here year-round.

The elderly woman stopped petting a calico cat on her lap and waved back. Her bright pink shirt contrasted with her white cloud of hair and brought out her piercing blue eyes.

"Tanya knows more than she's saying," he murmured.

Two energetic Australian shepherds bounded down from the porch before she could argue the point. She crouched for the hurtling fur balls.

"Hey, Beau. Hey, Belle." She laughed as the dogs jostled to give her frantic tongue baths. "Who brought you guys back from the vet's?"

"Sam picked them up," called Nan. "They got all the porcupine needles out. Would you believe some were lodged in the back of their throats?"

When she gestured for them to approach, they climbed the steps and Dani settled on the porch swing. Jack leaned against the railing, his arms crossed over his chest.

"Poor puppies," Dani crooned. "I hope you've learned your lesson." Beau whined and rolled over on his back, presenting his white belly. Belle swerved back down the porch after a butterfly. Her obsession.

"I'm Nan." The woman extended a gnarled hand in Jack's direction, and he shook it gently with an old-school, courtly kind of grace. "My, aren't you a tall drink of water. Are you single?"

"Nan." Dani stopped rubbing Beau's soft

stomach and shot the would-be matchmaker a warning look. Nan approached setting up couples like it was a competitive sport—one she indulged in with gusto every season.

"Jackson Cade." To her surprise, he didn't seem ruffled by her question at all. In fact, he gave Nan a warm smile. "And I'm single."

Nan's rocking chair picked up speed and she returned his smile. "Well, now. Dani here's single, too."

"That a fact," drawled Jack. He tipped back his broad-brimmed hat and studied her with amused eyes.

"He's our new wrangler," Dani blurted, heat creeping in her cheeks at the shrewd look Nan was giving her.

Nan's rocking chair slowed. "Diane and Larry didn't mention a new hire."

"It was a last-minute thing. They should be home soon, right?"

The cat on Nan's lap purred loudly as she scratched behind its ear. "They're about an hour out. Got a nice deal on a seven-year-old finished heel horse."

"Good," Dani observed absently, her mind flashing to Milly. The mare had been one of her best roping horses and they needed a replacement. When they put on their weekly rodeo, she'd always gave a show. Had relished performing as much as Dani did. No, more. She stopped petting Beau and straightened. "Hey. You haven't seen Smiley, have you?"

Nan rubbed the side of her nose. "Not that I'm certain."

"What do you mean?"

"Thought I might have spotted him a couple of days ago, but haven't seen him since. I heard rumours that he got into some trouble, though, so I must have been mistaken." She held up the glasses that dangled from a chain around her neck. "Whatever you do, don't get old."

"Who's old?" Dani avoided Nan's playful swat and kissed her soft, creased cheek. "Would you ask Diane and Larry to page me when they get in?"

"I will. Nice meeting you, Jack. I expect you'll be at the welcome-back square dance tonight."

"Same, ma'am. As for the party, I'm not much of a dancer."

"Dani here can teach you, can't you dear?"

Dani opened her mouth, thought better of her words and swallowed them. "I'm sure Mr. Cade's got more important things to do."

"Well, now." The corners of his mouth hooked up, the attractive half smile that got under her skin flashing at her. "Don't know if I can turn down such a tempting offer."

Nan's hand clap shooed the cat off her lap. "Of course you can't. I knew I saw something between you two."

"Goodbye, Nan," Dani said firmly, then shot her elder a significant look before traipsing down the steps after Jack.

Bella and Beau wove through their legs and Jack's hand came up, quick and warm around her elbow, his touch firing along her skin.

"Nan saw Smiley," he observed, as they passed an old-time stagecoach, which the guests still got to ride in. Chickens meandered through its spoked wheels.

"She thinks she did. Beau. Stop." The rambunctious dog quit jumping and took off after his sister.

"Tanya's hiding something."

She rounded on him, her patience wearing thin. "How do you know?" Overhead, an American flag hung from its rope in the still air. The fragrance of the newly planted petunias encircled them.

"I saw two glasses on her coffee table."

"So?"

"She said we were her first visitors."

Her mouth opened then closed. *Brain cells, get moving*, she ordered, but they just rolled in her skull, sluggish. He was too observant by half. "Tanya wouldn't lie. She must have used both of them."

"Is she a sloppy housekeeper?"

"No…"

"Food for thought."

"Corn bread," she blurted, not sure if she was doing the right thing, but suddenly needing to speak when the source of the cherry scent came back to her. "It's Smiley's favorite."

Jack nodded slowly and a smile lightened his eyes to dark amber with gold flecks. "I appreciate that."

"And her hair." Was she really saying this about her friend?

"Go on."

"It smelled like one of his cigars." Her chest burned at her admission…but she couldn't hold it back. There had to be reasonable explanations for this…

But another part of her worried. Was there a chance that she'd befriended the kind of people she'd come all this way to avoid… the sort of friends that brought out her old trouble-making self, the person she no longer was…or wanted to be?

"Can we get inside Tanya's cabin?"

"This doesn't feel right."

"Her employee agreement gives—"

"Consent to search," she finished for him.

"And my search warrant request is just waiting on official approval."

"Larry and Diane won't want a fuss made," she protested, feeling defensive of her friends. "I'll think of something when I drop by to see her later."

Jack nodded slowly, then chucked her under her chin. "Thanks, partner."

"I'm not your partner," she called to him as he doubled back and headed for the trail behind Tanya's house.

He turned and the gleam of amusement in his eyes got her heart thumping. "Right. Thanks, *boss*." After a long look he turned and disappeared into the forest.

She stared after him far too long, then let out a breath.

Honestly.

Mooning after a cowboy who was all kinds of wrong for her...and dangerous. Had she learned nothing from her mistakes?

CHAPTER SIX

DANI HUNG HER hat on a hook, dropped into her office chair and powered up her computer. Exhaustion pressed on her eyelids until they drifted shut. She stretched out her legs, crossed her boots at the ankle and tipped her head back to rest on the cushion as she waited for the old-school dial-up connection.

What a crazy eighteen hours. When she'd pictured her first season as stable manager, she'd never imagined everything would go smoothly, but she hadn't envisioned an undercover bounty hunter, a suspicious avalanche and friends who might be lying to her.

But haven't you been deceiving them, too? came the sudden question, echoing in her brain, louder than if she'd actually heard it.

Her lungs expanded as she took in a deep, stress-management breath. It wasn't the same thing. She hadn't actually intended to commit a crime.

In a flash, she was twenty-one again,

double-parked on a busy street in Oklahoma City, finished with her morning jumping competition, excited to see what mischief her boyfriend, Kevin, would coax her into today. Maybe they'd borrow that ATV they'd been eyeing the past few days and take it for a spin. The owners looked like they were away...

A loud bang on the passenger-side window jolted her out of her thoughts and Kevin's face appeared in the window.

"Let me in!" he yelled like some wild carjacker, and she immediately unlocked the door and hit the gas pedal when he hollered, "Drive! Fast!"

She thought maybe he'd gotten in a fight. He had a quick temper and she'd seen how easily he got riled. She wouldn't stick around for some offended mountain boy to stomp out and teach Kevin a few manners.

Her pulse raced as they blew through five intersections before he turned to her with a big grin and opened his duffel bag. At the stacks of cash spilling through the open zipper, she hit the brakes and got honked at by a car that swerved around her.

"Woooo-hooooo!" Kevin whooped. His eyes darted over her shoulder. "That's fifty

Gs. At least. We're going to take a vacation. I'll buy you something special, too. Promise."

Her insides froze. Her outside, too, for that matter, her hands awkward on the steering wheel.

"What did you do?" she asked dumbly, her thoughts tumbling over each other as she resumed driving, her body on a tense sort of autopilot. Sure they liked raising hell, but this...?

She wasn't that kind of person.

Later on, as she'd agonized over what to do, she'd seen a picture of herself on TV. A wanted woman with a misspelled name—in some ways anonymous. She'd vowed to turn herself in, but was stopped by a call from Kevin. After she'd dropped him off to meet his cousin, a bank employee who'd been Kevin's accomplice, the two men had been apprehended.

"You won't do me any good locked up," he'd said after he explained that he hadn't clarified the correct spelling of her name or given any details about her. "When I get out, I'll need a place to go, someone to help me out, and that's you."

"I don't want anything to do with you."

"Well. You won't have a choice because you'll owe me."

Muffled words sounded through the phone,

*as if he'd put a hand on it, and then his voice
returned, sharp as a knife.*

*"Look, my time's up. Just remember what
I said," he'd hissed. "You owe me."*

The line went dead before she could speak.

At the gargled shriek of her connecting
hard drive, her eyes flew open, rocketing her
from her past and into the present that didn't
feel so very different.

A whirring overhead fan stirred the muggy
air in the cramped space and didn't cool her
burning cheeks one bit. She needed to distract herself, and checking through her guest
preference sheets a final time wouldn't cut it.

A thirst to know more about Jack took
hold. Technically that wouldn't be procras-
tinating, since she needed to know about her
employees—real or otherwise.

Ahem.

Oh, who cared if she justified her actions?
She was curious and no one would know.

She opened her browser, typed his name in
and drummed her fingers beside the framed
family photos on her desk, waiting…waiting…
waiting…for the toddler-sized brain of her an-
cient hard drive to figure out what she wanted.

Her gaze drifted over her eclectic picture
collection. There was her father at age five

in black-and-white, pulling a wagon with a droopy beagle in it. Beside him was a photo of her younger sister, Claire, her glowing face bent toward her newborn son, Jonathan, now ten, cradled in her arms. That fiercely tender expression always made a lump rise in Dani's throat when she looked at it, remembering the miracle of that day.

Next to the photo of her sister was her much younger self atop a brown-and-white pony, her short legs just barely hitting the stirrups, reins gripped tight in her small hands, her huge smile scrunching her nose and eyes so that she was all freckles and teeth. Brownie… She traced her first mount's nose, nostalgia rising, the sense of loss increasing as her eyes drifted to a last picture: her mother at Port Aransas.

Her mom perched on the rear deck of a fishing boat they'd chartered, her arm slung with casual abandon over Papa's. Mama was laughing at the camera, at Dani, who'd been making crazy faces to get her to smile while Claire snapped the shot.

Remembering the I-love-you-you-fool look her mom usually wore around Dani, how her mother had always called her "baby girl," wrung her heart right out. She'd never be anyone's baby girl again.

She tore her eyes away and studied the monitor, the muscles on either side of her mouth tense as she kept her lips from wobbling, her mother dying again and again and again, as she did every time Dani looked at that photo. She wished she could step into it and have another one of her mama's lilac-scented hugs that warmed her right through.

Her bangs lifted at the force of her exhale, and as she scanned her computer's search results, a *Forbes* headline on the computer caught her eye.

New Heir to Cade Ranch: Jackson Cade.

Puzzled, she swirled her mouse on her *Pride and Prejudice* pad, brought the cursor over the words and clicked.

A picture of a beautiful vista, Rocky Mountains rising over grassy planes dotted with grazing cattle, appeared. Cade Ranch, the article chronicled, one of the biggest cattle ranches in Colorado, had been visited with tragedy when its owner, Jackson Sr., was killed in a private jet crash, leaving the first-born of six kids, Jackson Jr., to step in as CEO of this beef corporation at the tender age of twenty-one. The article went on to talk about business facts that made her eyes cross. She closed the tab, wondering.

Why would the owner of a lucrative ranch leave it to track criminals?

She glanced at herself atop Brownie. Lots of reasons drove a person from home. Could Jack's be one as dark as hers? A sympathy for him rose, which was ridiculous because she didn't know any actual facts.

Her curiosity still piqued, she resumed her search and another headline snagged her eye. *Jackson Cade Sets Passing Record and Clinches Division One Win.*

She clicked on it and a large shot of a teen-aged Jackson filled the screen. His jubilant expression as he thrust two fists in the air while being held aloft by screaming team-mates made her squint, marveling that this could be the same person as the remote, sober-looking man she'd met.

His unscarred face beamed at her, and the thought that he was almost too perfect-looking then, strange as that sounded, struck her. His scar brought his heavenly good looks back to earth, so that now he resembled a darker angel, a look that drew her much, much more than a Hollywood appearance.

But did her attraction suggest she might be falling into her old habits? She'd always had a weakness for sympathetic bad boys.

She'd sworn off relationships, but now another brooding hero had appeared, just like the ones in her favorite gothic romances.

Well. No, thanks.

She'd left tragic love stories safely between the pages where they belonged long ago. She wouldn't reopen that chapter in her life again.

JACK SLIPPED ALONG the edge of the clearing behind Tanya's cabin, sticking to the tree line, out of view. No sense in alarming Smiley's girlfriend in case she wasn't involved (doubtful) or warning her if she was (a much more likely scenario).

It'd been clear she was hiding something from the moment Dani mentioned Smiley. He hoped she'd get something more out of Tanya when she visited her friend later. Would she blow his cover?

He moved a sapling aside and stepped over a rotting tree stump. Something about Dani made him instantly reject the idea. She'd given her word, and while he didn't trust her, his instinct said that meant something to her.

He smiled as he pictured the spirited woman. She looked like the type who'd defend her friends till the end, who saw the good in people until they proved her wrong, which was just like…

His eyes dropped to his tattoo, and Jesse's wide-open grin flashed through his mind, making his own smile fade. He forced his mind back to the hunt.

When he glimpsed the dirt footpath that led off Tanya's clearing up to the copper mine, Jack followed it. He stepped lightly over protruding boulders and exposed roots as thick as his arms. Studying the dirt, he noted that the fresh prints lingering in the muddy depressions all pointed to Tanya's house. A one-way trip. He puzzled over it, doubled back, moved slower still, checking and rechecking the area as he ascended the hill.

The shadows cast by the slanting sun pooled in the depressions, the way he preferred for tracking, illuminating the minute distinctions. A square heel with a pointed toe. Boots. Size twelve or so. A slight notch on the back of the left heel seemed to appear more than once. The stride suggested a man of average height, his build slightly husky given the depth of the impression, his gait uneven, which might mean bowlegs, a limp or just an adjustment for the terrain. There weren't enough solid prints to be sure.

And where was the return set? Or a partner's? Smiley could be hiding alone in Tanya's house and waiting to slip back up to the mine to meet someone.

Everett Ridland?

If so, Jack'd be there to greet them.

In the distance, aspens gleaming in the late-afternoon sun half hid a jagged bluff. Overhead, a mourning dove quieted as he approached. It sped off its perch in a flurry of gray, leaving only the *rat-tat-tat* of a woodpecker to break up the forest hush.

Suddenly he was ten years old again, creeping through the mountains with his grandfather and Lance on one of their camping trips, committing to memory the slightest disturbances in the wilderness, identifying the passage of elk, black bear and deer, determining edible berries and roots, predicting weather and the direction of his quarry's travel by the shadows, by the moss, by some kind of sixth sense that seemed bred into his family's bones. The same knowledge, his grandpa insisted, that'd been passed on to him.

Too bad that sense hadn't been with him two years ago, the night he'd caught up with Jesse, fresh out of rehab, at a pool hall when his mother insisted he bring his missing brother home. He winced. The painful memory slashed deeper than the knife that'd left a gash that had taken over a hundred stitches to close.

Absently running a hand over the raised scar, he halted at the edge of the woods and stared at the small campfire he'd spied earlier this afternoon. A mound of rocks were in a heap at the bottom of a steep bluff. The tracks ended.

So. A one-way trip by one man. The pile of rocks suggested the avalanche was an accident, but he had to be sure. He scouted the cliff, found his first foothold and began pulling himself up. His fingers scrabbled on scrub brush, roots and depressions as he hauled himself upward, his breath harsh in his throat. At last, he heaved himself over the edge and lay flat on his stomach for a moment, dragging in air.

A cigarette butt swam into view, not more than an inch away from his face. He blinked at it. Processed. Pushed to his knees and studied the distinctive filter. He picked it up and lifted it to his nose. Inhaled. It smelled darker, browner somehow, than other brands. Camel Filters.

And in a breath, he was back at that pool hall, Jesse's knee banging against the underside of the hardwood table top at which they sat.

He'd looked thinner than ever, Jack recalled, despite their mother's nonstop cooking all week since his baby brother had been released from rehab. And his eyes had been bloodshot. Telltale signs of another relapse, Jack remembered thinking, resentment swelling as he envisioned more heartbreak ahead. His family had already gone through a lot since Jesse's addiction began in high school.

When Jesse had said he needed money for reasons he refused to reveal, Jack imagined the worst. He would forever regret how he'd shut his brother down, telling him he didn't want to hear about anything that involved drugs. He was sick of being his brother's babysitter.

His mother's cries echoed in his ear as he sniffed the cigarette butt again. Camel Filters, the same kind he'd seen one of Jesse's suspected killers smoking. Smiley had been caught with heroin, another connection.

He didn't recognize the bond jumper in his picture. The thick dark of that long ago night and the men's hoodies had concealed their appearances enough to make clear identification impossible. Smiley might be here with an accomplice, with Everett Ridland, and either man could be his brother's assassin.

Adrenaline spiked his blood. Made his head swim.

Could this be this be the chance he'd been desperately seeking to finally make things right?

Jack shimmied back down the bluff, dusted off his pants and spun around at the sound of approaching footsteps. A man in his mid-thirties, his broad face mostly shrouded by a beard, appeared around a bend in the trail, a leather saddlebag slung over one arm. He pulled up short, doubt crowding his already pinched features so that he looked cross.

"Who the heck are you?"

Jack set his hands on his belt, easing his shirt back slightly, ready to grab his gun from his shoulder holster if needed.

"New wrangler. Jackson Cade."

The stranger's eyes skimmed down to Jack's boots then rose. "Haven't heard of you."

"Dani hired me."

Stroking his beard, the intruder pursed his lips and said nothing for a moment long enough to make some folks uncomfortable.

But Jack used the time to size up the man. From the bright red on his neck and arms, he must spend a lot of time outdoors. His worn boots looked broken in...so a lot of walking. He looked slightly heavy, with a barrel chest that'd be handy in pinning down a foe in a brawl, and short, powerful arms that'd land a good punch if you were stupid enough to stay within reach.

His boots resembled the size and shape of the prints, though Jack would need a closer look to be certain. What was more, he had the height and build to be one of the suspects.

"What's your business here?" the man growled, with no pretense of welcome or friendliness. Just straight-up menace.

Well, good. Jack liked knowing where he stood.

"What's yours?"

"I work here," protested the guy, looking like he didn't get challenged much.

"Well, so do I." Jack lowered his head and met the guy's stare dead on from beneath his brows, enjoying his new acquaintance's deepening scowl and the way his eyes darted away, small fish scattering before a bigger predator.

Could this be the real person behind the Everett Ridland alias?

"I'm a groundskeeper and I've got to clear that out. This, uh, isn't a safe place."

Jack followed the man's point to the pile of rocks left by the avalanche. His doubts about the rough man settled some. Seemed like a legitimate reason to be here. Still. He had to check.

"What's your name?"

"Sam. Perkins. Not that it's any of your business," the groundskeeper huffed. "Now. I like to get on with my work."

Jack nodded slowly, considering. Why didn't he have any tools? He couldn't outright accuse the guy of anything exactly and didn't want to blow his cover. He'd run the name Sam Perkins by Lance later.

Out of choices, he said, "I'll leave you to it, then."

A few hundred yards down the trail, Jack doubled back, creeping through the thick new growth on the forest floor slowly, carefully, his breath a silent pull of air in his teeth. At last, he reached a vantage point, and peered around a tree.

What was Sam really up to?

But to Jack's surprise, he was gone.

CHAPTER SEVEN

AFTER SCOURING EVERY inch of the internet for more on Jack, Dani finally admitted that she'd gone too far when she looked up his astrological sign.

Sheesh.

Time to clear her head.

She stood in the doorway of the barn and dragged in a long gulp of air, her nerves steadying at the familiar scents of manure and freshly tilled soil, the afternoon warmth hinting at summer.

Shoving her hands in her pockets, she headed to Tanya's. A moment later she'd climbed the porch steps and knocked on the front door. Waited. Rapped again. Waited some more. Tanya's cat, Mittens, leaped off the porch railing and wound like a ribbon in between her ankles.

Cupping a hand over her eyes, she peered into the dim interior. The TV blared. A can of something sat by itself on the kitchen table. Maybe Tanya couldn't hear her.

She headed around back and ducked beneath laundry hanging from the clothesline. A sudden gust lifted the damp garments.

"Mittens, stop!" He threw his lithe gray body at her feet with every step. "Fine!" She squatted to scratch behind his ears and he rubbed his cheek hard against her palm, her leg, her foot before he slid onto the grass, tail lashing. His fierce purr practically vibrated the air around him.

Resistance is futile, she thought, chuckling. "Who's a pretty baby?" She skimmed her fingers along his soft stomach. "Who?" she cooed, because obviously all animals spoke the universal language of baby talk. "You're the pretty baby."

Long, jeans-clad legs stepped into her line of vision and she pressed her lips together, feeling her cheeks heat. She wished she could suck those words in like a popped bubble, but they rose around her, pink and sticky sweet.

She nearly groaned when she recognized the distinctive tooled leather boots. Jack. Brown eyes, rich as spring soil, gleamed down at her.

"Howdy."

An amused expression tugged up one corner of his handsome mouth and her heart jerked to a stop. She waited for her lungs to start breathing again. The shadow cast by a nearby aspen slanted across his slashed cheek.

"Hey." Mittens's tail lashed her feet when she straightened and tilted her face to stare at him.

"Did you talk to Tanya?"

"She didn't answer her front door, so I thought I'd try the back."

"And that's what you're doing right now?" His head swiveled from the house to the cat. An eyebrow rose and his mouth twitched as if he fought off a full-blown smile. "Nice detective work."

Smart aleck.

"What's this?" He swooped down and grabbed a cigarette butt from the ground.

"A car?" she ventured, unable to resist. Why did he bring out her sass? Darn those bad boys and her apparently undiminished need to flirt with them.

He didn't answer. Just pulled another cigarette butt from his pocket and compared the two. "Does Tanya smoke?"

"No." She averted her eyes, which had been

lingering much too long on his profile, when he glanced up at her, quick.

"Smiley?"

"Just cigars. He says cigarettes are the wine coolers of smoking."

"Huh."

"Sooo...what's the significance, *partner*?"

He shot her a considering look. "Spotted the same type of cigarette at the top of the ledge where the avalanche started."

His words knocked the air out of her. Something about Camel filters nagged at the edge of her memory. Then it hit her. Her ex...but he was thousands of miles away...behind bars. She forced down her panicked thoughts. "But Smiley wouldn't have intended me any harm..."

He shook his head. "This could be the other guy on the double homicide. Ever heard the name Everett Ridland?"

"No. And Smiley isn't a murderer."

"And he doesn't appreciate Very Berry wine coolers. Got it. Let's see if Tanya is in."

He followed her to the screened-in porch's door. "I can handle this on my own," she said over her shoulder and lifted her hand, then stopped. "It's open."

"All the invitation we need." He eased open the door into Tanya's kitchen and gestured for her to precede him. "Go in and call for Tanya like you think she's home."

"What if she's not?"

"Just got an email saying my search warrant's been authorized."

"You can't just go through her things," she hissed.

"This isn't exactly a panty raid, darlin'. Not unless you're into that, of course."

At his sarcastic drawl, she rolled her eyes and elbowed past him. "Tanya! Hey, girl," she hollered once she'd stepped inside the kitchen, feeling like a complete fraud and the worst friend possible. "You decent?"

She moved farther into the cluttered space, noting a newspaper open to the sports section beside a can of beer, an empty pizza box thrown on top of her trash can and the shade still down on the window above her sink.

The stale scent of strong cigarettes rose from a dirty ashtray beside the paper, cigarette butts crushed in the middle. Muddy tracks crossed the kitchen floor and she put her foot next to one, seeing how much bigger it was. Not Tanya's for sure… Smiley's? The smoker's? She ignored the questions. These were her friends. She knew them.

But you thought you knew Kevin, too.

And Jack? She couldn't trust her interest in him, either.

"Anything?" rumbled a voice beside her ear.

"Thought you were waiting for my signal," she said, her voice breathy.

"If I waited any longer, I'd be drawing Social Security."

"Ha-ha," she enunciated slowly, so he understood exactly how unamusing she found him—so he wouldn't suspect that she really did find him funny.

No more flirting.

He tipped his hat. "Never thought I'd hear you laugh."

"You didn't."

His lightbulb grin had her turning away, fast. "Tanya!" she called again. "Stopped by for that visit!"

She waved Jack back, hoping he'd return to the porch, but he waltzed right by as if breaking and entering—though he had a warrant...

Then again, bad boys didn't ask for permission. Or follow rules.

Shoot.

"She's not home," he announced, and his boots thunked on the wooden floor as he paced through the rooms, searching. When he headed to Tanya's bedroom, she hustled after him.

Jokes aside, she needed to protect her friend's privacy. He looked under the floral spread across the bed, and when he peered up at her, the lace hem fell across his hard-bitten face in a contrast so comical she almost did laugh.

"Would you know what size shoe Tanya wears?" He pulled out a large pair of boots with a distinctive star pattern on them. She knew those... Smiley's. But they could have been left here last year. Or Tanya might have held on to them after the breakup and planned to give them back.

"Same as me. Seven." She'd borrowed a pair of Tanya's heels once for a local wedding in the mistaken belief she could actually walk on stilts. Her toes stretched inside her comfy boots and wiggled at the remembered torture. Nope. She was a tried and true, square heel kind of gal.

He peered inside the boots and she heard him mutter, "Twelve."

A clatter at the back door made the air clog her lungs.

"Mittens," called a lilting, sing-song voice. "Did you leave this door open?"

"Tanya!"

Jack's large hand engulfed hers and he tugged. "Quick! Into the closet!"

CHAPTER EIGHT

DARKNESS FOLDED AROUND them as they squished into the tiny space and jammed shut the folding door. *Honey*, thought Jack, as he inhaled her scent, every one of his senses acutely aware of the soft woman pressed against him.

"Your hand is touching my belly," she murmured in his ear.

Didn't he know it. "Yours is on my—"

"Oh!" she exclaimed and jerked her hand from around him as if she'd touched fire. He held in a laugh and resisted the urge to brush his fingers along her firm abdomen.

With a jackhammer in his chest and a desert in his throat, he wiggled his hand free and dropped it to his side. He felt the back of the closet against his knuckles and the louvered door against his shoulder. If Tanya discovered them, they'd have some fast talking to do.

A cat meowed outside the door and the scratch of nails sounded on the panel.

"Mittens!" she breathed in his ear. His body clenched and he held himself still, wishing he was a statue and immune to this beautiful woman. What was that irritating thing she always did? Right now, he couldn't think of it. Or anything else.

In fact, her decision to follow him into the closet, rather than crying out a warning to Tanya, deeply impressed him. Dani was loyal to her friends, but that hadn't kept her from doing right. Most of all, in that split second, she'd trusted him.

"What are you after, kitty cat?" he heard Tanya coo, and the hairs on the back of his neck rose. "You know you're not allowed in there. Remember what I said about dresses not being scratching posts?"

Dani snorted in his ear.

"Are you catching a cold, Mittens?" Their breaths hung in the snug space as Tanya's voice grew louder. Tension snapped through him.

The cat meowed again and his dark shape seemed to rise as Tanya must have picked him up.

"Hey. Did you drag out these boots?" Tanya's voice dropped. "Too heavy for you, though. Come on. Let me get you some food."

Damn.

Dani's silky hair brushed his cheek as she turned her head. He registered the way her body seemed to curve into his, like she was made for him. His mind conjured all the wrong kinds of thoughts. How did the alphabet go backward? *Z, Y, X...*

Warm breath rushed against his jaw. In the dark, without his scars both drawing eyes and repelling them, he felt freer. He could imagine himself like any other man alone with a beautiful woman. His hands would tangle in her hair. He'd draw her closer still. Lower his mouth until it brushed hers and...

"What are you doing?" Dani husked, shoving at his chest.

He jerked his head back and banged it against a hook just as a cell phone buzzed. Their hands flew, patting pockets until they heard Tanya's voice, thankfully sounding some distance away, the almost kiss still dancing between them.

He'd nearly lost his head—and his mind. The case, his life's quest for justice, for atonement... those were his priorities; not chasing women. *Woman*, he mentally corrected. Dani. It'd been a long time since anyone caught his eye like this.

Besides, even if he could pursue her, who

would ever love him once his past came to light?

"Hello? Hello?" Tanya said, growing louder. "Hello? Can you hear me?"

Her footfalls padded on the wooden floor. Some muffled swearing floated through the louvered doors.

"Well, you don't have to shout," she snapped, and despite his suspicions about Tanya, he felt a smile come on. "Yes, I can hear you now. You know how this place is. The only decent signal is out by the road."

Good to know, he thought.

"So, where are you?" she asked after a pause. "I thought you were coming back."

Dani stiffened against him. Yes. Chances were she was talking to Smiley, which meant he'd tracked his target to the right spot.

He heard the pop and fizz of a can opening. His breath seemed to synchronize with Dani's.

"Yeah," Tanya said, after what sounded like a gulp. "*He* showed up." An uneasy note entered her voice. "Are you sure about that guy? Something's off with him."

The Camels smoker? The other hit man? His brother's killer? Air rushed from between his clenched teeth.

After a moment, she said, "Well, of course I was. What'd you think I'd do? I know how to mind my Ps and Qs. Besides. He scares me half to death. The way he stares. So cold. Like he's looking at your corpse."

Yep. Sure sounded like his man. His hands balled.

She paced the room now and her shadow moved against the door. Dani's fingers dug into his shoulders.

"He's not happy, though." He felt Dani jump a little when Tanya's words came right through the panel. Close. "He's looking for it. Seems dead set you've got it. Do you have it?"

It? What was "it"? Something related to the homicide? The object stolen from the Phillips' safe? He filed the question away to ask Lance…if they made it out of this closet without his cover blown. His blood pounded in his ears. Never before had a bounty been this critical. He wouldn't screw up what might be his only chance to make things right for his mother, his brother, maybe even himself.

"You'd better give it to him, then. What? What? Hello?"

A cat yowl rose and Tanya cried, "Sorry, kitty. Bad mama." Then, "I think I lost you.

If you can hear me, hang on. I'm going out back."

Her footsteps faded, then disappeared.

Jack eased open the closet door, peered around and pulled Dani out of the bedroom, through the living room and onto the front porch. He glimpsed Tanya's back through a rear window just before easing the door shut behind them.

They trotted down the stairs, not speaking until they'd reached one of the pastures. This one held mules that hung their heads through the fence slats, ears pricking forward then back, tails swishing. The two dogs, Bella and Beau he recalled, dashed away, then bounded forward and back in some ecstatic game only they knew the rules to.

At last they rounded the corner of a barn and Dani stopped and leaned against it.

"Who do you think Tanya was talking to?" Her large eyes met his and the weakening sun, skimming over the tree line, sparkled on the gold specks in her hazel eyes.

A muzzle pressed at his knees and he absently scratched the dog between its ears. "Not sure. Who do you think it was?"

"Smiley?" She squatted on her heels and buried her face in the other dog's neck. "It just doesn't make sense." He barely made out her muffled words.

"Why's that?"

"Tanya's my best friend. She wouldn't lie to me."

He picked up a stick and chucked it far down the dirt road that led up from the front gates. Lies. Honest folks hardly ever saw them coming.

"Do you think she's lying to me?" Suddenly Dani was in his face, her eyes blazing, her features tight.

"I think she's telling you as much as she can."

"What's that supposed to mean?" When he didn't answer right away, she touched his arm. "Is Tanya in danger?"

"I don't know," he said heavily, his mind turning over the facts. If Smiley was one of the two killers, and the other hit man had been in Tanya's house...

Her eyes rounded with alarm. When she whirled to leave, he grabbed her arm. "Let go! I've got to find out what she was talking about. I need to warn her."

"And how would you explain overhearing her? The Mays want me undercover. Are you going to blow that?"

The fight seemed to leave her and he dropped

her hand. The feel of it, soft and warm in his, lingered.

"No. Not yet. But if I think she's in trouble, I'm telling her," she warned. "Sometimes a good woman doesn't know she's in trouble with a man until she's in way over her head."

Both of the dogs loped up, growling and huffing, the stick held in both of their mouths as each tried yanking it from the other.

Jack's curiosity about Dani was even more piqued by her fervent tone. Had she gone through a hard time with a man? Been betrayed? Had her heart broken? This could be why she was driven to intervene on Tanya's behalf.

He waited for her to say more but she fell silent.

An ache reached up through the base of his skull. He closed his eyes briefly and said, "Fair enough."

He'd watch out for Tanya. If she was an innocent party in this, she didn't deserve the heap of trouble she'd just landed in.

A horn honked and an extended cab pickup pulling a horse trailer rolled past them. The driver and passenger, an older couple, waved.

"It's Larry and Diane!" Dani hurried after the truck and he followed. Beau and Bella raced ahead; their ecstatic barks filled the purpling air. By the time they caught up to the truck, the Mays had parked beside a small, empty corral.

A slightly stooped tall man with a wide-brimmed Stetson and a smile that creased his weathered face, extended a hand. He had wide-spaced features a size too small for his broad face, and ears that stuck out.

"Must be our, uh, new wrangler, Jack." He nodded to the other workers who'd assembled to greet their employers.

Jack appreciated the firm grip and the steady gaze of the man who looked like he'd spent most of his waking hours outdoors. If Larry was taken aback by Jack's scars, he hid it well. "Nice to meet you, sir."

"And this here's my wife, Diane." Larry put a hand around a petite woman with a long, salt-and-pepper braid that trailed past her waist. She wore a full denim skirt that reached the top of her boots, a leather belt with a silver-and-turquoise buckle and a tucked in, buttoned-up shirt. When her gaze flashed to his, her smile wavered and she swallowed hard.

He ducked his head to the right to hide the

worst of his scar and ignored the gasps of the staff around him.

"Howdy."

"Welcome." Her chin rose and she stepped close, her hand out. He shook it.

Good people, the Mays. He could tell.

Mountain Sky Dude Ranch was a clean operation and deserved protecting. He'd catch Smiley and his partner before they did any harm.

Suddenly he was glad to have to go undercover, to experience, once again, his old life of riding out every day, working with people, decent people, handling animals...

He caught one of the workers pointing at him and shook away the thought. His scar kept him from moving freely in the world and that's how it should be. Jesse couldn't enjoy life anymore, so what right did he have to it?

"We'll be happy to welcome you, proper, tonight at the square dance, and arrange for a chat later on," drawled Diane, her accent a little softer, more rounded than a Mid-Westerner's. A Southern girl. Mississippi. Kentucky, maybe. "But we've got to unload our new roper."

Dani stepped forward, her eyes bright. "I'll lead her out."

Larry swept off his hat to reveal buzzed silver hair atop a square-shaped head. "Good to see you, Dani. Thanks for holding down the fort." His blue eyes leaped from his stable manager to Jack.

"No problem," she said over her shoulder.

She pulled the pin out of the trailer's latch and opened the door. Inside, behind an angled metal gate, he glimpsed a sleek black horse shifting on its feet. His mind drifted to Milly, the skittish white who'd been too fearful to take an apple from him.

He hopped on the trailer behind Dani and automatically grabbed the gate as she slid under it, a lead in hand. The appreciative look she shot him fizzed in his blood like a Fourth of July sparkler. How she set him off.

"All good," she hollered a moment later. He held open the gate and she slowly led out the new roping horse. Larry gripped the door and a few oohs and aahs erupted from the staff. The mare was a beauty. Easy gait. Nice musculature. Willing disposition.

He swung open the corral gate and Dani led the horse inside, unclipped the lead and grabbed the water bucket. She ducked between the fence slats and straightened.

"She looks good. Her father was Sin City, right?"

Diane beamed. "She comes from a long line of champion ropers. Couldn't believe we won the auction, but here she is."

"No one stood a chance once Diane got started." Larry came up behind her and she swatted him away when he squeezed her waist. "The paddles just dropped."

A few of the employees leaned over the fence, some making useless clicking noises, others holding out treats to the new horse.

Dani nodded. "I read the sheet you faxed. A sweet deal. I'll settle her in and introduce her to the herd tomorrow."

Speaking of which, on the other side of the pen, a growing number of horses clustered on the abutting fence, checking out the new arrival. Milly, he noticed, stayed far back, her ears twitching as she kept tabs on this new arrival.

"What about Milly?" he found himself asking, though for the life of him, he didn't know why. The horse was rangy, but had a good frame. He could see the potential in her to be a strong riding horse again, darn it.

The jabbering crew quieted; Larry's pleased look faded. "We're making one last effort to find a home for her. Sorry, Dani, but we inquired at the auction and no one would take her, so it's still down to Old Man Graham. He's been hemming and hawing, but he said he'll have a decision by tomorrow. It'd be a very sad end for our girl if it doesn't work out. She's always been one of our hardest workers."

"And the best with kids," put in Dani, her voice growing quiet and tight. She shaded her eyes against the low-riding sun and stared out at Milly.

"Maybe she can be broken in again," Jack said, unable to stop his runaway mouth. What was he getting at? Milly wasn't his business. And he understood the hard facts about ranch life. Still, something about Milly getting a raw deal, how one kid's mistake could now end her life, didn't sit right.

"What do you mean?" asked Diane. Her eyes looked moist as she tore them away from Milly.

"If you can't settle her with Mr. Graham tomorrow, will you put off euthanizing her… let me work with her this week when I'm not busy with my, ah, job? I'll see if I can help her turn things around."

Larry settled his hat back on and cocked his head. He studied Jack in a way that reminded him of his father when they'd all lined up for bed as kids, ears and hands mostly washed.

"Well. That'd be kind of you. Don't know if I can impose like that, not when you've already got…" He trailed off and Diane settled a small hand on his arm.

"It'd be no trouble at all, sir." Jack felt himself flush a bit at Dani's small smile. It seemed to blot out all of the raised hands and whispered voices behind them. He shifted in his boots. Ducked his head a bit.

One of the horses whinnied and another took up the call. Milly lifted her head and everyone seemed to hold their breath.

"Then we'd be grateful. Thank you." Larry pumped his hand again. "And don't forget about the square dance tonight!" He hopped in the truck and drove away toward the main house, Diane by his side.

The employees hustled off, too, leaving him and Dani alone. He joined her at the fence, where she turned on a spigot and filled a bucket.

"Why'd you do that?" she muttered without looking up. Water swirled inside the plastic.

"Do what?" He grabbed the handle from her and waited as she unlatched the gate and headed inside. "Whoa there—ahhh—what's this horse's name?" he asked as the suddenly hot mare twisted her head and turned in a quick, prancing circle beside him.

"Cher."

"Cher?" He dumped the water in the trough and studied the black beauty.

"She comes from Las Vegas," Dani announced, a smirk teasing up the sides of her mouth, the one he'd almost kissed today.

He tipped his hat at Cher and followed Dani to the feed barn. "Guess that explains it."

"We've got an Elton, too. Wonder if they had the same owner."

"My favorite horse was named Sundance," he told her for no reason at all, except that Dani seemed to have a way of unhinging his jaw.

She shot him a sideways look. "Of course it was."

He mock frowned, more tweaked than offended, and he liked it. It'd been a long time since anyone had teased him. Flirted. "And what'd you call your English jumper? Crumpets?"

An unladylike snort escaped her and he smiled again. "Dolly. Broke her leg on the last gate. We had the championship up until then."

She stopped for a minute in the road and the

last drip of sunset surrounding them seemed to burn the brightest on her hair.

"Sorry to hear that. She sounds like a good one."

Dani studied him for a minute. "She had the biggest heart. I miss her."

They resumed their trek in silence for a moment, then Jack asked, "Stupid question, but how'd a Texas gal come to ride English?"

"Jane Austen." At his puzzled look, she continued. "Broke my leg the summer I turned fourteen. I was bored staying inside all the time, so I began reading and couldn't stop. Austen's one of my favorite authors. All her heroines wear these fancy riding habits. Polished boots. Top hats… It was so different than what I grew up with, and it kind of fascinated me."

He scuffed his worn boots in the dirt. Tipped up his cowboy hat. "This is as fancy as this cowboy gets." He shot her a sheepish look from beneath his brim.

After clearing her throat, she blurted, "So. You're going to work as a wrangler, bounty hunter and a horse whisperer?"

"Until I think of something else. Any need for a juggler?"

She rolled her eyes before she pushed into

the barn. "Not that I can imagine, but I hope you're a good square dancer. Male partners are in demand."

He leaned in the doorway and watched her confident, no-nonsense walk. It appealed to him more than any sashaying woman in heels.

The party tonight would be torture, but seeing Dani again would make it more tolerable. She was tough-minded and opinionated, which he liked about her, but the way she worried about her friends, the horses, the emotion he'd heard in her voice when she spoke of her mother, her mount, added up to a complex woman he wanted to see more of.

Much more than he cared to admit.

CHAPTER NINE

LATER THAT EVENING, Dani shoved back her bangs and frowned at her reflection in the freestanding oval mirror in the corner of her room. The light blue, off-shoulder blouse brought out the red in her blond hair and deepened the green in her hazel eyes. It looked nice, but maybe too nice. Like she was trying too hard. Wanted to catch a fella's eye.

Jackson Cade came to mind.

With a disgusted noise, she yanked the blouse off and tossed it on the growing heap of discarded, would-be square dance outfits on her double bed. A fan whirred on the slanted ceiling in the apartment she occupied at the end of the storage barn, turning in lazy circles while a moth banged against its domed light. Outside her window, crickets sang and stars clustered around the full moon like fireflies.

She had to stop thinking about him. Even during her earlier start-of-the-season meeting with the wranglers, her first as stable manager, she'd found her eyes drifting to him where he'd leaned against a wall in the back, his black hat pulled low over his dark eyes.

While handing out tomorrow's assignments, she'd imagined their almost kiss in Tanya's closet. It'd been the barest of pressures, more shadow than flesh, a stirring of air that'd somehow made her heart thump so hard she'd been dizzy.

Had she imagined it?

Maybe. Standing close to his lean, muscular shape had made her imagine all kinds of things she had no business considering. Other wranglers and staff seemed to be keeping their distance from the terse bounty hunter. They sensed trouble and avoided it. She needed to do the same because only an idiot ran straight at danger, a fool who hadn't learned from her mistakes.

Yet he'd offered to rehabilitate Milly, which meant so much to her. How did that reconcile with his desperado image? Was he a bad boy with a heart?

That sounded like an even more lethal combination.

One she had to guard herself against.

Her cell phone buzzed and a familiar, smiling face appeared on the screen. A signal! As always, she sent a silent thank-you to the capricious satellite powers that be and hoped it wouldn't cut out on one of her sister Claire's infamous teasers, like, "And you'll never believe this…"

"Hey, Claire!" Dani said. She tapped the speaker button and dropped her phone on the mound of clothes as she pawed through her choices. "I was just thinking about you."

"Me, too."

"Sisters," they both said, then, "Jinx," then, "Buy me a cola," then they laughed. It was basically their verbal version of a not-so-secret sister handshake. The familiar weight Dani carried in her chest lightened; her lungs moved easier.

She slid on a black tank top and stepped into a pair of worn jeans. "How've you been, girl?"

"Good. Real good, and…you'll never believe this…"

Dani braced herself, waiting for the inevitable static, but heard, instead, the sound of a bag being ripped open followed by noisy crunching. She sat on the edge of her bed, shoved her feet into her favorite pair of dark red boots, then stood. "Dad's okay?"

"The therapist has him knitting," Claire

mumbled, her mouth full, Dani guessed. The words sounded more like *The rest is kitten.* Luckily Dani had a lot of experience translating Cheeto. "She says it's good for his fine motor skills."

Dani laughed at the image of her John Wayne look-alike father holding a pair of needles, a ball of yarn at his feet. "He must love that."

"He's already knitted three baby blankets for the church." Then, after a moan, "Have you tried the cheese-fries-flavored Cheetos?"

"We're lucky if our convenience store has more than one flavor of chips."

The sound of a scandalized *tut* made her grin. "How can you live like that?"

"It's a burden."

"I would imagine. You just need to move home, that's all."

She leaned her elbows on her knees and clenched her eyes and jaw and fists—held everything clenched until she could speak without betraying herself.

"Dani?" Claire's voice sounded sharper now. A lull in the chewing. "Dani?"

"Yeah. Still here." Always here and not there...

Please let me get through this season with-

out incident. In six months, the statute of limitations would run out on her crime. Accessory to a felony. Without the threat of jail, she'd be free to visit Coltrane whenever she wanted. Now she only had to keep her distance from Jack in case he uncovered her secret.

Easy.

Right.

Dani grabbed a soft plaid shirt and slid her arms into it. "So, what won't I believe besides the taste of cheese-fries-flavored Cheetos?"

"They're the best I've tried yet." More crunching.

"You always say that. Remember the sweet pickle relish ones."

"I'm trying to forget. I had a stomach ache for a week." Claire's voice grew muffled, as if she'd turned her head away and was speaking to someone else, then, "Can you talk to Jonathan?"

She grinned as she pictured the red-haired, freckle-faced boy she'd watched grow up, mostly in pictures. "Of course." She left her overshirt unbuttoned, tied it at the waist and looked around for her hat.

"Aunt Dani?" Jonathan sounded excited. She could feel her expression go soft and gummy.

"Yes, honey. How're you?" The brim of

her hat peeked out from under the bed and she grabbed it.

"Fine! Guess what?"

"What?"

"Don't say anything, Jonathan!" she heard her sister warn.

"Okay, I won't." Then, in a whisper. "Mommy's got a wedding dress."

"Jonathan!" exclaimed Claire.

"What?" Dani fell backward onto the bed, her hat to her chest. Another milestone in her sister's life—missed because she lived so far away.

"I'm sorry, Dani. I was going to wait until you could come home again when your season ended, but with the wedding coming up…"

Dani nodded, tracking the fan blades as they circled, then said, "Wait. Did you set a date?" Her dismay turned to excitement.

"Yes! Tanner and I picked September 20. It'll be cool then, and you'll be through the season, right? I mean, you'll come." Claire's voiced dropped a bit.

Dani crushed her teeth together. "Wouldn't miss it." Unless she was in jail. She pushed the crazy thought aside, shoved upright and put on her hat.

"And you'll be my maid of honor…"

"Depending on the dress you pick out." She grinned, recalling some of the pictures of hideous bridesmaids' dresses her sister had sent as jokes.

"Something with a big bow," Claire mused.

Dani rolled her shirtsleeves to the elbow. "And satin. Really shiny. Like, if you look at it too long you'll go blind or start singing a Diana Ross song."

"Puff sleeves." Her sister began humming "Ain't No Mountain High Enough" and she could picture her. Smiling.

"Crinoline. Especially if it's hot out."

"Mint green or lemon yellow."

"Sounds perfect."

Claire's half laugh, half sigh came through the phone. "I just miss you so much…"

A beeping sounded and Dani stared at the now empty screen, a "disconnected" message where her sister's face had been.

Shoot. She'd been lucky to chat with her that long without the call dropping. Just in case, she tried the number, got nothing, tried again and gave up.

The familiar emptiness inside her swelled and she thought of Tanya. Normally, hanging out with her friend helped. Now, after what she'd overheard, she didn't know what to think of the woman who was like another sister to her.

Her mind drifted to the sketchy phone conversation. Had it been Smiley? On an involuntary shiver, she hugged her knees to her chest. It felt dead wrong thinking anything bad of her two friends…but she'd be naive not to be suspicious.

Could Tanya be in trouble? Manipulated by Smiley?

She finger-combed her damp hair, still wet after her quick shower a half hour ago. At the square dance, she'd corner Tanya. Get her to come clean without blowing Jack's cover. She didn't want her friend taken in by a guy who wasn't good for her.

Yet she couldn't tell Tanya everything… Another secret between her and someone she cared about.

More friends hiding illegal activities.

Same issues, just a different location.

Lord, no.

Things had changed. She'd changed, but the more time she spent around Jack and Tanya, the more she saw that maybe she hadn't…not nearly as much as she'd thought.

The digital clock on the night table caught

her eye. Nine o'clock. As if on cue, the opening strains of a fiddle twanged in the crisp air and she imagined the reunited workers excitedly gathering for their season kick-off event.

She had to move and stop fussing. That girl she'd left behind her in Oklahoma was gone and forgotten.

Mostly.

She twisted in front of the mirror. With her hair curling over her shoulders, her face makeup free, she looked like she always did, without the trail grit. Spit-shined, as her father liked to say.

There. Good enough.

A few minutes later, she neared the brightly lit deck beside the main house. White string lights stretched from poles at each corner of the long rectangular space. A three-man band sped through a fast-stepping tune that got a number of couples twirling on the large dirt area beyond the deck.

Joe, one of their maintenance men, sawed with his fiddle bow. One of the cooks, Pete, madly plucked his banjo while a groundskeeper, Todd, strummed a guitar. Nan sat on a stool by the mic, calling the dance. The fringe on her shawl swung as her boot kept time, the lights glinting on the rhinestones adorning her hat.

"Hey, Dani!"

She stopped to chat with different groups, catching up, listening with half an ear as she scanned the crowd for Tanya or Jack.

Her friend hadn't shown yet, but her midnight cowboy had made an appearance, barely. He stood in shadow, leaning against the side of a barn, alone. No surprise there. She wanted to ignore him, but something in the way others kept staring and whispering, his tense body language, propelled her to his side.

"Having fun?" she asked when she reached him.

He shot her such an agonized look she had to laugh. "How long does this thing last?"

Settling herself beside him, she leaned against the wood-slatted building. He smelled of woods after a thunderstorm, clean and elemental, and his crisp shirt filled her nose with the scent of fresh laundry. She breathed deep. "It just started."

He tipped his head back and his hat slid forward, covering his face. "Wake me when it's over."

Lifting the brim, she peered at him. His shadowed face was mysterious in the moon's glow, the light pooling beneath his high cheek-bones and highlighting the jagged ridge of flesh that sliced through his face. Insanely, her fingers itched to touch it. She dropped her hand.

"Beep. Beep. Beep. Beep." She did her best impression of an alarm clock.

He opened one eye. "Are you being annoying on purpose or does that just come naturally?"

"It's a gift." She shrugged, amused. "And you're intimidating."

Both eyes were open now and gleaming at her, sharp. "I like the sound of that."

She ignored the traitorous leap of her pulse and gestured to the chattering group. "You're supposed to blend in, not look like you're about to steal the payroll."

His eyes were smiling, his mouth only sort of. It did something funny to her heart. "Fair enough. What do you suggest?"

"How about getting out there? Dance." She blinked, astonished, as her own words fell around her ears. Why had she suggested dancing?

Because you want to spend more time with him.

Please let him say no...

And, eyelashes, stop batting.

His eyebrows rose and he slid his hand into hers. "I thought you'd never ask."

WHAT WAS HE DOING?

He'd come to gather information, Jack thought, not get lost in a pair of hazel eyes. Yet here he was, stepping out with the lithe woman beside him, her hand folded into his like some long-ago wish.

"Thanks," called the older woman he'd met earlier, Nan, as a song ended. She stood and waved at the cheering crowd. "Now, y'all go on without me for a bit while I wet my whistle."

The trio swung into an instrumental version of Blake Shelton's "God Gave Me You" and Dani stepped into his arms like she belonged there. Or maybe it just felt that way.

His arm rose up around her waist and one hand settled on the curve of her back. His other fingers laced with hers. As soon as he touched her, he wondered how he'd gone this long without doing it. He was aware of her every breath this close. Her skin was as soft as it looked.

The lilting music faded. The other couples disappeared. Under the star-studded sky,

Dani shone the brightest. She was as lovely as a warm wind in the shade. Her pretty face shone up at him from beneath her cowboy hat—big eyes, full pink lips that curved in a way that made him itch to kiss them.

And she had adorable cheeks, round as crab apples. Dimples on top of freckles, which shouldn't even be allowed. Rosy skin like a fresh peach. A long neck that arched, proud and strong. He steered her around the dance floor and she followed his lead, stepping backward easily, trusting him not to let her stumble.

Suddenly a gust of wind blew through, and he snatched Dani's hat as it lifted off her head. Settling it back on, he couldn't resist reaching out and wrapping one of her curls around his finger. The honey-and-vanilla scent of her rose around them and his arm tightened, bringing her closer.

"So, tell me about Carbondale. Do all your siblings work on the ranch?" she murmured through her smile, her eyes never leaving his. She had the kind of smile that could have been in a toothpaste commercial. Wide and genuine.

"No." He twirled her beneath his arm and drew her close again, their feet picking up the tempo without faltering.

"What made you leave?"

Jesse's thin, worried face bloomed in his mind. "Work." That was all he'd say on the matter, though something about Dani made him want to open up and believe that speaking his hurt out loud wouldn't cut him straight through. They moved slower now, closer. His fingers tightened around hers.

A line appeared between her eyebrows. "Is this one of our monosyllabic conversations?"

Despite himself, he felt a laugh come on. Held it back. "Maybe."

She looked up at him through her bangs and flattened her smile into a smirk. "That was two. Two syllables. Don't hurt yourself there, cowboy."

This time he did laugh and she joined him. She had the kind of full-on belly laugh that shook her shoulders, loosened her joints and made him want to make her do it again.

"So tell me about your ranch."

"It's called Cade Ranch. It's been in the family for almost a hundred and fifty years. Not much has changed, except now all our Angus beef is grass fed."

And Jesse was gone.

He was keeping both his eyes mostly shut, and his heart wrenched as he pictured their spot in the center of the Rocky Mountains, the places he and his siblings rode, fished, camped. Every corner of the property reminded him of Jesse and how he'd failed to protect him.

She whistled. "That's all the thing, huh. My family's ranch is modernizing, too."

The wistful note that'd entered her voice drew his gaze and made him wonder if they had more in common than the ability to get under each other's skin. He ran a thumb along the veins in her wrist. "Do you miss it?"

A strange look crossed her face and she stumbled slightly. He steadied her, and her face fell for just a second against his shoulder, against the sleeve of his shirt. "I wish I could see it more."

"Don't you go home much?"

"No," she said shortly and seemed to stiffen. Sore subject. It made him wonder. "How about you?" she asked quickly. "Do you go home much? What made you give up ranching for bounty hunting?"

He opened his mouth to answer, then shut it. Her eyes searched his and it seemed like she could read his mind. His heart. She felt right in his arms, like she was born to be there and he was meant to hold her. He wished his life was different and he was the kind of man who could spend more time in Dani's world.

When he looked away, a familiar man caught his eye. The groundskeeper from the trail. "Does he go by Sam Perkins?"

She followed his point. "Yeah. Why?"

"Not Everett Ridland?"

"Jack. What's going on?"

"Nothing. Will you bring me over? Get a conversation going?" He didn't wait for an answer, just tugged her after him until they stood before the bearded man.

"Hey, Sam," Dani said, sounding a little winded. "I wanted you to meet our new wrangler, Jackson."

The broad-faced man studied him for a long minute, turned his head and spat on the dirt at Jack's feet. "Met him before."

He felt the fight rising up in his throat and put his hands in his pockets. Pressed them into fists. "Wasn't much of a meeting."

"Enough for me," ground out Sam, his hostile tone setting Jack's stomach on edge.

"Where'd you run into each other?" Dani asked brightly, and Sam's expression grew guarded, his small eyes sinking deeper into the thick folds of his skin.

"Off of Coyote Trail. Was up there to clear

out the rocks from the avalanche." The tip of his nose grew red and he jutted his chin. "Is this some kind of interrogation?"

Dani blinked at him for a moment, the surprise clear on her face. "No. I, uh, didn't mean to pry."

"Keep that in mind next time." And without another word, Sam turned on his heel and strode away.

"That's strange," she muttered to herself.

"Is he always that friendly?"

A short laugh escaped her. "No. Tanya can't stand him. What Smiley sees in him, I'll never guess. Those two are thick as thieves..." She trailed off and stared after the man.

"That's interesting," he said slowly, considering.

"Not as interesting as the fact that I never let groundskeeping know about the avalanche."

He turned her by the shoulders slowly. Lowered his voice. "Did anyone else know?"

"Diane and Larry. I told them after they got in and they promised to get it taken care of. When did you say you ran into Sam?"

"Before we went to Tanya's. The second time."

"So Sam wouldn't have known unless..." Her voice dipped and her eyes widened.

"Unless he'd been there when the avalanche happened…"

"Do you think he caused it?"

"Looks suspicious. Tell me what you know about him."

"Like I said, he's a friend of Smiley's. Worked here before I came on. Pretty much keeps to himself. I think he's from Oklahoma."

"Thanks. I'll see if I can catch him." He tipped his hat and headed in the direction Sam had taken, the sight of Dani staying with him as he hustled away.

She was girl-next-door pretty without even trying. Her prickly personality kept a man on his toes. Interested. But even more important, he liked how she'd been helping him and letting him take the lead, following him into that closet, giving him inside information about Sam and Smiley.

He wished he could stay with her longer, but the groundskeeper needed sorting. The man was connected to Smiley. He felt sure of it in his gut. But were they his brother's killers? The same pair that'd gunned down the Denver couple, too?

He wove through the crowd, looking for his target, but the man seemed to have vanished. Circling the area twice, he came up empty-handed and returned to his spot beneath the barn's eaves.

The glint of a holstered gun caught Jack's eye. Sam Perkins stood off just a bit to his right, leaning against a tractor, tipping back a flask as his eyes scanned the crowd. The move revealed a 9mm, otherwise concealed under his jacket, holstered on his hip.

Same weapon that'd been used in the Phillips' homicide. Same caliber that'd killed Jesse.

He and Sam were about to get real friendly, real fast, he thought grimly. The moment he stepped out of the shadows, though, Sam spied him and disappeared around the corner of the barn.

His breath harsh in his throat, Jack hustled after him, then pulled up short, peering into the dark where Sam had vanished into an empty field. His blood fired. The guy had run from him. No doubt about it. Why?

Jack headed into the night to track down his new quarry. Sam's suspicious actions raised a big red flag. It was clear he was hiding something and Jack wouldn't rest till he got to the bottom of it, wouldn't stop until Sam led him right to Smiley.

CHAPTER TEN

"HEY, DANI!" ONE of her youngest wranglers leaned against her office doorway. He was treetop tall, with an endless length of denim-clad legs and an animated face.

"Morning, Blake." She swallowed a yawn and tapped her fingers on the warm side of her coffee mug. "Did you just get in? I didn't see you at the staff meeting or the square dance yesterday."

He ducked his head of loose, brown curls, resembling a surfer more than a cowboy. "Sorry about that." He adjusted his puka necklace, its shell pendant settling at the base of his throat. "Some last minute stuff I, uh, couldn't get out of. But I'm glad to be here now." His face burst into a wide smile she immediately returned.

"How was Oklahoma State?" She blew at the steaming surface of her coffee and took a cautious sip. The roasted brew killed off a few thousand taste buds, but at least it woke her up. She'd tossed and turned last night, thoughts of Jack chasing away sleep.

He'd opened up more about his old life, yet it'd only increased her curiosity, an interest she couldn't afford to indulge. This was her first season as a stable manager, and a successful season meant she'd turned the corner on her past for good.

Only Jack's investigation, and her budding feelings for him, challenged her ambitions and her assumptions. This peaceful spot no longer felt like her safe haven with him around. The sooner Jack caught up with Smiley and straightened things out the better.

Blake blinked, his long lashes seeming to bat right at her. "Oh, I decided to drop out of college."

"You did?"

"Yeah. Just wasn't for me." His smile faded. She wondered if he'd actually flunked out, given how disappointed he seemed.

Which was none of her business, she reminded herself firmly, downing more of her coffee. Blake had had a great first year with them last season and she'd been glad when he'd let her know he was coming back. End of story.

"I messaged you with today's assignment

and posted a print copy outside on the bulletin board."

He tipped his head back against the wall. "I didn't get Mr. Clark, did I?" he groaned.

"No. I'm taking him," she said heavily, her fingers tightening on her mug handle. Reginald Clark had been coming to the dude ranch's opening week for years and was always their most demanding guest. He'd used all caps on his preference sheet when he'd written: NO ORIENTATION TRAIL and SMILEY FOR FLY-FISHING. And what the Denver high roller wanted, he usually got... but not Smiley this year.

The groundskeeper doubled as a fishing guide, but with him gone, someone else would have to step in. Someone with a thick skin... maybe body armor. She wouldn't have some junior wrangler reduced to a stuttering, crying heap on her watch.

Nope. She'd just have to take charge of his party herself and bring Jack along to teach him the ropes. Better she bear the brunt of Mr. Clark's wrath than risk one of her staff members quitting before the season really started. As for Jack, he didn't scare easily. Or at all. Since they'd start on a more advanced trail, it'd also give him a chance to see more of the property.

"I gave you a party of five. Two best friends from their sorority days plus their kids. They used to come with spouses, but I think they're both divorced now."

Impossible as it seemed, Blake's smile only widened. No. He twinkled.

"Don't get any ideas," Dani insisted, immediately wondering if it'd been a good idea to put her resident Romeo with two newly single women.

Oh, well.

She'd keep an eye on it.

"Who's got ideas?" His innocent shrug was anything but, and it made her laugh.

"Behave."

"Who's behaving? That doesn't sound like fun," piped up a voice behind Blake, and a slim girl in cowboy boots and a Stetson bigger than her cat-shaped face ducked under his arm. She'd dyed her blond hair to a shade so black it looked blue and had braided it into thin, swinging braids.

"Morning, Jori Lynn. We're all following the rules this season, right?"

Dani shot her legendary troublemakers a warning look. There was always a group of college-age kids working here every season and they got up to minor mischief, like she had at their age. But she knew all too well how slippery that slope could be.

Jori Lynn elbowed Blake, who returned the favor and she gave an exaggerated *"Ouch"* before asking, "Wanna see my new tattoo?"

"No!"

"Yes!"

She and Blake spoke at once, and in an instant, Jori Lynn whirled, raised her shirt hem and revealed a cowboy-hat-wearing fairy atop a rearing white stallion. Fairy dust trailed from her raised wand and spelled out *BELIEVE* in scrolled letters across Jori Lynn's lower back.

Dani bit back a smile.

"Sweet." Blake reached out to touch it but yanked his hand away at Dani's cleared throat.

"I like it, but you're going to have to keep that covered up," Dani warned as she stood. "And, I'm sorry, but the necklace has to go, too, Blake. You know how Larry and Diane feel about dress code."

"But my tattoo's pretty and I brought crop tops," Jori Lynn wheedled, then launched herself at Dani, hugging her like a bear even though she was built like a bird. "I missed you so much. Didn't get to catch up with you at the square dance and at the meeting, I was…"

"Busy flirting?" Dani finished for her, recalling her giggling with Max, another wrangler.

Jori Lynn shot her a you-got-me look so comical Dani chuckled.

"I heard every word except the name of that hot new wrangler. He looks dangerous. Wonder where he got that scar." Jori Lynn gave a delighted little shiver.

Dani wagged a finger at her. "No, Jori Lynn. Off-limits. He's older, one, so I know your mama wouldn't approve. And, two, I don't think he's the kind for casual flirting."

Jori Lynn clucked her tongue and a gold piercing appeared in the middle of it. "Didn't look that way to me last night. I saw you two dancing. The way you were staring at each other could have burned down the barn. Go on, now. What's the real reason he's off-limits?"

Heat crept into Dani's cheeks. "That wasn't anything."

Yes, it was, came the traitorous thought, along with the remembered feel of his lean, hard body so close to hers. The easy way he'd laughed and teased. Jori Lynn had it right. Despite the scar—or maybe because of it— he was gorgeous.

Dani raised her mug.

"So, where'd he sleep last night?" Jori Lynn lifted pencil-thin eyebrows.

"You didn't see him in the men's section when you came in this morning, Blake?" Dani nearly spilled her coffee on the guest preference sheets stacked on her desk.

"Um. No," Blake said, without looking up from his phone. Mechanical chirping erupted as his fingers flew.

"Huh…" Dani finished off the rest of her drink, thinking fast. He'd said he wouldn't bunk down with the employees and hopefully that was all it was. She tried to curb her rising concern that he might have found trouble pursuing Sam Perkins. What Jackson Cade got up to wasn't her business.

Still, the need to see him seized her. He hadn't picked up his assignment sheet for today, so she had that excuse to look for him as she headed over to Tanya's house. Not that she needed an excuse. She was his boss, sort of, which legitimized all their communications.

She almost groaned out loud. Who was she kidding?

"Did you get your assignment, Jori Lynn?"

The young woman held up a sheet and peered at it, frowning. "Why do I have smelly Franklin?"

Dani held in a smile, picturing the large, placid chestnut with gas issues. "We don't have a lot of female wranglers and you know how he is with men."

"Okay, but someone else is taking him next week." Jori Lynn practically breathed fire.

"I'm making a note." Dani scribbled the reminder on a sticky note and placed it beside the twenty others that surrounded her monitor.

"Are you coming to breakfast?"

"In a minute. I'm going to stop by Tanya's first and see if she's on break. Go on ahead."

"I've been dreaming of her corn bread!" The two stomped outside and were nearly out of the barn when a thought occurred to Dani. She turned off the screen, grabbed her hat and hurried after them.

"Don't forget to take out that tongue ring, Jori Lynn."

The girl stuck it out, pink and curling. "Shoot. Didn't think you'd notice."

"It's the Mays you don't want noticing, okay?"

"Yes, ma'am." Jori Lynn gave her a half salute, then said, "Save me a seat, Blake," before she dashed down the path, back to the staff quarters.

"Catch you later," Blake called as Dani veered away up the road to Tanya's cabin.

"If I don't see you, have a great day and let me know if you have any problems." She patted her walkie-talkie.

She wondered if Jack had remembered to pick up a radio, which then made her think, where was he?

It was a beautiful day, the air so clear she could see each jagged mountaintop against the pristine sky, and pick out every needle on the pines that lined the pasture's wind breaks. The air felt freshly scrubbed in the early morning light, and pollen drifted on soft air currents, the atmosphere unfiltered and promising.

Her heart beat a little faster when she spotted Jack and Milly in the round pen, a separate, fenced area connected directly to one of their pastures. He looked impossibly handsome, with his broad shoulders filling out a light denim shirt, slim jeans over brown cowboy boots and a matching hat that emphasized his jaw.

He tapped Milly lightly with a training stick and walked left in a circle, holding her lead. "Come now," he coaxed, his muscular body moving effortlessly.

Dani reached the fence and leaned on it, watching, holding her breath so as not to distract either party. Milly was showing incredible trust right now, but that could change to fear and aggression in a flash. If Jack wasn't vigilant, he could wind up hurt or worse. How had he gotten Milly to let him this close?

A horse whisperer, indeed.

It touched her that he'd followed through on his vow to work with Milly, even though they still hadn't heard if Mr. Graham would take her. Clearly Jack was a man of his word and he didn't back down easily.

Milly lifted her regal head and her nostrils flared. Her eyes rolled then settled on the intent man beside her. When she shook her head, her white mane swung. A blowing snort sounded and Jack repeated his request, not pushing.

Milly continued to brace.

Jack tapped her again, this time moving her sideways and, to Dani's shock, Milly shuffled a few steps before turning to look at the tall man, giving him her eyes instead of her hooves.

Progress.

"Good," Jack said in a deep voice that sounded commanding, yet warm and reassuring. It loosened her joints and she marveled at the tender and patient side of this formidable man.

He applied more pressure by walking closer, edging Milly sideways again, laterally softening her, flexing her, making her supple and calm so she was bending through the middle and getting her hindquarters underneath her, using them as dirt clouds rose around her shifting hooves. Dani recognized the strategy: trigger the horse's thought process; get her to think before reacting.

And it was working. To Dani's surprise and joy, Milly stopped bracing and Jack lessened the pressure, putting distance between them. He rubbed the stick's soft leather tip along her back. "Good girl.

"Left, now," he ordered, moving slowly in that direction as he brushed the training rod along her hindquarters. Milly jerked at her lead, then settled once Jack stopped. They eyed each other.

"Come on, girl. Left, now." The low lull of his voice was soothing.

Milly's tail slashed the air, but she looked more uncertain than frightened…a positive sign. If Jack could make progress with her, could she return to being ridden? Roping?

Lord, Dani hoped so, but it seemed such a distant wish, one she'd already made so many times, she was afraid to dare hope. She'd tried working with Milly since the thunderstorm incident, but hadn't gotten anywhere. Many nights she'd gone to bed exhausted, fighting back tears for not being able to rehabilitate the horse with such a big heart. It brought back memories of Dolly and the crushing blame she felt when she thought of the jumping accident.

It was amazing that Jack, with his stern face and terrifying scar, was the first person Milly had responded to in a long time.

"Come, now," Jack urged again, moving close and leading her left. Milly followed, her head up now, looking jumpy but slightly calmer.

"That a girl," Jack said when she completed the circle, the approval in his voice raw and pure. It brightened the sun.

He continued applying small amounts of

pressure when she hesitated, taking it away when she complied. The white horse gradually moved a bit faster, smoother, following his directions, her ears flicking but not flat.

At last he stopped, removed the lead and held out an apple. "Good girl," he crooned, the rich timbre of his voice reassuring.

After a moment's hesitation, Milly extended her neck as far as she could without stepping a hair closer, nipped the fruit from his hand and scooted away, trotting to the opposite side of the pen, where she stared at Jack steadily as she chomped her treat.

"Nice work!" Dani called and Jack glanced up. The effect of his deep brown eyes snatched the air from her lungs and she felt light-headed at the steady power of his gaze.

"Didn't expect you here." He ambled over and leaned his wrists on the top of the fence, his strong, broad hands dangling close to her. For a moment she remembered how it'd felt to hold his hand, the pressure of his fingers against her back. Her pulse raced when he swept off his hat and smiled. It made his eyes squint like the sun was in his face.

"I wanted to give you this." She handed over his assignment sheet. "We're going to team up this week. The horses that need to be saddled are listed in their riding order. Have them in the corral at eleven."

He studied the paper and spoke without looking up. "Do stable managers lead tour groups?"

"They will to teach a new wrangler. Plus, uh, this guest can be a little difficult."

His lips twisted, his expression wry. "So you thought of me?"

She smiled. "You're difficult, so that should work."

A low chuckle emerged and she found herself leaning toward him until she caught herself. "Do you think Milly has a chance? We'll hear from Mr. Graham later today, I hope, but there's no guarantee he's going to take her."

"She's got a ways to go," he said, looking at her, his dark eyes warm. He lifted his arm, and for a second she thought he was going to touch her face, but he just ran his fingers through his short, wavy hair. "I'll keep working with her. See how it goes."

Dani backed up as he ducked between the slats and joined her. This close, the scent of him curled beneath her nose: horses and leather, clean male skin with a tinge of sweat. "That's really nice of you."

He shrugged and settled his hat back on. "She deserves another chance."

The powerful simplicity of his words rang inside her and made her think of her own past. The mistakes she'd made. If he knew about them, would he think she deserved a second chance?

She shouldn't be worked up about what he thought of her, but she was. She liked him. Maybe she had from the moment she'd stared at him down the length of her rifle and he hadn't flinched.

But given his thirst for justice, he'd never let himself have feelings for her if he knew what she'd done.

Who she was: a fugitive from justice.

And there was no way she'd let him find out...

Though the more time he spent snooping on the property, asking questions, investigating employee backgrounds, the greater the chance he'd uncover her past. The incorrect name on her Oklahoma arrest warrant meant a search using her real name shouldn't bring it up. The only other thing linking her to the bank heist was a police composite sketch and her ex, and he was safely locked up...

So no need to worry, exactly...

But she did.

She did.

"She used to be our best roper," Dani said after a moment. "We hold a rodeo twice a month and she always put on a show."

Bella and Beau appeared, capering and sneezing with excitement, as she and Jack wandered back to the main road. He slanted his gaze at her and ruffled Beau's ears. "My siblings and I used to do a bit of roping."

"Are you any good? Bella. Stop." But the shepherd only leaped at her knees harder.

A smiled meandered its way around his broad face and landed in his eyes. He pulled an apple from his pocket and winged it toward a pond, where it dropped with a splash. Joyous barks erupted and the dogs plunged out of view. "Depends on who you ask."

What was it about that confident, no-need-to-boast side of him that appealed to every last one of her feminine sensibilities? "If you're still here at the end of the week, you could ride Cher in the rodeo. Let me form my own opinion."

He stopped and turned. "I'd like to ride Milly."

He was staring at her, she could feel it, waiting for a response. How much she wanted this for Milly, a horse that, in some ways, reminded her of herself: promise derailed. "I'd like to see that."

A shuttle van filled with guests bounced by. It kicked up pebbles as it headed to the main house for check-in. Jack's arm swept around her shoulder and he scooted her to the side of the road. "I'll do my best."

She ducked her head, moved away slightly and switched subjects. "Where did you sleep last night? The wranglers said you weren't at staff quarters."

"I mentioned I wouldn't be bunking there."

"And I mentioned you needed to blend in."

"Not my strong point."

They resumed their trek. A pair of ducks, followed by their offspring, waddled in front of them, quacking to each other, until they swerved down the bank and disappeared into the swaying reeds lining a large pond. "So where did you rest?"

"Over there." He nodded at a rise topped with trees that would have given him a good view of the entire property. He took another apple from his pocket and tossed it with one hand, caught it with the other.

"Outside? Why?"

"Surveillance."

"You mean of Sam, Smiley and Tanya?"

He shrugged. "They're on my list. Either Sam or Tanya could be helping Smiley hide. Either one could lead me straight to him."

She yanked to a stop and gaped at him. "Who else? Or should I ask who *don't* you suspect?"

"That would be the quicker one to answer."

"So you believe everyone's guilty until they prove themselves innocent?"

He smoothed her bangs out of her eyes and peered down at her. "Guess I'm never disappointed that way."

"It's not all black-and-white," she insisted, thinking of her own situation, trying not to focus on the devastating effect the brush of his fingers against her temple was having on her.

"It is in my world."

"That's a pretty narrow place to live. And dark."

He stared at the mountains for a long moment. "Yes," he said quietly. "Yes, it is."

And something in his tone made her switch topics and resume walking. The apple arced overhead again.

"So are you going to sleep in the staff quarters? The other wranglers are already talking about it."

He caught the fruit and sent it up again. "Wouldn't want my snoring to keep anybody up."

"And just when I thought you couldn't be more unattractive," she joked, knowing how impossible that would be…

He stopped tossing the apple. Hurt flashed across his face, then disappeared so fast she might have imagined it…but deep down, she knew she hadn't.

"If that's all, I'll be heading up to breakfast." He refused to meet her eyes and a muscle moved in his jaw.

"Jack." She laid a hand on his tense bicep. "I'm sorry. I didn't mean…" Ugh. She needed to slap herself upside the head. How could he know how attractive she found him? That comment had been nothing but a joke. "It's just that I don't…"

She trailed off as he stopped and studied her, his level gaze rattling her as she tried again. "It's not that I don't find you…"

His lips quirked and a light appeared in his eyes.

"I mean I think you're very…"

A full smile creating deep indents in both cheeks bloomed. Her words tumbled to a halt and she glared at him. Suspicious.

"Are you laughing at me?"

He placed a hand over his heart, trapping hers with it, so that her palm rested against his chest. "Only on the inside," he said solemnly.

She yanked her hand away. "You're awful. You know that?"

"Might have heard that once or twice. Never to my face, though." He rubbed his jaw like she'd just clocked him.

"Maybe it's time you did." She whirled, fuming, and laughing...on the inside...she had to admit.

His deep chuckle floated after her as she stomped up the road to Tanya's. The excited voices of arriving guests rose and fell in the distance: kids shouting, adults calling. Trilling. Vibrating. Breaking the long silence that'd hung over the dude ranch these past eight months.

And suddenly she felt as if she was awakening, too, more alive than she'd felt in years.

Her new stable manager position. It'd be easy to believe that it'd had this effect on her, but deep down she knew something—or someone—else was responsible.

CHAPTER ELEVEN

"HOWDY, JACK!" NAN waved at him from a table beside the windows lining one of the walls in the ranch's private dining room for staffers. The thick, greasy scent of a breakfast buffet wafted in the room and a line of domed warming trays, overflowing with food, steamed at the far end. Staff sat shoulder to shoulder, chattering and laughing, at rectangular tables. Neither Sam nor Tanya were in sight. "Come join me."

He ambled over, doing his best to ignore the forks pausing in midair as he passed, the wide eyes. Some of the wranglers he'd met yesterday gave him curt nods. "Good morning, Nan. You're looking lovely."

She swatted the air and shook her head. "Don't waste your flattery on me." She shot him a though-the-lashes look. "Though it is appreciated."

He chuckled. Charmed, despite his unease at being around so many people. He'd hoped to grab something quick and head out to tack his horses. "Looks like a fine day."

"Good weather to kick off the season." Nan's white topknot bobbed as she nodded, smiling. "Diane put on quite the spread for the employees on their first day. You should grab some corn bread." She held up a golden square and the buttery smell made his stomach grumble.

"Now that I can't refuse." Suddenly the idea of sticking around gained merit.

Nan was a gold mine of information about the history of the dude ranch and its employees. He could probably learn more from listening to her than he could spending days pouring over employee records, a task high on his to-do list, and he needed help. He hadn't picked up anyone's trail as he'd finished searching the upper quadrant of the grid he'd made of the property. Something inside him screwed tighter, tighter at every minute that passed without him finding his quarry. "Can I get you anything?"

"Aren't you sweet. I'm really quite full, but since you're on your way, maybe just a little something." Her lashes fluttered. "Three pieces of bacon, a couple of sausage links and a scoop of hash browns."

"Is that all? Can't let all that food go to

waste, now," he couldn't help but add, keeping his face neutral. It'd been a long time since he'd talked for the fun of it; he'd forgotten how good it felt.

"Well…make that two scoops of hash browns!" She made a shooing motion and he joined the buffet line, beating back an impolite grin, and grabbed two plates.

A young woman, wearing the largest Stetson he'd ever seen, scooted ahead and turned. Her heavily made-up face reminded him of the ceramic dolls his mother collected, and her enormous blue eyes shone up at him, sincere and avid. No shrinking violet here. "You're our new wrangler, right?"

"Jackson Cade."

"Jori Lynn Daniels." She held out a pair of tongs, laughed, then thrust her hand out, instead. He shook it. "I'm a wrangler, too, but in the off season I'm a student at CU Boulder. Planning on being an architect."

She placed a few bacon strips on her plate and shuffled down the line. "Always knew that was what I wanted to be ever since we built this tree house that fell down on account of a tornado and broke my Barbie Jeep. I never did get another one, though I cried and cried. Maybe that's why I plan on owning a pink car someday. I'll sell Mary Kay if I have to. Hey, you ever build a tree house before?"

He felt a bit motion sick as she switched topics, and she rushed on without waiting for an answer. "They're the best places in the world to be alone and just think. The silence. I just love it." She chattered on without the least bit of irony.

After scooping up scrambled eggs, she handed him the serving spoon. "Yep. Peace and quiet—it can't be beat." She nudged a tall fellow ahead of her with a mess of hair that looked like it'd gotten into a fight with a brush and won. "Isn't that right, Blake?"

He turned and rolled his eyes at her. "Wouldn't know with you around."

"Hey," she protested, pouting. "Blake, this is Jack, our new wrangler."

"Nice to meet you." Blake flashed a peace sign, then his huge smile froze as his eyes lifted from Jori Lynn and settled on Jack's face, sticking there for a long minute before the girl cleared her throat.

"Same," Jack answered, ladling potatoes next to his bacon and eggs as well as onto the plate he was making for Nan. He turned away to hide his cheek, sparing the kid.

"Blake was at Oklahoma State, but he

dropped out like an idiot because some dumb girl broke up with him. Why do men always go for the ones who don't really want them?" She drew out the question and something seemed to pass between the youngsters, a charged silence. The young man muttered something under his breath and left the line.

"Well. Any who..." She speared a couple of sausage patties and handed over the fork. When he reached for the pan, his shirtsleeve rode up and he heard her gasp. "Hey! Nice ink." She lowered her voice and poured batter into a waffle maker. "Though we're not supposed to show them around here. The Mays are really conservative and Dani is..."

"Right here," came the spunky voice that immediately made his pulse pick up. "You were saying?"

Dani's freckled nose scrunched and for an insane moment, he wanted to dab a bit of the whipped cream sitting beside the waffle maker on its tip.

Jori Lynn waved at the steam rising off the waffle maker when she lifted its lid. "Oooh. It just got hot all up in here."

"I bet," drawled Dani, and she shot the cheeky wrangler an indulgent look as she hustled away. "Looks like you're already making friends."

"Getting my ear talked off, more like." He felt himself staring into those hazel eyes that seemed to shift and change colors every time he looked at them. One minute they were green with some brown, the next a yellow-green, then olive, then green again with bronze-gold.

"That's what makes Jori Lynn one of our best wranglers. You need to talk to people. As in more than one syllable at a time. Cough-cough." Dani slid a sausage patty atop a mountain of eggs, the only feasible spot given that every inch of her plate was already full with the most outrageous combinations. Jelly on top of bacon...?

"Right." He waited for his waffle to finish and caught her sprinkling something over her cream cheese bagel.

"Are those Froot Loops?"

"Yeah. You want some?" She grinned, un-apologetic, that brash, in-your-face attitude of hers making the tension in his shoulders un-coil, his gut warm.

"What do you recommend I put them on?" The timer dinged and he retrieved his breakfast.

"They'd make a good waffle topping," she

proclaimed in that first-testament tone of hers that made him smile.

He placed the waffle on his plate, poured syrup over it and sprinkled fruit loops on top. Warm, sweet steam puffed around him. "Never considered the combination."

"Stick with me, kid, and you'll learn lots." She twirled an imaginary moustache, the goofy gesture endearing, her shining eyes taking his breath away.

"About Froot Loops?" he repeated, skeptical, trying to keep her here, glad they'd be riding together later.

"You can never know enough about your basic breakfast cereals." She shot him a sassy grin and strode away, cutlery in hand, napkins left behind.

"Hey, uh, you done with the cereal?"

"Oh," he started, realized he'd been staring at Dani and moved off the line. "It's yours."

He watched Nan flag down Dani and the strawberry blonde slid into a seat opposite the woman. A moment later, he joined them, sitting close enough that the sides of their legs touched, knees bumping. Dani was saying something about not being able to find Tanya, and Nan looking concerned.

When she glanced over at him, the line between her brows lessened. "Oh, thank you, darlin'." Nan took the plate he slid her and tucked into the hash browns.

"Is that unusual?" He handed Dani the napkins he'd grabbed. "Shouldn't Tanya be here, cooking?"

Dani spread the paper on her lap, her movements jerky. "Sometimes she takes a break when the food comes out but I didn't see her up at her house and she's not in the kitchen."

"Never known that girl to miss a day of work." Nan fidgeted with her beaded necklace. "According to Diane, Tanya's under the weather. Sure hope she's okay."

"I hope so, too." Dani stared down at her plate. "I'll check in on her when I get back from my tour this afternoon."

Nan chewed off the end of a bacon slice, considering, then pointed the lower half at him. "So tell me a little about yourself, Jack. You look like a man of mystery and I love solving them. Always thought I would have made a good sleuth. No one ever notices the little old lady reading in the corner."

She chortled to herself and Dani laughed. He was taken by the soft roundness of her face, at the way she smiled when she liked something, with her lips just turned up at the corners, at the way she smelled, like the Christmas cookies he used to snatch as a boy, warm off the pan.

Looks were the least interesting thing about her, though. She worked hard at her job, evidenced by the customized itinerary sheet she'd passed him, one of the many he spotted other wranglers stuffing into pockets or reading as they ate breakfast. Guest preferences took top priority, but she also considered her staff and even the horses, if the specific lineup she'd given him, matching mount to rider and putting them in order, was evidence. Despite what must be a hectic first day of the season, she'd also taken time to check in on her friend and sit with Nan.

He liked Dani Crawford, a woman who could go from goofy to deadly in the blink of an eye.

Yes. He liked her a lot.

But nothing could come of those feelings, he firmly reminded himself, crushing down the happiness she gave him. What right did he have to one moment of it with Jesse gone?

"Not much to tell." He was always uncomfortable at recounting his life, wondering how to begin a story without a happy ending.

"Oh, Jack's being modest." Dani slapped him

on the arm. "He's a juggler. You should see him with apples, though I'd like to see what he could do with bigger fruits… Pineapples? Watermelons? Pomegranates?" She tapped her chin.

Nan lowered her glass of orange juice. "You mean professionally?"

"I think it's more of a hobby." Dani ignored the dirty look he shot her, shrugged, and bit into a peach. She was so pretty with her hair pulled up in a high ponytail that swung in a curl at her shoulder blades. "And he's also a roper. He's working with Milly and planning to ride her in the show this week if Mr. Graham doesn't take her."

"Well, now, that's a thing." Nan shot him an approving look that reminded him of how his mother used to look at him—before. He glanced down fast, his throat swelling. "I'm sure Larry and Diane will be appreciative, since I overheard Mr. Graham's call this morning. Milly doesn't have another home to go to. And since she's too old to be bred, the Mays might have to make a tough call…" Nan sniffled and looked away.

"No!" Dani frowned and she smacked the side of her fist on the table, making her plate jump.

He steadied her tipping cup of juice. "I'll do my best to make sure that doesn't happen."

Dani brought up her napkin and pressed it to her eyes, nodding, unable to speak, it seemed. The need to save Milly, for the horse's sake, and Dani's, powered through him.

Nan reached across the table and patted Dani's arm. "See? Jack will take care of it."

"Thank you, Jack," Dani said, then lowered the napkin, her wobbly smile plucking at his heart.

He forced his eyes away from her. "Have you worked here a long time?" He cut into his waffle and lifted a dripping mouthful, Froot Loops sliding on top. The sweeter-than-sweet bite made his back teeth ache, but he forced it down when Dani hit him with an I-dare-you stare.

"All my life." Nan nibbled on a corn bread slice, her expression far away. "My mother got into trouble, as they used to say in the day, and Larry's parents were kind enough to take her on. Of course, it didn't hurt that they'd just lost their cook and my mama made the best green chili this side of the Mexican border. I'll make it for you one of these days when my arthritis isn't bothering."

"That'd be kind of you, though I wouldn't want you to go to any trouble." Jack swallowed another bite of the cereal-covered waffles and followed it, fast, with a sausage chaser. It really was awful, but with Dani watching, he wouldn't wimp out.

"No trouble at all," promised Nan.

"The Mays sound like good people to work for."

"Oh, yes. We've got a lot of return employees every season. Why, Smiley's uncle, William, he worked here for over forty years."

At the name, Jack perked up and Dani leaned forward. "I never knew that," she said.

"Uh-huh. William was the salt of the earth. Smiley's parents never could control him, or so they said, so they sent their son up here every summer to get him out in the fresh air." She put a hand to the side of her mouth and lowered her voice. "Or to get him out of their hair. Anyways, he seemed happy enough, and Larry and Diane were glad for Ben to have a playmate. I guess they were a pair."

"Well. We'd better get going," Dani said as she stood. "But we'll stop by and catch up again soon, okay?"

"Y'all have a good day." Nan trotted out a smile and Jack returned it. He pushed back his chair and hustled after Dani.

He caught up to her at the duck pond.

"You'll need to cover up that tattoo," she

said out of the side of her mouth, her eyes straight ahead, hair swinging as she walked.

The memory of his brother shot him straight in the chest, the way it should, when he looked at it. "You mentioned that."

"And you haven't complied."

He rolled down his plaid shirtsleeve. "Anything else, ma'am?" he asked.

Her assessing eyes ran over him and every fiber of his nervous system leaped awake.

"You could use a haircut."

He couldn't resist pushing back the bangs that hid too much of her eyes. "So could you."

She snorted as pink rose in her cheeks. "Are you ready for today? We're heading to a more remote part of the property and into the Pike National Forest. We sometimes encounter park visitors or workers, so there's no telling who we might see."

"I intend on scouting for evidence of Smiley as we ride. It'll give me a starting point for my search this afternoon."

She studied him for a long moment and nodded slowly, as if coming to some weighty decision. "I'll be on the lookout." The corners of her lips twitched when his mouth dropped open.

After a few steps ahead, she turned, adding over her shoulder, "Partner."

CHAPTER TWELVE

"THE PEAK TO your right is Shawnee Mountain, the tallest mountain in the Front Range at 1,350 feet," Dani narrated for the tour group behind her a half hour later.

Her back swayed as Storm rounded a turn, the familiar rocking motion and the speech she used on the North Fork trail returning to her like old friends. If only the jitters that'd seized her after her impulsive decision to tell Jack she'd be his partner would disappear.

Where had that impulse come from?

She was the last person who should help him. Tanya and Smiley were her friends. Plus, she had a ton of work to do, not to mention the hypocrisy of a wanted woman helping to search for a man running from the law.

But she couldn't deny how much she enjoyed having him around.

Scrub brush and saplings broke up the rocky outcropping to her left. Rosettes of yucca spiked beside indigo larkspur and wild primroses, whose pink petals surrounded yellow eyes. The soft, fresh air carried a hint of evergreen and her lungs expanded farther and farther.

If she could inhale a perfect weather day like this, she would, to steady her jumpy nerves. Instead, she was conscious of Jack, riding behind the tour group, and the decision to join forces.

The intimacy that created.

She breathed deeply again, wishing the fresh-scrubbed air would cleanse the stain of her past, a mark she'd grown used to until Jack's glaring presence spotlighted it again.

Now she couldn't stop seeing the imprint of her old ways. Could her impromptu offer to be his partner in crime fighting come from a need for redemption? A wish to erase that blemish at last? Maybe. But most important, she needed to help him finish his business here, to get rid of him, despite her growing feelings.

"We've heard all this before," complained Mr. Clark, who'd been in a bad mood since she'd told him that she and Jack, rather than Smiley, would take him fly-fishing later this week. "What else is there?"

She mentally counted backward from ten.

What did he expect after visiting here, at the exact same time, for so many years? Maybe they should have arranged for a meteor strike to shake things up. Then she could have said, "If you keep your eyes open folks, you'll see the large gaping hole where western Colorado used to be."

Ugh.

"Well. We're coming on a great view of the Continental Divide." The horses clomped onto an arched wooden foot bridge over a creek off the north fork of the South Platt River.

"Cool! I want to swim. I want to swim!" hollered Mr. Clark's eight-year-old son, Dakota.

She twisted around in her seat and her breath caught when the child leaned sideways out of his saddle. His otherwise Zen quarter horse, a large, placid animal named Tiny who was extremely good with kids—usually—sidestepped, the whites of his eyes showing.

"Straight in the saddle," barked Jack, and the boy snapped upright.

Phew. If Mr. Clark was difficult, his kids were downright impossible. His older girl, Cheyenne, used to be a terror. Now a teenager, she'd sunk into a silent sulk that closely resembled a catatonic state.

At the crest of an incline, Dani pulled up

Storm at a wider part of the trail and waited for the group to catch up. "The spectacular landscape of this forest was shaped by continental and alpine glaciers, and it's a great place to take some pictures."

"Are you kidding?" She turned to see a frowning Mr. Clark. He had close-set, sunken eyes, a blond comb-over and a broad face the color of an artificial tan left on ten minutes too long. "We've got dozens of these pictures."

"Reginald." His wife spoke up, a bone-thin woman with an immobile face. Her skin was so tight she looked like she'd been shrink-wrapped.

"What?" When he gestured, a gold watch flashed on his wrist. "I'm paying for this. I've got rights!"

To be verbally abusive? Apparently that's what he thought, since his wife subsided and Dani's pinned-on smile began to feel maniacal. Since her spontaneous promise to Jack, she'd found it hard to concentrate and project an easygoing, cheerful, tour-guide persona.

"Happy to escort you back to the ranch, Mr. Clark," Jack drawled, the firmness in his voice making the offer sound more like a threat.

Everyone turned to look in his direction, and even Cheyenne stopped playing with the ends of her hair.

"Well, no. This is what I came for," sputtered Mr. Clark. His mount, Reba, bobbed her head, and her tail flicked at the gathering flies.

"Good to hear," Jack said. His warm brown eyes clamped on hers and she returned his quick smile.

"How much longer do we have to do this?" griped Dakota. He scratched at a scab on his knee until a trickle of blood oozed from it. To Dani's dismay, Mr. and Mrs. Clark acted as though they didn't notice.

"We're going to stop in a few minutes for our picnic lunch," she said smoothly, reaching behind her for a Band-Aid in her pack and passing it to Mr. Clark. He looked at it, shrugged and handed it over to his wife, who shoved it in her pocket.

Okay, then.

She squeezed her knees and urged Storm forward.

"What are we eating?" whined Dakota. "Because—"

"Bugs," Jack interrupted, and she smiled

to herself at his shut-it-down tone. The kid quieted. Then laughed.

"Bugs, huh? Like ants? I saw once on TV that they dipped them in chocolate. Hey this could be like *Survivor*. Can I vote Dad out of the tribe?"

"Hush, Dakota," murmured Mrs. Clark halfheartedly, her voice faint, as though she was phoning it in. Long distance. Overseas, even.

"Or maybe we can pretend we're the guy on that show *Wild*," came Dakota's megaphone voice, so loud it roused roosting mourning doves. "That's a cool show."

"Nature sucks," Cheyenne snapped with the absolute authority only teens could muster about huge, sweeping topics they knew little about.

"Did you know that if you lick an aspen leaf it'll stick to your face?" she heard Jack say.

Dani's mouth dropped open. Where was her monosyllabic midnight cowboy? Who was this sincere, knowledgeable man, at ease in the saddle and with others?

She heard a whinny that sounded like Tiny and peeked over her shoulder to see Dakota yanking on the reins as he bounced in his saddle, a sweeping vista of the Platt River valley below. "I want to try that."

"Ease up, bud," Jack said. Then, "If you peel off ponderosa pine bark, it smells like butterscotch."

"Butterscotch is pretty cool," muttered Cheyenne.

"Oh!" hollered Dakota. "Please can we stop? Please!"

"We're coming up on our picnic spot in a few minutes." She turned in the saddle and met Jack's eyes. Some unspoken communication, an understanding, a camaraderie, flickered between them, subtle but strong.

Partners.

The horses kicked up small stones and dirt clouds as the path dipped downward. Sun rays spiraled through the green canopy overhead that kept them cool on such a bright day.

"We're entering the Pike National Forest, which borders on the ranch and Highway 67."

She pointed to a large, log-hewn cabin with a gift shop sign hanging from hinges beside its green door. "The cabin you see there was owned by Samuel Pike, who donated a great deal of the acreage that is now protected forest. This preserve serves as a refuge for mule deer, mountain lions, elk, black bears, prairie rattlesnakes and, at higher elevations, big horn sheep and mountain goats."

"Heard all that before," complained Mr. Clark, and Dani pressed her lips together for fear her mutinous thoughts would tumble right out of them. He acted like he hated this spot. Given all of his money, why did he come here?

"And someone's got to get Smiley for me," her cantankerous guest continued. "We have an agreement to meet this time every year. I expected to see him."

"What kind of agreement?" Jack asked, his tone too casual to her ear.

"It's a…a…business arrangement. Services. You know."

"Just fishing?" Jack asked, his tone bland.

"Well. What else would it be?" Mr. Clark blustered, and then an awkward silence descended. Hoof beats and birdcalls rose in the sudden quiet. Why did he sound so defensive? Could Mr. Clark have something to do with Smiley? Was he the person Jack suspected Smiley had come to meet?

Dani shook the ridiculous thought away. Now she sounded as suspicious as Jack. Mr. Clark might be a pain in the butt, a rich and entitled one, but certainly not the criminal type.

The next thought stopped her cold. She hadn't thought that about Kevin, or Tanya, either. And Tanya had looked guilty of something. Tonight she would speak to her friend alone and get to the bottom of it, for Tanya's sake and for Jack's...and her own.

"I want to do something fun!" the boy complained again.

No one answered.

"Let's pull up here for a moment," Jack called, and she turned to shoot him a puzzled look before bringing Storm to a stop beside a clump of aspens in a small clearing.

She dismounted, let Storm loose since it was frowned upon to tie up horses in the national forest and helped Dakota off Tiny, who appeared slightly spooked, given the battering he'd been getting on this ride.

Cheyenne slid off her horse in a boneless move and slumped against a large boulder jutting from the ground, her cell phone already in hand, her face covered by her tangle of long hair as she jabbed at the screen. She stopped then held the phone aloft in search of the ever elusive signal.

Overhead, eagles rode air currents, and a squirrel froze in place a few yards away. Bees hovered over a patch of fragrant mouse-eared chickweed.

Mr. Clark jumped down from his horse, making it sidestep, and he held out a hand to his wife, who sort of tumbled off her mount. Her designer sunglasses flew and she jerked out of his arms to grab them. She was relieved when the Clarks disappeared from view, arguing, oblivious, like the rest of the family, to the natural wonders surrounding them.

Jack held his palm against the dry bark of one of the aspens, then strode back to Pokey. Dakota grew silent and even Cheyenne thrust her cell in her pocket and watched. Jack pressed his hand against Pokey's back end. When Jack stepped back, a chalky white outline of his hand stood out on the horse's buff coat.

"Wow!" Dakota jumped up and down and raced to an aspen. He pressed his hand against it and bolted straight at Tiny, whose ears flattened. Jack caught him neatly around the waist, checking his forward momentum by sweeping him off his feet so that he hung in midair, arms outstretched.

"Slow and easy around horses, squirt," Jack said with warm humor and patience. He was good with kids. He set the boy back down and they walked together, sedately, up to Tiny. A squall of affection erupted inside her at the endearing sight.

A few minutes later, Mr. and Mrs. Clark still hadn't returned from their private talk. Handprints covered the horses and Cheyenne stood a bit away, inhaling a piece of ponderosa pine bark, her eyes half-closed as she said, "Butterscotch."

An aspen leaf stuck to Dakota's face and he slapped another onto Jack's cheek as the man sat patiently, tolerating the assault.

"Are you a bad guy?" asked the boy, peeling back one of the leaves and touching Jack's scar.

He studied his hands a moment, and her chest tightened at the way this question seemed to shake him. "Maybe," he said, without looking up. "I haven't always done good."

The boy sighed and rested his head on Jack's shoulder. "Me, neither. Does that mean I'm bad?"

Jack seemed to have trouble speaking, and when his voice emerged, it sounded hoarse. "No. No, it doesn't."

What bad things had Jack done? Did he have regrets, like she did? Something had propelled him from ranch owner to bounty hunter and she burned to know the reason. She sensed a dark story, and a sudden wish to share her own with him rose.

But she couldn't trust him. Not a man who saw things in black-and-white. His life's mission revolved around ensuring others faced judgment.

He'd never understand.

"I don't think you're bad, either." Dakota clambered atop a boulder and stuck a fist in the air, the other on his cocked hip. "You're one of the good guys!"

Jack's head still hung but his eyes rose. "How do you know?" His strangled words pressed on her heart. How often had she asked this question of herself?

Every day.

"'Cause I can tell!" Then, with the lightning quick leaps only kids can make, Dakota hurtled off the rock and shouted, "Can we eat? I want peanut butter and jelly."

Jack stood. "Back on the horses, then."

To her amazement, both children hustled to their mounts, checking for Jack's approving nod, as if they wanted to impress him. She shared the sentiment, not that a bounty hunter would ever look favorably on an on-the-lam bank robbery getaway driver.

Nope.

Better to keep these growing feelings to herself.

She called for the Clarks, got them situated and they took off again, the tour going smoothly, thanks to Jack.

"You'll see another of the old copper mine shafts ahead." Dani returned to narrating. "The mines in this area…"

"I want copper!" exclaimed Dakota.

Dani and Storm passed a bush and a long dark stick, poking through the bottom branches, caught her eye. Storm's ears shot up, then lay flat as she hesitated, assessing the threat, breaking her gait slightly then resuming when Dani clucked to her, reassuring her that it wasn't a rattler.

"Cool! A snake!" Dakota's exclamation behind her was followed by a horse's whinny. In a flash of dark brown, Tiny bolted, spooked by the same stick that'd frightened Storm, taking the boy with him. They disappeared down a steep ravine. She hadn't even known the drop-off existed this close to the seldom-used trail. Her heart leaped in her throat.

A loud "Hyah!" sounded and Jack sped by, leaning low, his head against Pokey's neck.

They flew down the embankment and vanished.

"Dakota!" Mrs. Clark cried, twisting in her saddle. "Dakota!"

The horses sidestepped, still spooked by the noise, and Dani jumped off Storm and moved between the animals, making reassuring sounds, settling them before they had another runaway.

"Jack will get him," she said over the loud heartbeat drumming in her ears, feeling that it was true. Something about his steady, quiet confidence, his skill with animals and people, the way he made her feel safe, filled her with certainty that he'd protect the boy. "No harm will come to him."

Mr. Clark turned the shade of a newly unearthed beet. "And if anything does, I'll sue..."

His wife collapsed in his arms. "Dakota," she sobbed.

Cheyenne turned in a circle and looked lost until Dani put an arm around her and pulled her close. "Is Dakota going to be okay?"

"Yes. Jack will get him."

And her words seemed to summon the bounty hunter, who emerged trotting Pokey over the ridge line, leading Tiny, Dakota pale

and shaken in his arms but otherwise un-
harmed.

After a flurry of hugs and scolding from
the Clarks, Dakota turned to Jack, his eyes
shining. "See? I knew you were a good guy."

Jack ruffled the kid's hair and she looked
up at the warmth in his face and smiled at
him.

Her midnight cowboy was a very good guy.

Did she dare give in to the feelings? Trust
in her wiser—she hoped—instincts after all?

CHAPTER THIRTEEN

DANI KNOCKED ON Tanya's front door a few hours later. Again. Worry rose in her past the high-water mark.

Tanya could not fall prey to the same kind of guy Dani had, or make poor decisions that'd haunt her the rest of her life. Dani had been so determined not to think about her past, about Kevin, that maybe she'd missed the signs that her friend was in a similar situation.

Jack's heroic actions had inspired her, and she understood she needed to make up for her mistakes. And that included helping Tanya.

Please. Answer the door...

"Tanya? It's Dani. Can I come in?" She raised her hand a fourth time, then lowered it when her friend appeared in the entrance. Her dark hair tumbled in messy waves around her flushed cheeks and smudges of mascara rimmed her lower eyelids. In an instant, relief rushed through Dani. Tanya was okay. Safe.

"Hey, Dani." Tanya lips twitched into a scant smile. "How are you?"

"Good, but I'm worried about you, girl." She touched Tanya's cold wrist.

"How's everything?" Tanya repeated, louder and her eyelid twitched.

"Good," Dani repeated, and this time Tanya nodded, though her eyes darted every which way. "I didn't see you at work or at the square dance." Dani's voice was breathy. She closed her eyes for a moment, gathering herself. "Heard you were under the weather."

A coughing fit erupted behind Tanya. She glanced over her shoulder and Dani peeked, too, spying a familiar, fair-haired, mustached man, seated on the couch, waving cigar smoke from his face.

Smiley!

Emotions twisted through her. Elation at seeing her old friend okay and well. Anger that he'd been hiding out and forced Tanya to lie for him. Fear—she had to admit it—that maybe he was caught up in something bigger than a drug bust. She couldn't wrap her head around a double homicide.

"Hey, Smiley!"

He pressed his hand on the plump cushions and leveraged himself to his feet, moving like every bone in his body ached. "Come on in, Dani. Shut the door behind her, darlin'." He clamped a cigar in his mouth and waved Dani closer.

Tanya hustled to obey. The curtains were closed against the bright daylight while a weatherman warned about a band of storms ahead this week. A coffeemaker sputtered in the kitchen.

Her eyes swerved between Tanya, who fidgeted with her leather bracelets, and Smiley, who leaned on one leg, then the other, grimacing.

A strange feeling of disorientation took hold, as if she'd landed in some alternate universe with complete strangers who only resembled her friends.

"You are a sight for sore eyes, Dani. How've you been?" Mittens and a cloud of cherry-scented cigar smoke trailed Smiley as he came in for a hug then guided her to an armchair.

A part of her recoiled at his touch, but another part, the one that knew him as her friend, hugged him back. Who was he? Drug dealer? Murderer? Neither? She felt the same stomach-dropping sensation she got whenever she rode the county fair's Freefall ride. She itched to grab the cell phone in her pocket and call Jack but didn't want to make any suspicious moves.

She raised her chin, met Smiley's stare head-on. Smiled. Or made her best attempt. "It's good to see you, Smiley. Been wondering where you were at."

He stepped back and cocked his head. It was a shade too big for his narrow shoulders, Dani had always thought, his eyes a smidge too small for his nose. "I've been around."

She forced a confused expression, which wasn't exactly hard to do, considering... "Huh. Well. Then Larry and Diane were right not to fill your position yet. They said there must have been a mix-up." She nearly bit her lying tongue in half.

Smiley and Tanya exchanged a long look and her breath caught. Had she poured it on too thick? Tanya knew her better than anyone.

Still. This was for Tanya. She had to make sure her friend was okay.

A tense moment passed as the coffee machine dripped into silence. "How about a cup of joe?" he suggested. Then, before she could answer, he said, "Tanya, will you fix us up?"

Her friend scurried into the kitchen, leaving them alone.

Smiley grabbed hold of the back of the

couch and lowered himself, wincing. Had he gotten beaten up by the guy who'd been looking for him? Searching for "it," whatever that was…

"So. You haven't heard anything?"

She assumed her most concerned look, which, again, wasn't hard to do since she was worried. Truth time. Or some of it. "About your arrest? Oh. Thank you, sweetie." She accepted the offered mug and blew on the rising steam before sipping. Half coffee, half cream. No sugar. Tanya remembered.

The color had leached out of Smiley's cheeks, leaving him a putty color. "That's a miscarriage of justice right there."

She set down her mug. Leaned forward. Went for her Daytime Emmy award. "Well, of course it is. You? Drugs?"

She'd never suspected Kevin capable of robbery, either.

Smiley ran a hand over his fair hair, the shade so light it made him look bald. "Glad you see it that way. So Larry and Diane understand?"

"I'm sure they'd like to hear your side of things." She crossed her ankles beneath the coffee table and nearly felt her nose to see if it was growing.

"That's why I've been hiding out. Been too embarrassed to see them since I didn't think they'd believe me." His wet brown eyes rose, and the deep sadness in them made her question the situation all over again, her stomach sick over the twists and turns her mind took.

"When's your trial?"

His cigar trembled as he brought it to his mouth. After a couple of puffs, he said, "A month ago."

A crash sounded and Dani glanced over to see Tanya staring at a decorative table she'd knocked over, a yellow vase in pieces on the floor. A jar candle rolled away.

"I've been telling him to turn himself in," Tanya insisted as she rushed into the kitchen.

"And why haven't you?" If Smiley wasn't guilty or caught up in a bigger crime, then there had to be a good explanation.

"Because I did have the drugs."

"What?" Dani gasped. Did a guilty man confess to his crimes voluntarily?

And you haven't confessed, either, or *turned yourself in*, piped up the small voice that been growing louder with Jack around. Surely if she settled Smiley and Tanya's situation, she would have repaid her karmic debt.

"I know. I know," Tanya said, returning

with a broom and dustpan. "How many times have I told you not to do your cousin any favors, Smiley...huh?" She swept the shattered pottery with quick whisks.

Smiley bowed his head and spoke to the hands clasped on his jittering knees. "I should never have agreed to deliver that package without checking."

"Your cousin's trouble." Tanya frowned at Smiley and headed back to the kitchen. She hunched so that the vertebrae in her back poked through her thin T-shirt.

"What's his name?" Dani set down her mug before she dropped it. "Have I met him?"

"He's been in and out of juvie and jail since we were kids. My parents didn't want me hanging around that side of the family so they sent me up here for the summers. I never believed them, but I do now." Smiley puffed his cigar, blowing rings.

Doubt seeded itself in her mind. Spread its roots. Much of his story matched Nan's account of Smiley's childhood spent here at the ranch. Could this all be a mix-up?

"Told you to stay away from him," Tanya hollered, then returned with a plate of chocolate chip cookies.

Smiley picked up a treat, studied it, then set

it down again. He reached over and rubbed Tanya's knee. "They look good, darlin', but I ain't hungry."

"You've hardly eaten." Tanya's voice rose and she handed him back the cookie. "You're making yourself sick over this."

Obliging, Smiley bit into the cookie and chewed as if he'd bitten into wood. "Can't sleep, either." His eyes appealed to Dani and a flutter of sympathy went out to him. She knew what it was like to be framed. Hadn't she felt justified in running? If Smiley was telling the truth, then he wasn't any worse than she was. The only difference: he'd been caught.

Did that make a difference?

"I'm so sorry, Smiley." Dani got to her feet, eager to find Jack so he could make sense of this. "What are you going to do?"

"He's going to turn himself in. Tonight."

A stream of smoke curled from his nose and mouth. He set the cigar in the ashtray. "Or first thing in the morning. Tanya's finally talked sense into me. Guess I just panicked."

Impulsively, Dani leaned down and kissed his cheek, then Tanya's. "You're doing the right thing and this will all get straightened out. I'm here if you need me, okay?"

Hypocrite. Hypocrite. Hypocrite.

She'd never been brave enough to face the music head-on and, strangely, a part of her envied Smiley. Hopefully, he wouldn't have jail time once he explained everything and would be a free man without jumping at shadows as she had all these years.

"Thanks, Dani." Smiley picked up the remote and clicked to a baseball game. "Hopefully, I'll see you soon."

Tanya walked her down the front steps then stopped. Her thin eyebrows met over her nose. "He's a good man, Dani. I would have told you about this before, but...well. Please forgive me."

A maintenance man peering under a nearby gator's hood caught Dani's eye. She stepped closer and lowered her voice. "It's not for me to forgive. But you shouldn't have been hiding him. I don't want you getting into trouble."

Tanya nodded, but her mouth wobbled. She'd chewed off most of her lipstick, Dani noticed. "I love him, Dani. When he showed up looking wild, said he'd been sleeping outside for fear of getting caught, my heart went out to him. Then that cousin of his started calling." Tanya gripped Dani's elbow. "Once he turns himself in, we'll set it to rights."

Dani pulled Tanya in for a hug and sighed at her softie of a friend. "Yes. And you know I'm here for you."

"Thank you, Dani," Tanya whispered. "I'll find you when I get back from turning him in and let you know how it went."

They pulled back, squeezed each other's hands, then let them drop. "Sounds good. Hang in there, sweetie."

Tanya climbed the stairs and turned. "Don't have a choice, now, do I?"

Dani stared at the shut door for a moment, her faith in her friends fading slightly, doubts returning.

Tanya said Smiley was reporting tonight or in the morning.

But what if he didn't? He could be leading a double life—like she was—and hurting Tanya in the process.

There was only one thing to do.

Traitor.

Squashing her guilt, she pulled out her cell phone once she'd walked out of sight. A frustrated noise escaped her when she failed to get a signal.

Jack.

He had to grab Smiley in case he changed his mind.

As hard as it was to reconcile, the man she called friend might be someone else entirely. A dangerous person.

Maybe even a murderer.

JACK BREATHED IN the aromatic scent of sagebrush, the thick sugary pine, aware of every breath he took as he headed down a hill to the dude ranch. It was a warm, windless night and the forest was still and lonely. He could taste the sweetness of the spring air on his tongue and the bitterness of fruitless hours spent searching and finding nothing.

At first he'd been excited to catch the trail left by a guy he'd spotted in the woods earlier, when he'd ridden after Dakota. The man resembled Sam Perkins in size and coloring, but he hadn't gotten close enough to positively identify him. After the tour, he rode back, hoping it'd lead him to another campsite, or better yet his bounty, but he'd come up empty. The guy's tracks, similar in size but not the same shape boot as the previous prints, had appeared with someone else's beside a fishing spot, then vanished again.

Another false lead when he couldn't afford even one. He'd already spent more time on this bounty than any other to date and he suspected the cause.

Dani.

She teased, irked and challenged, keeping him off-balance. He wanted to stop thinking about her so much, but the more he thought about that, the more he thought about her. A vicious cycle that kept going round and round, too fast for him to jump off.

While riding on the tour earlier, he'd struggled to keep his focus on the surrounding brush, his eyes straying to her bright face, his ears tuned in to her soft belly laugh that yanked a chuckle out of him every time.

Enough.

No more mooning over his charming "partner." His brother's killers, and the redemption he sought, could be within his grasp and he needed to let go of Dani if he had any chance of catching it.

A few more steps and he emerged from the forest onto the back of the Mays' property. Only the first stars hung faint and distant in the darkening sky, and rose-bottomed clouds on the horizon echoed the recent sunset. The distant sounds of the outdoor barbecue mingled in the smoke-tinged air.

"Jack?" Larry's silhouette appeared in the

doorway of the main house and he jogged down the front steps. "The sheriff called for you earlier. Said he's been trying to reach you on your cell."

Jack pulled out his phone and scrolled. "It's not getting a signal. Would you mind if I called him back on your phone?"

"No, of course not." Larry smiled broadly and ushered Jack inside. "Heard about what happened on the trail with the Clarks today. Good work saving that boy."

"I was in the right place at the right time." He doffed his hat and followed the older man.

"Mr. Clark is one of our most demanding clients. And he tends to like causing trouble." Larry pointed at a strip of wood with a row of hooks. "You can leave your hat there."

Jack hung his Stetson and turned. "What kind of trouble?"

"Heard he throws his weight around in Denver. Has his fingers in lots of pies."

"As in illegal activities?" Jack asked. Bella appeared, followed by Beau, and their nails scratched and skittered against the wood floor, tapping out a frantic rhythm in time to their beating tails.

"There are rumors."

They passed through the kitchen and entered a dim hall as Jack turned that over. Hit men had killed the Denver couple, a professional job without a clear motive.

"He told me he requests Smiley every year." Bella appeared and swooshed through the entrance ahead of the humans. Jack flicked on the light switch. "So he would have been counting on seeing Smiley."

Larry scratched the back of his head and completely ignored the rushing canines, who stuck their noses in potted plants and began digging. "You think he'd planned to meet with Smiley for something beyond fishing?"

"Not sure what to think, but it's worth considering."

"Suppose it is. You're a good man to have around, Jack."

The weight of Larry's appreciation was suddenly too much and Jack looked away. Not everyone in his own family would agree with the dude ranch owner's sentiment. There'd been a time when he'd been less of an asset. Much less.

"So how are things going?" Larry pulled his pets from the plants and they flopped to the floor, draping themselves over his boots.

Jack leaned against a filing cabinet.

"Followed a fellow that resembled Sam

Perkins up to Eagle Rock then down to the ravine on the other side. I'd spotted him off trail earlier."

Larry nodded. "That is a popular fishing spot, and if Sam finished his duties, I wouldn't be surprised if he'd headed there. Although...we always make the joke that it'd be the perfect place to dump a body."

Jack pushed away from the cabinets and straightened. "Why's that?"

"It's so deep, some claim it's bottomless."

"Good to know."

"Well, I should head back to the barbecue." The dogs bounded to their feet and followed Larry to the doorway. "How about I bring you back a plate?"

"That'd be nice, thanks."

Alone, he sat at the desk and dialed Lance.

"Covington."

"Heard you were looking for me."

"Glad you called." Some kind of timer dinged on Lance's end. "Did that background check you requested yesterday on Sam Perkins."

Jack placed his elbows on the stacks of envelopes littering the desktop. "What do you have?"

"Nothing. He's clean. Owns a registered

9mm and has a concealed handgun permit. As long as it's not loaded, he's not breaking any laws. No alias. Not Everett Ridland...not that I can prove, anyway."

Jack's molars clenched. His best lead shot down today and none going forward. "No prior arrests? Convictions?"

"Nope. Son of a—" Muted swearing came through the phone. Then, "Someday I'm going to arrest whoever makes these TV dinners. Temperatures this hot are a felony manslaughter waiting to happen."

Jack angled in the flex-back office chair, waiting. Lance and his feud with packaged meals was too long-lived to raise an eyebrow at.

"Anyway," continued Lance. "He might have been an idiot, but we can't hang him for being a jerk. If we did, we'd have to string up half the state."

A short bark of laughter escaped Jack. "Okay, then. I'll move him down the list, but he's acting suspicious so I'll still keep my eye on him." He thought of the two men who'd been seen with his brother. Sam was the right height, build, and with his hood hiding most of his face that dark night...he couldn't rule him out.

"Good." More chewing, then, "If someone

up there's helping Smiley, he might have also assisted him in the double homicide. Explore those leads when you can."

"Right. So how are things going on your end? You got anything that could help me here?"

"Not much," Lance said, his voice clear again. "Got the Phillips' credit card reports in. No strange transactions, though one looks a little off."

"How so?"

"They bought a couple of tickets to Madagascar for another couple. I'll know more when I check the flight manifest and see if I can track those two down. If it's somehow connected to Smiley, I'll let you know. Oh. And I, uh, heard from James."

Jack pinched the bridge of his nose and felt a headache throb at his temples as he thought of the second oldest brother in his family.

"You there?" Lance asked.

"Yup."

"They're wanting to know if you're coming home for the reunion."

"You didn't give them my answer the first time?"

"Jack. We're celebrating your ranch's one

hundred and fiftieth anniversary. You should be there."

"So should Jesse. Night, Lance."

Going out into the cool night again, he climbed the incline he'd camped out on last night, unfurled the sleeping bag he'd left wedged between a large branch and the trunk of a juniper and stretched out, his fingers laced behind his head.

Dani.

He needed to be objective about her. To-morrow, after he'd completed more of his grid search for Smiley and a possible accomplice, he'd see what she had to say about Tanya. Other than that, he'd keep his distance. Focus his attention where it belonged: on catching Smiley and anyone who'd lead him to his bounty. Including Sam.

He stared into the night, lying under the fir tree, under the few stars visible in a cloud-ing sky, on the green grass, in the world… wondering what configuration the stars would have to take for him to bring this all together.

CHAPTER FOURTEEN

DANI CLIMBED THE small hill to Jack's lookout for the third time that night. The stars and moon were mostly hidden by a growing number of scuttling clouds and she felt like she was swimming in darkness, her body breaking the air as if it were water.

When her foot slid on the nylon shell of a sleeping bag, she peered into the gloom. He'd come back; but where was he? Had he encountered trouble on his scouting? Was he hurt? An unfamiliar panic rose in her, her thoughts so loud she felt as though her head might explode.

A twig snapped underfoot as she paced forward. Then the moon broke free of its cover and she spotted him. His tall shape was blacker than the air; it seemed to hold all of the light and give none of it away. Relief weakened her joints. Her knees dipped slightly.

"Did you speak to Tanya?" he asked before

turning, startling her, the rich timbre of his voice melting into the warm evening.

Faint moonlight and shadows played on his face and pooled along the ridge of his scar, making him look more like a desperado than ever. Strange that, despite this, she felt protected at the sight of him. Less anxious. How much had changed since their first encounter.

"Smiley's there." She bit back the sense of betrayal, knowing she was doing the right thing. At least it'd guarantee Tanya stayed safe.

In two strides, Jack reached her. "You saw him."

"I spoke to him four hours ago and I've been calling you ever since but there's no signal. Tanya's convinced him to turn himself in."

He blew out a breath. "He confessed to the drug possession charge?"

"He said he was carrying a package for his cousin."

"That's convenient." Jack rolled up his gear and stashed it in a tree. "I'll make sure he explains that to the judge. Thank you."

Her stomach fluttered at his appreciative look, then he strode down the hill. When she hustled after him, he stopped at the base.

"What are you doing?"

"Going with you."

"Sorry, sweetheart, it's too dangerous."

She spotted the faint outline of his Glock beneath his shirt. What if Smiley was armed and panicked? He could resist being brought in despite his assurances. A chill ran through her as she imagined Tanya caught in the middle of a standoff with Jack, a dangerous-looking man whose actions, she didn't doubt, more than backed up his lethal appearance.

"Tanya's there."

"Dani, please go back to your room."

"Not unless it's to grab my rifle."

"I won't put you in jeopardy."

She returned his steady gaze and planted her feet, bracing. "I'm not taking a chance that anything happens to Tanya, *partner*."

One side of his mouth hitched. "What are the chances of you changing your mind?"

"Not even your Glock could do much persuading."

"You don't scare easy," he said quietly, reaching out to straighten her collar. A gentleness flowed from Jack's eyes and hung there a moment.

"And I don't back down." She nodded and

he nodded back; her heart tumbled at his lop-sided smile.

"That is one of your more irritating habits."

"I aim to please." His deep chuckle warmed her through and they walked the rest of the way to Tanya's house in an expectant silence that seemed to swell the air around them.

Moments later they reached Tanya's door and Jack knocked.

Nothing.

Dani cupped her hands around her eyes and peered in the window. Through a slit in the curtains, she saw only darkness and no movement.

"Do you think she's home and not answering the door?"

Dani glanced sideways at the driveway. "Her car's gone. They must have headed to the sheriff's office."

Jack banged on the door with the side of his hand. Somewhere in the distance, Bella and Beau barked.

"Do you have to do that so loudly?"

"It's called a police knock because it's meant to wake the dead."

"Tanya's not dead," she said, fear gathering her lungs in a bundle and squeezing. Her mind flashed to Tanya insisting Smiley was a good man. Had he followed through on his promise or had something happened to her friend?

"Let's see if the back door is open."

They headed around the house and tried the handle. Locked.

Jack pounded on the door again.

"Look. Window's open." She pointed to a small window that she knew led into Tanya's bathroom.

"Too small."

"Not for me." She hauled an empty paint bucket over and turned it upside down.

"Dani. No."

"I wasn't asking permission." Before he could answer, she stepped up on the bucket, pushed the sash the rest of the way up and shoved herself inside. She landed in a heap in the shower unit.

"You okay?" Jack's fierce question echoed in the small space. She leveraged herself up onto her elbows and stood, wincing as she flexed a sore ankle. "Dandy."

"Go directly to the back door and let me in."

"Got it."

"If you're not at the back door in thirty seconds, I'm breaking it down."

"Got it."

She tiptoed down the hall, peered in Tanya's bedroom and saw that her bed was still made. Otherwise, the room was empty. Her breath came faster. *Please let Tanya be all right.*

Mittens sprang from the back of the couch and trotted toward Dani as she halted in the living room doorway. Fear rushed through her. What if Smiley was here…alone…had done something to Tanya? Would he take this opportunity to do something to her, too?

She tiptoed through to the kitchen, noticed Tanya's purse wasn't in its usual spot by the toaster and continued on to the enclosed back porch.

Jack scowled at her when she opened the door. He was silent for a moment, then in a voice ragged with emotion, said, "What took you so—"

He cut himself off and pulled her close, his heart thundering against hers, and she melted in his strong arms, loving the way his embrace seemed to banish every last one of her fears. But just as quickly he let her go, steering her behind him, his gun suddenly flashing in his hand.

"They're gone."

He whirled, lowering his weapon.

"Tanya's bed hasn't been slept in, plus I

don't see her purse. They must have gone to Denver."

After a quick inspection of the house, he joined her on the front porch and they headed down the lane. Crickets droned in the scrub grass and a wild rabbit emerged from the brush, spied them and froze.

"Didn't see anything of his," Jack observed. "No clothes. Toothbrush…"

"I didn't get the impression he'd been staying here. In fact, he looked kind of beaten up."

He slanted a sideways look at her as they passed the duck pond. A few solitary birdcalls broke the night's quiet. "Cuts? Bruises?"

"More like moving stiffly."

As they walked, he rubbed his chin with his thumb and index finger, his expression inward. Considering. "Could be from sleeping on the ground. But where?"

"Tanya mentioned he'd been camping but I didn't want to alert Smiley by asking too many questions. I went up to your look-out right away, but you weren't there."

He swore under his breath and his quickening pace stirred up the dirt road. "Was out searching the property for Smiley and the Sam Perkins look-alike I spotted when I grabbed Dakota."

Her pulse jumped. "Did you find him?"

"No. I tracked prints to Eagle Rock then down into the ravine."

"That's a popular fishing spot. A lot of the staff go there."

"So Larry said." Jack pulled out his cell phone and studied it. "I need to call the sheriff's department."

"I have a landline in my office."

Minutes later she left Jack ensconced in her office and slipped back outside to give him privacy and herself some distance.

Overhead, stars put on a show in the clearing sky and she focused on the brightest: the North Star. She'd followed it here, to Colorado, and now she wondered if it'd led her to Jack, too.

He'd been worried about her earlier at Tanya's house. She hadn't imagined it. That dark concern in his eyes, his deep voice, had nearly unglued her, and if he hadn't let her go, she would have kissed him.

The barn door swung open behind her and she turned. Her eyes, now adjusted to the weak light, drank in the sight of him, and a yearning to unburden itself seized her heart.

"Did he report?" she asked, her voice catching in her throat.

Jack shook his head. "Not yet. They'll call if he does."

"So you'll be leaving then?" Disappointment welled up in her, alongside concern for Tanya. Could be they'd stopped for a bite to eat…gone to a hotel…

His eyes searched hers. "Once I have confirmation, there's no reason for me to stay."

Silence swelled between them and neither seemed to breathe. "Right. No reason." *Except me*, she almost added.

Crazy how just days ago she'd wanted him gone, and now…now…her future, while nearly secure, stretched on, empty and dark when she pictured him no longer in it.

He stepped close enough so that she had to tip her head back to look at him. "Let me see you back to your room."

"No need." She backed up, battling the irrational letdown at the thought of never seeing him again.

"I want to." He dug into her with his eyes, like he was begging for something.

"Okay."

They strolled to the pasture across from her quarters in the storage barn. A white horse caught her eye and she stopped. "What about me—ah, Milly?" She nearly swallowed her tongue. Or bit it in half. Sheesh. Could she be more obvious?

If she thought about this objectively, she should be happy he'd be leaving. With him gone, she'd be out of danger of discovery and could run down the clock on her statute of limitations.

Yet the thought of the dude ranch—her life—without him filled her with melancholy. What if...

Jack leaned on the fence and studied the horse, who stood in a distant corner, her nose in the grass. When Dani joined him, he angled his head and his eyes searched hers. "She's got heart," he said, his gaze on Dani. "Spirit."

"You can't just give up on her." Her voice came out rushed, breathy.

"I don't want to." He turned more fully and gathered her hand in his, studying it as he brushed his thumb across her knuckles, making her shiver.

"So stay."

His eyes rose to hers, the expression hard to read in the dark. "I'm a bounty hunter, not a horse whisperer. Besides, being around people. It's not my thing."

"You're people." She reached up with her

other hand and lightly touched his hair. Brushed it out of his face. It felt smooth and sharp at the same time, like she could feel each strand under her fingertips. "Good people."

He pulled away. "You had me pegged right that first night."

A rush of something, everything—her old panic, her new fears, an awareness, a need, a caring for this man—was so strong she had to hold on to the railing. "That's not true. I was an idiot, and everyone likes you. Jori Lynn, Nan, Larry and Diane. And you worked wonders with those kids today."

"They don't know who I really am."

"What do you mean?"

He averted his face and spoke to the distant hills. "Nothing."

When he shoved off the fence and looked ready to bolt, she swiftly changed the subject. "Don't you have more leads to chase down here? What about the other guy? The one in the double homicide?"

"Technically, my job is to catch Smiley. If he's turned himself in, that's it."

"But it's not," she insisted. "You found those cigarettes at Tanya's house and Sam Perkins… he's got a 9mm. Plus he could have caused that avalanche."

"All things I'll look into if Smiley doesn't turn himself in." Crickets buzzed in the tufted grass and Jack folded his arms across his chest. "Sam's background check didn't show anything, but that doesn't mean he's clean. Criminal history information isn't stored by Social Security number, and one of the most common ways for a criminal record to slip through the cracks is through the use of a maiden name, additional name, misspelled name and/or an alias."

"So, then, I guess there's…uh…not much you can do, right?"

Jack rolled his eyes to the sky, as if he searched for the hiding spot there. "My next step would be to search a database of warrants and composite sketches to see if he resembles one."

A faintness stole over her. Could her picture and warrant be in that mix? *No. No. No.* It was her worst nightmare come true—her past catching up with her at long last. "That sounds like a lot of work."

"If Smiley's turned himself in, there'll be no need for me to search it." He stared at her for a minute longer than necessary but not as long as she wanted. Not even close. His voice deepened as he said, "Guess this could be goodbye."

"Oh." Her eyes felt raw and she looked skyward, blinking fast, marveling at this rush of emotion for a man she'd met only days ago. If he found her picture on that database, he'd despise her and that thought was more than she could bear.

Without warning, he laid his thumb on her lips, as if seeing whether she would pull away. She didn't. He leaned closer. She wanted to drop her gaze from his but couldn't. Before, Jack had just been a threat to her secret. Her security. The safe life she'd constructed in this hiding spot. Now all Dani could see were his big dark eyes, the palms of his strong hands, the way his torso shifted under his T-shirt.

Her mind swerved in unexpected directions. She wondered, briefly, what it would feel like if he were to kiss her. She made a small, involuntary sound at the thought.

His lids lowered and he leaned his head into hers. When their lips were almost touching, he cupped the side of her face, the caress achingly tender, and slid his fingers into her hair.

He angled her face upward and brushed

his mouth against hers, softly at first, then he lifted her chin and deepened his kiss so that her body trembled. She kissed him back—tentatively and then with a fierce passion, her hand stealing up his neck, her eyes closing. She could feel his heart drum through his shirt, the rush of his breath mingling with hers, the strength of his body as he drew her closer still until she clung to him, her head spinning.

His lips traveled along her jaw and she dug her fingers into his shoulders, needing his strength because her muscles were suddenly limp. Never in her life had a kiss—or a man—affected her this way.

Jack's hands dropped to her waist and tightened there. In the still air, their breathing was the only sound. Blood throbbed in her veins, pulsed at the base of her throat. She buried her face in his neck and inhaled the clean male scent of his skin. It reminded her of a forest after a storm, strong and pure and good.

Yet he'd denied Dakota's claim that he was a good man. And the sadness she glimpsed in the corners of his eyes suggested there was more to Jack than an ex-rancher turned tough guy bounty hunter. One she might never get to know.

"You take care of yourself," he said softly into her hair. Then he pulled back.

Her heart beat erratically as she watched him stride away. She touched her lips, remembering the firm pressure of his. When she'd looked into his sorrowful eyes, a door in her heart had blown open. And when they'd kissed, she'd seen that on the other side of that door was the sky.

The more time she spent with him, the harder it became to hold in her secrets. He made her want to be open and vulnerable. To earn his appreciation honestly, as the person she was, not who he imagined her to be: someone with a spotless past.

Was there a chance he would understand, accept her, care for her, just the way she was?

If he found her picture in his composite sketchbook database, or her warrant, the choice to reveal all would be taken from her.

And so might the man who'd captured her heart.

CHAPTER FIFTEEN

WHEN DANI STEPPED inside the hay barn the next morning, a shadow moved and she jumped.

"Hey Dani-girl. It's been a long time."

Dani's senses scrambled. White noise raged in her ears. With every heartbeat came a sharp longing to run, but where could she go that her ex wouldn't follow? He must have tracked her thousands of miles from home and it wasn't likely he'd leave empty-handed.

"Kevin." She took in the familiar bulk of his muscular frame, his messy dark hair, the stubble on his square jaw, a nose like a knife and assessing blue eyes, just as sharp. A smirk twisted his full mouth—like he knew a joke you weren't in on. She let out a long breath. It felt as though she hadn't fully exhaled since she'd last seen him. In fact, she hadn't breathed easy at all since then.

"What do you want?" she demanded, but her body seemed to have detached itself from her voice, and her words floated from her mouth, faint and faraway. His familiar aroma—coffee, a slight tinge of tobacco and leather—rose around her. It transported her to the lowest point in her life.

"That's all you've got to say after all this time?" One side of his mouth hitched and his eyes swept to her toes then lifted, the familiar drag of his gaze making her skin crawl.

Calm yourself. Concentrate on filling your lungs, draining them. Filling them again and again and again.

But the roar remained, the buzzing of a thousand bees, very close. She sidestepped to get a view of the open door behind him, but he moved with her, blocking the sun, escape. "We said all we needed to each other in Oklahoma," she forced out. What if Jack saw him here? Asked questions?

Disappointment weighed on his features, turned them down. The right pocket of his jacket bulged with something. A gun? "Now, I wasn't expecting the red carpet. Although I damn well should have gotten it. Didn't I keep your correct name and your date of birth out of it when I got arrested? You got a clean record because of me. This job…"

She nodded mutely and her gaze darted

around the barn, looking for something to defend herself with. The sharpest thing she spied was a black cat's claws as it sat in a patch of sunlight, lifting first one paw, then another, to clean itself. From outside came the faint rumble of a passing truck. *I could scream,* she thought wildly, trying to hear her own thoughts over the rush of blood in her ears.

He stepped closer and she smelled cigarettes on his breath. "You never did thank me for that."

She let his words hit her full-on. Took them right on the chin. "I never asked you to keep quiet about me."

He angled his head and his eyebrows, rose. "But you benefited from it. Nice place." He pushed the door shut behind him and leaned against it, his relaxed posture somehow more threatening. "You've come a long way since our bank-robbing days. Guess that means I made an honest woman of you."

His deep chuckle startled a couple of roosting barn swallows. With a flurry of wings, they swooped, circled and glided before settling on another rafter.

"Honest? You made me a criminal," she blurted, outrage torching her fear, licking in her veins suddenly. "If I'd known you were going to rob a bank, I wouldn't have driven you."

Silence, broken only by the distant cooing of nesting birds in the loft, descended.

Kevin lowered his face and studied his black boots. They shuffled on the sawdust-covered floor. "I regret involving you," he said at last. "We were a regular Bonnie and Clyde, but that part of my life's over."

"What?" She gaped at him. "We were never Bonnie and Clyde." At his sudden squint, she fumbled. "Not anything big. Not like that."

"No. Not like that. Look, I came all this way. Please just hear me out and then I'll go. Promise." He crossed a finger over his heart in a gesture that took her back to their old days together and softened her a touch.

"Fifteen minutes. That's all you've got. Follow me." She led him farther inside the barn to her small office.

He leaned against a file cabinet. She dropped into her desk chair, her knees weak. The hum of her oscillating fan filled the cramped space and the blades stirred the thick air. It lifted her bangs off her forehead.

When Kevin made to take a pack of cigarettes from his breast pocket, she shook her head at him. Even if it wasn't a fire hazard and a big no-no in a stable, she would have stopped him. The strong scent of his cigarettes had always made her slightly light-headed and she needed all of her faculties right now.

Why, of all times, had he shown up now?

He dropped his hands and spread them wide. "I'm a changed man, Dani. I had a lot of time to think while I was locked up. I never want to go back in there again. Not ever."

She pinched the bridge of her nose and squeezed her eyes shut, as if she could ward off the oncoming headache beating at her temples.

"Did you skip out on your parole?"

"No." His boots clunked on the particle-board floor as he paced. A hollow sound. "Got out over a month and a half ago and been searching for you ever since. Once I traced you here, I petitioned to have my parole transferred to Colorado."

"Traced me? How?" She met his small eyes and dropped her gaze to the half-full coffee mug left over from last night. The faint whiff of stale brew didn't fortify her. Not a bit.

She'd never imagined he could locate her a world away from the English riding circuit, all the way to another state—another world, it'd seemed like when she'd first moved here. With their relationship based more on thrills than heart-to-heart conversations, she'd never mentioned anything specific about her family... where they lived in Texas, what they did...

"Facebook."

"I don't have a Facebook account."

"But your family's bull ranch does." He stood in front of her desk and lifted a horseshoe paperweight, turned it over in his hands. Her mouth fell open. "I popped your name into Google and, low and behold, there was a tagged picture of you with the location set here, at Mountain Sky Dude Ranch."

A punch to the stomach couldn't have knocked the air out of her faster. Of all things. Facebook pictures. Her family's business page, part of the new push they'd made to modernize. Claire, her sister, must have put up the photo. It'd never dawned on her, when she'd emailed it, that Claire would use it publicly.

Her head felt like it'd float right off her shoulders and the springs in her chair squeaked as she tilted backward, unsteady.

What a comedy of errors. One that wasn't funny at all. Changed or not, she had to send Kevin on his way, fast. It would all come out, especially with Jack digging for anything suspicious he could find on guests and staff alike.

Suddenly it was more than a guilty conscience threatening to reveal her long-held secret. The very real danger of past wrongs coming home to roost stood across from her.

Kevin could jeopardize everything: her job, her friendships and this blooming thing—whatever it was—between her and Jack.

She licked dry lips. "So are you saying you need money? I don't have much on hand, but I can see if…"

Kevin's thin mouth pursed. "I didn't come here looking for handouts. Like I said, I've changed." He peered at her for a long moment then blew out a breath. "But maybe I just need to prove it to you."

"What—" She cleared her throat. "What do you want?"

The muscles in his forearms corded as he gripped the edge of her desk and leaned close. Lowered his voice. "What I want is a job."

Dani's foot stopped swinging. Her breath quickened. "I can't give you a job!"

He let go of her desk and straightened. He wasn't a tall man, but he filled the room with a kind of on-edge energy.

He fiddled with the ribbon on one of her

jumping bows tacked in a collage on the wall opposite her desk. A tiny smile tucked itself into the corners of his mouth, almost hidden, not quite. He slanted his gaze at her.

"I remember when you won this."

"Kevin, that was another life."

He let go of the ribbon, grabbed the chair opposite her desk and whirled it around to straddle it. "Well. Help me to start a new one, like you did. I did my time. Kept my promise. Now you keep yours."

"But I didn't promise..." How had she missed his manipulative side? She'd been vulnerable when they met—freshly grieving the loss of her horse, her dreams of winning enough competitions to fund college over— but her judgment of character couldn't have been that off, could it? She hadn't wanted to think too hard then, either. She had no one to blame but herself.

How she wished Jack was here.

How fortunate that he wasn't...

Kevin's eyes darkened. "You didn't turn yourself in, either, so you took advantage of the vow I gave. I could have shortened my sentence if I'd shared your correct name." He rubbed the dark stubble on his jaw and stared at a spot over her shoulder. "The way I see it, you owe me, even if you don't want to help out an old friend."

"I think driving the getaway car was all the help you deserve." She moved restlessly and toppled her coffee mug, spilling cold liquid over her cluttered desk. "Now look at what you made me do!" She yanked some napkins from a drawer and began blotting.

"You never asked if I would drive for you," she said, without looking up, swiping furiously at the brown puddle, brushing away Kevin's help. "Didn't give me any warning. That was unfair and low."

She stood and dropped the wet napkins in the trash, fingers shaking, and frowned at him. The toughness drained from his face. Once again he was the handsome horse handler who'd had a special way of calming even the most spooked jumpers.

"It's Amy," he blurted. "You remember my little sister?"

Dani nodded, recalling the weekly letters he'd sent home to the girl, along with cute gifts Dani'd helped him pick out at every tour stop. Amy must be sixteen by now...

"Go on."

"My ma died and made me Amy's guardian. I can't go back to my old ways now and need honest work. But it ain't easy getting hired with a felony on your record. When I saw you were working here, I thought you'd help me get a job."

Surprised, she dropped back to her chair. "I'm sorry to hear that," she said slowly, reconciling the bank robber with the caring brother turned guardian who stood before her, wringing his hands.

Which was the real Kevin?

Could he be both?

"Look. Maybe I don't deserve your help after putting you on the spot to begin with." His voice broke. "I was a self-centered son-of-a-gun and a young fool. I—I apologize for that."

Her neck ached like she'd gotten whiplash. Fear, anger, and now sympathy fired through her. Kevin had never meant anyone harm. Hadn't done anything terrible before the bank heist. Maybe that'd been a one-time thing and he was truly sorry. She sure had regrets and had given herself a second chance. Wasn't it uncharitable to deny him one?

Her antagonism crumbled. She let out a huge breath. "I appreciate hearing that." His head lifted and the dimples on either side of his mouth popped. Something in his eager expression reminded her of Beau and Belle when they spotted saddled horses. "But I've already hired everyone for the season. There aren't any more vacancies and I have no reason to request more staffing from the owners."

His face fell and he seemed to deflate. He shook back the swoosh of hair that fell in front of his eyes. "A condition of my parole transfer is having employment or Amy and I have to go back."

There. A simple way to get rid of him, but somehow her heart wouldn't let her cut him off so coldly, to kick a man down on his luck, or put his sister in harm's way.

She wondered if she'd regret it, but she said, "A friend of mine owns a bar in Shawnee. The Rusty Roof. His bouncer quit on him. I could give him a call. He served time himself and made over his life. He'd probably be understanding."

He lunged across the desk and captured her hands. Squeezed. The dents in his cheeks reappeared. "That's my girl."

"I can't guarantee anything," she protested. Her stomach churned.

He hooked his thumbs in his jeans' belt loops and leaned back on his heels, the move so familiar it melted the time they'd been apart clean away. "If you set up an interview,

I'll get the job." His even white teeth flashed, his expression earnest.

"Do you and Amy have a place to stay?" She nearly kicked herself for asking. She was not getting involved in his life again.

His lashes fell to his high cheekbones and he shifted on his feet. "Me and Amy are in a hotel in Shawnee, but we could rent somewhere. I got money."

"Money?" Her blood ran cold. Had he ripped off another bank? "How much? I thought you were paroled just six weeks ago." Her chair rolled slightly, back and forth, as her feet pressed against the floor.

Kevin chewed on his full bottom lip as he pulled one of her state magnets from the side of her file cabinet. "My ma left us a small sum. So. You got an address for this place?" He turned Texas over in his hand and the familiar shape arrowed through her heart. "I'll hitch a ride back and stop in today."

After scribbling the information down, she handed him the sticky note.

"Much appreciated." He pressed the Texas magnet flat against the side of her cabinet and his eyes burned into hers. "If you'd like to look me up, I'll leave my address at the bar.

Otherwise, I won't trouble you again. Sure was good seeing you, Dani."

He peered around her office and his mouth curved. "It looks like you done good, just like I thought you would when I didn't share your name. Take care now."

"You, too. Give Amy my best."

She stared at the empty door frame long after he disappeared.

Had she done well?

She paced outside and stood on a small hill that overlooked the pasture, her eyes drifting to the milling herd.

Suddenly, she envied Kevin just as she did Smiley. He'd served his time and could move on, free of the guilt that weighed on her heart every day. Better still, he'd rescued his sister. Had he even rescued Dani with his decision to withhold her correct name and birth date? Maybe he'd been motivated not to make her pay for the mistake he'd made.

"Who's that?"

She jumped at Jori Lynn's voice beside her and followed her finger pointing to Kevin.

"Actually," Dani mused, watching her ex stride through the front gate, "I'm not entirely sure anymore."

CHAPTER SIXTEEN

"You're up, Jack."

He studied the tight harness that looped around his legs and back, and cinched over his stomach, then up at a cable that looked too thin to carry a one-hundred-and-eighty-pound guy. It attached to a line that stretched over the tops of hundred-feet tall pines.

Zip-lining.

Why would anyone voluntarily do this?

But with word coming in that Smiley hadn't reported to the sheriff, and Tanya sharing the news that he'd disappeared on her last night when she'd gone on a convenience store run, he needed to stay here and continue his hunt.

And avoid getting too close to Dani again.

What had he been thinking last night when he'd kissed her?

That it might be your only chance.

That you didn't want to say goodbye.

Fool.

He gave the ride operator a thumbs-up and

leaped off the wooden platform. The world melted into green, brown and blue flashes of color as he hurtled through the air. When his hat lifted, he snatched it, and a shout swelled in the back of his throat, his adrenaline firing through every nerve.

A bump in the line slowed his momentum; Dani and the Clarks, who'd gone first, appeared, waiting as he stumbled to a stop on a second wooden platform.

"Wooo-hooo!" Dakota held out one arm to the side and strummed the air with his other hand, mimicking a guitar. "You rock, Jack!"

He waved away the operator, unhooked himself and returned the kid's fist bump. "You went first."

"I'm not afraid of heights anymore!"

"Knew you could do it."

He met Dani's approving gaze and it felt as though something warm dropped into his heart.

"I want to ride again!" Dakota clamored, tugging on his father's long shirtsleeve. The man was entirely too dressed up for the humid weather. Was there truth to Larry's speculation about Mr. Clark's ties to organized crime? He looked polished in his designer clothes, yet sitting behind a desk didn't mean you never dirtied your hands.

Mr. Clark squinted at his phone and made a shooing motion. "I'm getting a signal. I'll meet you all down there in a minute."

"Let's go," Dani urged, her wide smile brightening the day several shades, her natural, relaxed way with the kids making Jack, strangely, long for home. "I've brought some fresh lemonade and magic bars for us."

"Can I stay, Dad?" wheedled Cheyenne. She shook back her dark hair. "I want to post some selfies."

"I think the world can go a few days without more pictures of you," snapped Mrs. Clark, hustling her daughter down from the platform.

Surreptitiously, Jack nudged off his hat, followed the group, then turned back to the stairs as if he'd forgotten it. The topic of Mr. Clark's private conversation could yield some clues on the man who raised his suspicions.

He'd ascended halfway when Mr. Clark's thunderous voice clapped overhead, making him pause. "What do you mean you can't meet me?"

Jack eased up another step and cocked his head, eavesdropping.

"No. You listen to me. We had an arrangement. You were supposed to be here and…"

Jack's pulse picked up steam.

Boots clomped on the platform as the man paced. "Well. That's not my fault. I knew I shouldn't have worked with an amateur on this."

Was he working on something with Smiley… if it was Smiley…?

"Look," Clark bellowed. "You've got to take care of this, Sam. Got it? Good. I'll contact Jim and stall him. But no more screwups."

Sam? Sam Perkins?

Silence descended and Jack cleared his throat as he noisily climbed the last few steps.

Mr. Clark jumped when Jack's head appeared. "You shouldn't be sneaking up on people."

"Just getting my hat," he said easily. He grabbed his Stetson and followed a grumbling Mr. Clark down the stairs. He needed to keep a close eye on him in case he had a tie to Smiley, and suddenly he was glad to have the irascible man in his tour group. It put him in the perfect position to spot anything amiss.

Later that evening, Jack polished off a plate of crispy fried chicken in the outdoor eating area beside the main house. He hadn't eaten in hours, not stopping for a break as he'd finished searching the southwestern quarter of his grid. He was exhausted. Not physically... just with the wear and tear, the grinding work of unrewarded effort. He didn't need instant gratification, though it'd be nice for a change.

Larry lowered himself onto the bench seat opposite Jack. "How's it going?"

"Cleared the southwest of your property. No sign of Smiley. Heading out again in the morning. Thought I'd do some desk investigating in the meantime, if I could borrow a computer."

"Sure. Why?"

"There's a database I'd like to look through to see if any faces on composite sketches or names on warrants match your guests or staff. Some might be using an alias or have a record you're not aware of."

"You can use the one at the main house, though Dani's got one, too, don't you?"

Jack turned around and spied Dani. Her eyes met his and dropped. Her teeth appeared on her bottom lip, worrying it. Did he make her nervous? He should never have kissed her, yet he couldn't bring himself to regret it. Not one bit.

"Go on ahead, Blake," she said to the tall guy Jack had met at breakfast the other day.

Larry waved her over, then gestured for her to lean down. "Jack's finished his ground search for the day and needs to look up some files this evening. Composite sketches. Warrants. Would you lend a hand and give him the guest list and employee names?"

"No problem," she said, though her closed-off expression suggested it *was* a problem. Why? She looked as jumpy as a black cat on Halloween.

"Follow me," she said, and he walked beside her, conscious of some distance between them despite her shoulder brushing his, their hands bumping.

"Dani, I—" he began, once she'd logged him in to her computer. He was ready to apologize for the kiss, but she'd already disappeared through the doorway and into the equipment barn.

He wanted to go after her. Explain… Explain what? That'd he'd been unable to resist kissing her last night, even though he knew full well nothing could come of it? Normally, he'd never behave like that, but Dani had a way of making a man forget his shadows.

And then there was her behavior. Even if

he was in a position to offer a woman his heart, Dani's secretiveness reminded him of his brother. Jesse had acted like that when he lied and covered things up. Did Dani have something to hide?

A part of him mistrusted her.

He shook his head and got to work. A couple minutes later, after inputting his parameters— gender, age, ethnicity, coloring—he scrolled through pictures, his gaze drifting to Dani as she sorted horse blankets and organized gear, her movements jerky, her back straighter than he'd ever seen it.

An hour ticked by. Then two. Dani had moved on to paperwork in a corner of the office. She was sitting in a wooden chair, which she had pulled as far from the desk as possible, and her knees were tucked beneath her chin, her arms wrapped around them, her eyes drifting over a printout.

He gazed at her, wanting to watch her forever, knowing that when she noticed, she'd probably leave. They hadn't exchanged more than a word or two all day and it bugged him. A lot.

The heck with it.

She glanced up, fast, when he pushed to his

feet, ready to hash it out, but a high-pitched whinny stopped him.

A second whinny got Dani out of her chair and a third made them shoot out the door. They raced to the pasture, where the sound of rushing horses and thundering hooves grew louder and louder.

They pulled up short to see several horses sprinting out of an open gate. Dani grabbed her walkie-talkie and urged all wranglers to report to her.

"What's going on?" A few workers ran up, including Jori Lynn and the guy he'd seen Dani with earlier. Blake.

"Horses are out. Let's saddle up and herd them back. Blake, you stay here and inventory. Jori Lynn, bring in as many as you can that are close. Jack and I will ride out and get the outliers. Update us as the horses return."

For the next hour, he and Dani rode the property, herding, roping and communicating effortlessly through eye signals and hand gestures. There was a kind of graceful rhythm to their movements that reminded him of herding cattle with his siblings, memories returning sharp and pressing so that he realized how much he missed it, missed them, missed home.

Bella and Beau joined in, running at the

horses' heels, their playfulness replaced with the same intensity he witnessed in Dani. Gone was his sparring partner, and in her place was a driven horsewoman who would have made his hard-to-impress mother nod in approval. She doggedly retrieved horse after horse, circling her rope overhead and dropping it with impressive accuracy around horses' necks, pinpointing the leaders that other horses would follow, causing the least amount of stress to the animals.

A couple of hours later, the light completely gone and thunder rumbling in the mountains, Dani's walkie-talkie crackled to life.

"Head home, Dani. Weather's approaching."

"But we're still missing Cher and Pokey." She pulled her hat off and wiped her brow with her sleeve.

"We'll keep looking in the morning."

"Got it."

Back at the pasture, they untacked their mounts and turned them loose. Larry met them just as the sky opened up and threw down its first volley of rain. They ducked back inside the barn. "Can't see how this could have happened."

"Who came in last?"

Blake stepped up, his expression woeful. "Me. I secured it."

Dani put a hand on the young man's arm and smiled kindly. "Thanks, Blake."

Jack waited until Blake left before he spoke. "Thieves?"

"Could be. Had a couple of reports today of guests missing wallets and jewelry." Larry shoved his hands in his pockets. "Stuff like this just doesn't happen out here, but Blake's a good wrangler. He wouldn't make a mistake like leaving the gate open."

"Well. We know Smiley's still in the area, probably on foot."

Dani shook her head at the same time Larry said, "No."

"Could be he got spooked when Dani stopped by and he wanted to head deeper into the back country."

"But why two horses?" Larry wondered out loud, then his face fell even further. "Two hit men, right? You said there might be someone with him. Helping?"

"Right. Tanya's accounted for. Who's seen Sam?" Jack shook out his wet hat.

"I did," Larry said, "early this morning when he was taking down a dead tree, but not since."

"Would you mind if I use the phone? I'd like to let the sheriff know about this."

"Sure." Dani plucked the handset from the cradle. Their fingers brushed as he took the phone.

"Tell the sheriff I'm going to hold off on filing a report on the horses or the missing items for now. Want to wait just a bit to see if they turn up," Larry said, before ushering Dani out and closing the door.

Jack cradled the phone with his shoulder and studied a picture of a grinning Dani, her smile so effortless it was hard to imagine her wearing any other expression. It made him smile, too.

"Any evidence this could be more than just an accident?" Lance asked when Jack finished relaying the day's events.

"The last wrangler to bring in horses swears he shut it and Larry seems to trust the kid. It's storming here, but if it clears, I'll head back out to search. If they were stolen, the thieves did a good job of covering their tracks since there are lots of hoofprints."

Swearing came through the phone, followed by, "What about Smiley?"

For the next few minutes, they caught each other up. A safe-deposit box key had been found in the Denver victims' home, and Lance was working to locate which bank it belonged to. Meanwhile, he was a bit skeptical regarding Reginald Clark's involvement with the case. The guy had been thoroughly investigated before and nothing illegal was found.

As he listened, Jack studied the large number of show-jumping ribbons that covered one of the walls. Many were for first place. Why had Dani given up what looked like a promising career in competitive show jumping?

"The guy's a jerk, but like I said..." Lance concluded, breaking Jack from his thoughts about Dani.

"If that were a crime, we'd have to bring in half of Colorado," Jack finished for him, smiling. "And what half am I in?"

"Haven't decided. Are you going to the family reunion?"

"Lance..."

"I still need a date."

"Can we stop talking about your love life? It's depressing."

"That it is." Lance sighed. "Anyway. Better get some shut-eye. Only have about a hundred-and-fifty-three more banks to canvas tomorrow."

Jack ran a hand through the damp hair at his brow. "Don't get discouraged."

"Me?" Lance spoke through a yawn. "I'm just getting started."

Dial tone.

Jack put down the phone and steepled his fingers. His cousin had the right attitude. Detective work wasn't easy. You didn't have to be the smartest. You just needed to be more stubborn.

He had plenty of that to go around when it came to getting what he wanted.

And, he realized, that included Dani.

CHAPTER SEVENTEEN

JACK SMOOTHED A brush over Milly's coat the next afternoon after tying her up in the pasture. Shoals of blue-and-gray clouds swam through the sky. The grasses tossed and shimmied. It had been a beautiful day, but clouds were moving in from the west in a dark, forbidding line.

Milly arched her neck and munched the apple he'd given her, ears forward, her stance relaxed. Every spare minute had been spent doing things to gain her trust, from grooming, petting and feeding her treats, to progressive training. Earlier this morning she'd finally accepted a blanket on her back and was following his direction signals.

The musky scent of her rose around him as he stroked the brush across her face and forelock. Warm breath rushed over his fingers. When she pranced lightly, her hooves struck one of the puddles left over from last night's storm, spraying his boots with muddy water.

She was starting to show promise. Seeing her improvement filled him with pride, a transformation he sensed happening in himself, too. Lately he'd become more at ease with people and he credited Dani with those changes. She'd pushed him from day one, never buying his excuse that he wasn't good with people. Maybe he'd judged her too quickly, and maybe he'd judged himself too fast, too…a fault of his, he now saw.

He thought of the way she chewed her cheek when she concentrated, the flutter of her hands when she got excited, the light in her eyes when she caught him by surprise and her snappy comebacks that kept him off-balance. He never wanted to forget any of it. Or forget her.

Something loosened inside as he imagined his life differently, with her, as if he'd been wearing something too tight around his chest for a very long time, a garment that'd never release him as long as his brother's murderer roamed free. Would Jack find the killer here at Mountain Sky Dude Ranch? Everything was a dead end. Progress followed by setbacks. Still, he would see this through, never stopping until every lead dried up.

Though he didn't want to leave Dani.

"Good girl," he murmured to Milly after a final pat, then he returned the brush to the equipment barn. The smell of roasted pork wafted from the outdoor dining area and his stomach rumbled, the aroma reeling him in.

At breakfast, Nan had mentioned plans to make her green chili dish for tonight's pig roast. After an early start looking for Cher and Pokey, scouting for Smiley and a horseback ride up Shawnee Mountain, he was famished. He needed to refuel before resuming his property search. One particular spot deep in the woods, Spark Canyon, had become virtually inaccessible after the rainfall. Hopefully enough water had drained out of it by now for him to search its caves.

He peered up at the sky, noting the darkening clouds still hanging on the horizon. They looked far off, but in Big Sky Country distances could be deceiving. The sooner he set out the better. The forecast predicted storms the rest of the week.

The outdoor eating area he approached was a blur of activity. Kids chased each other, shrieking, around crowded picnic tables. Chattering guests lined up at the buffet table, laden with steaming kettles, platters of grilled corn on the cob and sliced pork, bowls of coleslaw and a stack of chocolate brownies. His mouth watered at the tantalizing scents.

"Howdy, Nan." He returned the older woman's smile and accepted the fragrant bowl of chili she passed him. In a checked apron that matched the rosy color of her cheeks, her white hair in a low bun, a sparkling brooch pinned at her throat, she matched the festive atmosphere.

"You look like you need filling up." She ladled another scoop of the green stew into his bowl. "There's blue chips and other fixings down there, but don't go adding any hot sauce, now. My chili's already the right amount of hot."

"That I believe."

Her eyes twinkled and he found himself relaxing, barely noticing the crowd surrounding them, their chatter falling away, the few, sideways glances he still got on occasion vanishing. "Thank you."

He tipped his hat and stepped to his left to add shredded cheese and sour cream. He ladled salsa beside a pile of chips, firmly passed on the hot sauce (though it was his favorite), then stopped by the brownies and the slouching server behind them.

"Hey, Tanya."

Dark circles shadowed her eyes and she

shoved her messy hair back. "You want some whipped cream?" She held up a can, and when he nodded, she squirted a lopsided mound that mostly slid off his dessert.

"Much appreciated."

Tanya waved without looking and her lowered head seemed too heavy for her shoulders.

Clearly she hadn't been sleeping, he thought, returning Larry's and Diane's smiles, giving Dakota a fist bump and waving back at Jori Lynn as he headed to an unoccupied table. Was Smiley back and keeping her up? What information might she be hiding? He needed to mention it to Dani.

He dug into his chili, mulling this over as the first bite exploded on his tongue, catching him off guard. Then it torched the back of his throat. A blistering cough erupted and he groped for his pop, his eyes watering.

"I like a man who can handle his chili," he heard Dani say behind him.

"I can handle it," he gasped, and another hacking fit overtook him, a final chili-pepper flare. His fingers contacted the cool metal side of the can and he gulped long and hard.

Her hand settled on his back. Patted. "Easy, cowboy. Don't hurt yourself." He could hear the smile in her voice and his mouth twisted in the same shape, despite the fact that he was dying. Clearly.

"Who's hurt?" he managed at last. Dani grinned down at him; freckles seemed to bloom across her cheeks as she inhaled and suddenly he couldn't tear his eyes away. "I can take third-degree burns."

"Good, because Nan's watching. Look."

He turned and waved at the intent older woman, then popped another full spoonful in his mouth as if he had a death wish. The corners of Nan's eyes creased in approval and she returned to serving guests.

Dani shook her head and her long bangs fell adorably into her eyes. "You might have poured that on too thick. She's going to send you a second helping."

"God help me," he mumbled around his mouthful of food. His cheeks bulged and every part of him resisted gulping it down.

"Swallow," Dani ordered then sat beside him, wearing a cheeky grin. Darn her for looking like she enjoyed every bit of his misery.

He shook his head. Anymore of this and it'd blast a hole straight through his gut.

Buckshot would be preferable. A nobler end than death by chili.

"It's only going to hurt more the longer you hold it. Now be a good boy…" she teased, and if he hadn't been dying, he might have actually laughed. Blake passed by and flashed a peace sign, Belle and Beau tight on his heels.

"Bah," he gasped, after finally forcing down the stew. "Where does she get those peppers? Hell?"

Dani's hazel eyes danced with some private joke…on him, he suspected, irritated, and feeling more pleased to see her than he cared to admit.

"Probably. Did you put hot sauce on it?"

He stared at her a moment, then shook his head. "And make it hotter? I'm too young to die."

Her expression was serene. "Actually, the hot sauce is so much milder that it diffuses the spice."

"What? But Nan said…"

"Yeah. She just says that so you won't mess with her flavor."

He gaped at her, taking in the thick braid that revealed her animated face. For an insane moment, his fingers itched to loosen it, to touch the flowing silk. "Well, that's kind of her."

"I think so." She winked at him. "She just gave me loads of entertainment."

Unable to resist, he captured her right hand. "Never a dull moment with you around, either."

"Oh," she said, smiling, all shiny cheeks and full lips.

He cleared his throat to break the spell and released her hand. "Have you spoken to Tanya?"

Dani's expression grew clouded. "She looks exhausted."

"Smiley?"

"I don't know." She peered over at her friend and said, "I'm going to speak to her."

"Good. I'm heading out for Spark Canyon. Catch me in the corral before I go and fill me in."

She squeezed his arm. "See you in a few. Oh, and you might reconsider the salsa."

He stared at the dripping nacho in his other hand. "Why?"

"Nan admits it's hotter than her chili. We all call it Suicide Salsa. Your call."

"Good to know."

"See? I don't really want you to suffer. Much."

"That's debatable."

As soon as he said it, she laughed. And whenever Dani laughed, something broke inside him—had since the beginning—and made him want to make her do it again. It brought out the mischievous boy who'd served lunch detentions for clowning around in school…the boy he'd buried two years ago.

But she was resurrecting him.

He shook most of the salsa off the chip, then bit in, wincing but determined not to look like he was in excruciating pain—or in his final death throes—with Nan watching.

At Dani's over-the-shoulder salute, he found himself grinning stupidly, happiness exploding in his brain like fireworks.

It'd been long time since he'd felt a part of things. Had been included or *let* himself be included. Had he been using his scar to hide out from the world, rejecting it before giving it a real chance?

Dani was making him see lots of things differently. Especially himself.

DANI WATCHED A family of six swarm Tanya and her brownie bar, her mind returning to the reassuring conversation she'd had with Ray, the owner of the Rusty Roof.

Kevin had secured a job there as a bouncer

and seemed to be working out fine. He got along well with customers and had made a couple of friends on staff.

All good signs that he'd been telling the truth about wanting to turn over a new leaf.

So, why was she still skittish?

Jack.

He'd missed bumping into Kevin by minutes. If they ever met, she'd not only have to introduce him, but reveal their shared past. Then again, given Jack's database searches, he might come across her crimes on his own.

Was there a chance he might understand?

Given his black-and-white thinking, it seemed doubtful, and given how little time he had left on the ranch, she wanted to make the most of it with him.

At last the large group moved off the dessert line.

"Nan, can you spare Tanya for a minute?" Dani tried catching her friend's eye but the other woman suddenly got busy wiping up her dessert station.

Nan waved a hand, shooing them. "Line's mostly gone through. Go on, you two. I've missed seeing you together."

"I'm happy to stay and help," Tanya offered.

"No need. We can manage."

"Fine." Tanya untied her apron, folded it and smoothed the seams, turning it, pressing it, into a smaller and smaller square.

"Tanya," Dani prompted, knowing her friend's stall tactics too well.

"Coming."

They rounded a corner of the house and stopped at an octagonal white gazebo. The dizzy, drunk fragrance of primroses engulfed them as they sat beneath hanging baskets dangling from a dozen or so hooks.

"How are you?" Dani gathered Tanya's hand in hers.

Tanya ducked her head and her hair fell in her face, obscuring most of it. "Okay."

"You don't sound okay." Concern spiked, and Dani slid closer. She wrapped an arm around her friend's tense shoulders. "I'm here for you, sweetie. What's going on? Did Smiley come back?"

Tanya shrugged and circled the toe of her boot on the floor's wood grain.

"You know he's in a heap of trouble that's only getting worse the longer he stays away."

"I keep telling him to turn himself in, but he won't… I mean he wouldn't…"

"Did he have anything to do with the horses going missing last night?"

Tanya began to cry. "No."

Dani dabbed the tears with her shirtsleeve, her heart filling with lead. "Is that what you know or what you feel?"

Tanya groaned. "I don't know what to think. Smiley isn't some druggie. I would know. But he ran off instead of turning himself in."

"Do you still love him?"

"Yes," Tanya whispered, her voice low. She lifted her hat and tucked strands of hair behind her ears.

"If you see him, tell him he's in big trouble. Larry and Diane are going to get the police up here if we don't find Cher and Pokey soon. With officers on the premises, and Smiley wanted on an outstanding warrant, he'd be much safer turning himself in voluntarily. What if something goes wrong and he gets hurt?" Dani kept back the part about the double homicide, since that wasn't proven… and wasn't information she had permission to share.

Tanya dropped her head into her hands, and her voice, when it emerged, sounded muffled and wet. "I'm worried to death about that."

Dani held Tanya tight. It broke her heart to see Tanya in the position Dani'd been in with Kevin. If only she could open up and share her story with her closest friend. The burden of her secret weighed on her, heavier than ever.

"I'm sorry about Smiley. If you see him, will you get him to do the right thing?"

"Either he will or I will."

They exchanged watery smiles. "Love you, girl." She squeezed Tanya and they rose.

"Not sure I deserve it, but I love you, too."

CHAPTER EIGHTEEN

A SHORT WHILE LATER, Dani led Storm to the corral where Jack finished cinching up a paint horse. He looked up, his eyes widening when he took in her saddled horse and the rifle holstered on it.

"What are you doing?"

"Coming with you."

"No." He held up his hand and closed his eyes, as if that would help him not to hear her.

"It's a free country, Jack," she exclaimed.

His lids lifted. Brown eyes blazed. "It's my responsibility."

"And mine! I'm the manager. I should be looking out for the ranch and protecting the staff and guests." She clutched her elbows, arms crossed, feeling like she needed to hold herself together in case she flew apart. Kevin's appearance had left her feeling unsettled, and despite reassurances from Ray and Kevin, she still didn't believe that her life wasn't about to get turned upside down, especially given Jack's internet searches.

"Are you thinking about Tanya?"

"We need to get Smiley before he contacts her again. Who knows what he'll try persuading her to do?"

"If he's got the horses, I'm not sure he'll come back." Jack moved around his horse and hopped into the saddle in one seamless move.

"We can't guarantee that."

He turned his mount in a neat circle. "Nope. That's true. But with guests missing wallets and jewelry, someone's up to something."

She stepped up into Storm's saddle and squeezed her knees, guiding her horse forward then pulling her to a stop beside Jack. "I can handle myself." She patted her rifle.

He studied her for a long moment, then nodded. "Yes, you can. Let's go."

They rode hard for the first half hour, slowing as they moved through denser terrain. Treetops swayed overhead and tiny raindrops fell, too soft to be a storm, too substantial to be a mist.

"Did Tanya share anything with you?"

"Just that she's worried about him. She promised that if he returns, she'll either convince him to turn himself in or do it herself."

The horses picked their way up a rocky incline and the air seemed to grow denser, pressing around them. "Well. That's something."

"Tanya's a good person. She's just gotten caught up."

Jack studied her out of the corner of his good eye. "It's been her choice not to come clean or break away, though."

She flinched at that. "Sometimes it's not that cut-and-dried."

"In my world it is."

His judgmental words made the urge to confide in him wither. He'd never understand. That much was clear. Rain began to fall. "Maybe you need to turn up the color dial. We aren't living in black and white."

He opened his mouth to speak, then snapped it shut when a man appeared in the distance, followed by another, riding in and out of the trees. Putting a finger to his lips, he spurred his horse and she followed, her heart pausing.

At this distance, she couldn't make out details as the strangers rode along the far ridge, although she recognized the horses. Same size, color and markings as Cher and Pokey! Both of the trespassers wore cowboy hats pulled low, one brown and the other black. Dread trundled up from her gut.

Suddenly a crack of lightning exploded close by and the man in the black hat turned.

Smiley!

The bright flash faded and the men hurried down the ridge line and disappeared. Leaning low over their horses' necks, Dani and Jack gave chase, then pulled up, no sight of their quarry as they peered through the now steady curtain of rain the clouds pelted at them.

Jack's clenched jaw looked made of granite and his white knuckles shone against his reins. "Son of a— He's still here."

Lightning forked again, and thunder roared fast on its heels. The horses shifted nervously and she patted Storm's neck.

"Steady, Storm." Rain fell into her mouth as she spoke.

"I'll come back for Smiley. Let's take cover!" Jack shouted as the wind picked up, lashing the trees so that they swayed and creaked. If one of them toppled over, they'd be crushed.

"There's a mine shaft up ahead. Follow me."

She urged Storm on and they scrambled up a short bluff. Cold water slid down her collar. In seconds, the pummeling rain had soaked her through as it bore down in solid, unforgiving sheets and drowned out any sound.

At last, they dismounted and tied their horses beneath a rocky overhang before ducking inside the mine's entrance, weapons in hand. No one had boarded up this small, forgotten shaft, and water dripped from the ledge, trickling down its walls, creating rivulets that wound down the sloping dirt floor.

"What are you doing?" she asked, after she'd stowed their guns, shivering in her wet shirt and jeans.

Jack pried a piece of wood up from the old tracks that curved around a bend. He'd taken off his hat and the hair at the nape of his neck was plastered to his skin. "Gathering firewood."

"You don't think this will clear up soon?"

As if on cue, another crack of thunder sounded and the rain continued hammering.

"Doubtful. I need to get you dry. You could catch pneumonia."

"So could you." She dug her fingernails into a soft, rotting plank. It gave way faster than she expected, making her stumble back a step when it jerked free.

"Careful," Jack warned. He'd already pulled up five boards and was midway through liberating another. "The rusted nails could give you tetanus."

Pneumonia. Tetanus. Sheesh. "Do I look like some hothouse flower?" She heaved up another, sweat on her brow.

Warm brown eyes settled on her face. Drops of water sparkled on his eyelashes. "No. Not that. A blanket flower maybe."

Another hard yank and the wood came loose. "A blanket flower?"

"It's tough. Pretty. Red-gold, like your hair."

She fingered the dripping end of her braid and couldn't stop her goofy smile. "You think I'm tough and pretty?"

"Let's say I'm glad you were with me when we encountered Smiley and his partner. Much better odds."

Every ounce of blood rushed to her cheeks. "Thank you."

"You're welcome."

He hoisted an armload and she followed. "What can I do?"

"Grab as much of that dead grass as you can."

"Got it." She hustled away, needing some distance, her thoughts fluttering like trapped birds.

She grabbed the old, dry grass that lay on the floor and stuffed it between the wood pieces he'd piled in a tepee shape by the entranceway. He took a couple of stones from his pocket and, over a piece of the grass, began striking them. They sparked, he leaned down and blew on the pile, waving the tendril of smoke that rose until a flame leaped up.

She found herself drinking him in, his broad chest and strong arms, his square shoulders. She remembered his mouth hungry on hers, his big hands in her hair, the heat coursing through her, how it had made her feel—

"You're a regular Boy Scout." She forced a light tone, though it quivered just a little, betraying her.

"Eagle Scout," he corrected, his eyes gleaming as he blew again on the flame once he'd placed the smoldering tinder inside the wood stack.

It took a couple more tries to get a steady burn, but eventually the fire took hold and smoke drifted outside, caught by the blowing westward wind. The heat drew her and she settled beside it on the dirt floor. She listened to the rain humming against the mountain. Watched it drip past the mine's entranceway.

Jack lowered himself beside her and held out his hands to the strengthening fire. He looked into her eyes. His were so brown they looked black.

"So, you were an Eagle Scout?" *Ask questions. Indulge your curiosity, not this insane desire that has your lips puckering like a girl at her sweet sixteen party.*

He squinted into the shadows. "Sure was. It's a tradition in my family."

"You mentioned siblings."

"Right."

The fire strengthened and flames curled around the wood, flickering orange and red. Purling off the rocky overhang, the rain became a waterfall that blurred the outside world, leaving just them.

She put her damp sleeve over her mouth and shuffled closer to the heat when a shudder ripped through her. It was a bone-deep chill. She hadn't noticed it during the adrenaline rush of the chase or while they were gathering firewood.

At the sound of wet cloth dropping to the ground, she spotted Jack's T-shirt... which meant... Before she could process the thought, his bare arms wrapped around her. Every nerve leaped awake. The clean, male scent of him rose from his warm skin and a thrill entered her chest at the feel of his arms, strong and sure around her.

Kevin had never affected her this way. He'd made her feel rebellious, and his antics had kept her too keyed up to think about the loss of her mother, her horse or her future. Jack, on the other hand, made her feel safe and happy.

He was a far cry from Kevin.

If anything proved how much she'd grown, her feelings for Jack were irrefutable evidence. At first, she'd worried her old habits of falling for a bad boy had returned. Now she understood that she'd seen past his hard outer shell to the good, solid man underneath.

"What are your siblings' names?"

"James, Jared, Justin, Jewel..."

When the rise and fall of his chest against her back stopped, she angled around to peer up at him. He looked stern, yet incredibly, incredibly sad, his features as hard as the rocks that surrounded them.

"You'd mentioned four brothers and a sister."

"Jesse." His whisper came in her left ear; his breath smelled like crushed mint. The fire popped in the quiet, a shower of sparks in the dim, then near silence apart from the steady percussion of rain.

He cleared his throat. "I have—had—a younger brother named Jesse. He died."

She touched his arm. "I'm so sorry. Was it long ago?"

"Two years."

A previous conversation returned to her. "That's when you became a bounty hunter."

"Can I?" he asked, reaching for the rubber band on her braid. She nodded. He slid it off, the whole time holding her eyes. He undid her heavy, wet braid slowly.

"Did it have something to do with Jesse?" she asked.

The sensitive skin at the nape of her neck tingled at his touch. "Yes."

He'd freed her hair now and spread it across her back, smoothing it with repetitive motions. Her eyes drifted shut and her blood became a warm golden flow through her arteries.

"What was the connection? You don't have to tell me if you don't want to." She added that last part in a rush, hoping she wasn't pushing him, but, oh—how she wanted to know this man.

His hands stilled on her hair. "I do." The

surprise in his voice caught her off guard. "I want to tell you, though you won't like me at the end of it." The break in his voice cracked her heart, too. Who was she to urge him to open up while keeping her own past a secret?

"Doubtful."

Jack fell silent and they listened to the fire hiss and crackle. The rain continued to pummel the earth. The horses nickered to each other. Otherwise, all was quiet.

"Jessie was a cute kid."

"What was the age difference?"

He laid his cheek on top of her head. "Nine years. I'm the oldest, so it was my job to look out for my siblings after my dad passed."

She could almost feel the grief pulsing inside him. "So you were responsible for Jesse."

She felt his nod and scooted sideways to turn and look at him. The heat of the fire now roared up her arm.

"He had his share of troubles. A sports injury got him hooked on painkillers. After the refills ended, he turned to heroin."

"That's hard to quit."

"He tried. Many times. My mother would always get her hopes up when he'd go to rehab, then cry and cry when he'd fall into his old habits."

"What about you? How did you feel?"

He stared at the fire for a moment, then looked up at her, the muscles in his jaw working. "Angry. Not at first. But after years of it, I got tired of seeing Mom put through so much pain. She didn't deserve that."

"No. But it's what mothers do. I mean, they worry about us." She thought of her own deceased parent.

After the bank heist, she'd been relieved that her mother wasn't around to see how low she'd fallen. Now she wondered if her mother would have been more accepting and supportive, and if her father and sister wouldn't have felt ashamed of her. Perhaps her wish to keep them safe from Kevin had been an excuse to run from her problems rather than face them.

"He'd been out of rehab for a couple weeks when he went missing. My mother wanted me to find him and bring him home."

"Did your other siblings go with you?"

"No. Just me. I was supposed to protect him." His voice dropped and he was silent for a moment, stone-faced.

Finally, he continued, "I found him at a pool hall. He asked for my help and I told him I wouldn't give it if it had to do with drugs. When he got up and left, I knew I was right."

"You must have been disappointed."

"I was furious. He was going to break Mom's heart again. And Jesse…we'd gotten him enrolled in college. He'd always wanted to be a smoke jumper—you know—those forest firefighters, but it looked like he wanted drugs more."

"Did you guys fight?"

"I got into it with some lowlifes I saw him with behind the pool hall. Since he'd asked me for money, I knew he was looking to buy drugs. I got jumped when I tried stopping the deal. One of them had a switchblade."

He pointed to his scar and she reached up to trace it, her fingers exploring the ridges and valleys that marked him as a man who defended his family, who stood for what was right and good… Everything she did not.

"That's a horrible cut."

He caught her hand and brought it briefly to his mouth, pressing a kiss on her fingertips. "I deserve it for leaving my brother with them."

"He didn't go with you?"

"He told me to get out of there, but I could have refused to go to the hospital without him…made him with come with me."

He stopped for a moment, his voice thick.

He brushed his thumb slowly across her cheek. His touch was so tender, it startled her. No one had ever touched her like this before, looked at her the way he was looking at her right now, deep into her.

"I called him a jerk. Told him to fend for himself. Said he was a waste of my time. A waste, period, and not to bother coming home. I was in pain. Shock, too, maybe. But it's no excuse for me not keeping my temper."

He shook his head as if he shook away tears, and a heavy weight settled in her heart. She brushed the slight damp from the corners of his eyes and he gathered her close, his heart thudding against hers.

"Is that the night Jesse died?"

"Yes."

She nestled closer. "You don't have to tell me."

"I need to," he said, the words seeming ripped from a dark place. "I was supposed to protect him, but instead, I went to the ER and got stitched up. I left him, and in the morning the police told us he'd been shot and killed on a back road. His killers got away."

It took her a minute to register what he'd said, to understand the depth of his pain, his guilt—justified in his mind but not in hers.

"That's horrible. I'm sorry, Jack. But that wasn't your fault."

"Yes. It was. I was supposed to keep him safe." She could hear the heartache in his voice.

"He chose his path." Just like she'd chosen hers, spoke the voice that'd been pestering her, louder and louder and louder, since Jack's arrival.

"I was his big brother. All his life he looked up to me, and I left him to face those guys. To die…alone." He dropped his head into his hands and his shoulders bunched.

"Is that why you left the ranch?"

He nodded. "Everywhere I looked reminded me of Jesse, of how I'd let him down. I took off right after the funeral."

She studied the belt buckle tattoo on his forearm, her heart swelling with the burdens he carried. "That's Jesse's."

"So I'll never forget. Not that I ever will."

"Did they ever catch the guys?"

A hard look flashed in his eyes. If she didn't know him as well as she did, she'd have been petrified. Or maybe, knowing him as well as she did, whoever he was thinking of should be petrified.

"Not yet. Since it was dark and they wore hoodies, I didn't get a good enough look to visually identify them. They stayed in a nearby motel and one of the names on the register, Everett Ridland, was an alias used by a bond jumper."

"Is that why you became a bounty hunter? To find them?"

"I did it to make up for what I'd done."

"You want forgiveness." Oh, how she understood that...and the need to distance yourself from your wrongs. She and Jack weren't so different, except that he was fighting to make things right while she simply hid.

She wanted to confide in Jack. Needed to.

"I want retribution," he said. "My brother deserved better. I won't stop until I catch his murderers."

"And you won't go home," she added, thinking of her own self-imposed exile from Texas.

"Not until I've gotten justice for Jesse."

"Do you think the people that killed the Denver couple killed Jesse?"

He stared at the fire like he'd seen a ghost, then shook his head. "It's possible. A 9mm gun was used in both. Smiley's ma says she drove him and a guy named Everett up here. Oh, and one of the guys behind the pool hall was smoking Camel Filters cigarettes."

"The same ones as in Tanya's apartment!" A cold chill settled between her shoulders, pressing like a blade. Kevin smoked them, too...but he had nothing to do with this... "Smiley could be involved with Jesse's killer, which means Tanya's in major danger."

"She might be. I'm going to double my watch on her house when we get back."

Something inside her lurched at his protective tone. "Then she'll be safe."

"How can you trust that after hearing my story?"

"Because I do."

The words settled in the air between them. "You're nuts," he said, looking at her, his dark eyes both shiny and sad.

"Probably. But I'm also right. And Dakota was, too. You're a good man, Jack."

It touched her deeply that he'd opened up to her this way. He was brave. Yes, he'd made mistakes, wasn't perfect, but who was? He acted like he didn't need anyone, but she saw clearly that he did, and she wanted to be that person. Very much.

Only...how could that be possible when she kept such a big secret? One this law-abiding man would frown on? Here he'd opened up to her, shared his darkest secrets, and she still hadn't told him about her ex. Guilt and regret rose in her throat, cowardice and bile following.

"I wish that were true." The need for forgiveness in his voice sent a shudder right through her because she felt that way, too.

She touched his scar again and his eyes closed.

"It is." All her feelings for him—hot and beautiful in her heart—dissolved on her tongue, strange, new and inexpressible.

He twined his fingers in hers, his thumb circling the center of her palm, slowly, and Dani disintegrated.

"Jack," she said, voice tight.

He opened his eyes and peered at her strangely, then his eyes widened and sparked, as though he read in her eyes what was in her head, her heart, before he quickly glanced away.

Before she could think about it, she rose a little on her knees, reached for the back of his head and kissed him. He hesitated for just a moment, then shifted forward and kissed her back with a low groan that fired her blood.

His hands came up, firm around her waist, and he gathered her close against him so that she felt the rapid rise and fall of his chest, breathed in the musk of his skin. Mouth slanting against his, she lost herself in this moment. The scent and taste and feel of him. It was like tiny fireworks going off all over her, bits of her she'd thought dead reigniting.

He chased the world away. Evaporated time. Past, present, future—gone, so that none of it mattered, nothing should matter, but them, holding each other this way. For once, the muffled ringing that'd filled her ears since she left Oklahoma muted and she was free, adrift, awash with emotion that made her eyes tear and her heart swell.

He picked her up off the cold dirt and she fitted herself to him, his bulk and strength, the heat from his skin seeping through her shirt. Searing her. Setting her on fire. She kissed his face, his ears, his scar, especially his scar, her fingers in his soft dark hair. When he rained kisses down her neck, the world began to spin and she clutched his shoulders, sensation after sensation washing through her, nearly knocking her off her feet.

And then he pulled back, his eyes on her, his expression a silent question she couldn't answer. Instead, she reached up and kissed his scar, wanting him to know that it made him beautiful to her. How much he meant to her. How every atom of her wanted to be here with him.

He angled his head and kissed her once more, slowly and tenderly.

Their shallow breaths filled the space and they stared at each other, chests rising and falling, his brown eyes black in the dim light.

"Dani, I—I can't promise you anything. I've got to find those guys and I'm no good to anyone until I do… I might not be, even then."

"It's okay. We were caught up in the storm. The moment." She went for an off-hand tone, missed completely. When she whirled away, he turned her back gently, his tender expression making her ache.

"If there was anyone I would get involved with…"

She placed a finger on his lips, then managed to stay quiet for a dozen heartbeats as she struggled to say, finally, "I get it. I'm not interested in a serious relationship, either."

Liar.

"Let's forget this ever happened," she added.

He shook his head slowly. "Impossible," he said, then pulled on his partly dried shirt, doused the fire and guided her outside, where the rain had slacked off.

Dani eyed Jack's swaying back as he rode ahead, checking the path for obstacles or lurking strangers.

She did get it. She was the last person he should be involved with... Another wanted person, just like his brother's killers. Worse, a criminal and a coward. She could never be with Jack, have anything permanent because she kept this big secret.

She didn't deserve him.

CHAPTER NINETEEN

JACK RUBBED BLEARY eyes the next night and clicked on another composite sketch. A white male, aged twenty-five to thirty-five, with a shaved head, brown eyes and a wide moustache that knit into his muttonchops, stared back at him.

Jack was dead tired after a long day leading the Clark family, searching the southeast corner of his property grid for Smiley and working with Milly. The Spark Canyon caves were still inaccessible after the storm. Dani's office chair creaked as he leaned back and laced his fingers behind his head, studying the wanted man on her monitor.

Who are you?
Where are you hiding?
What else have you done?

He held up a picture he'd snapped of Sam and compared it to the drawing. Right age. Face shape. But the nose was off, and the eyes, too. Nope. Not this one, either. He needed a hit, bad.

Sam's alibi for both this afternoon and the horse incident weren't corroborated. Smiley's friend was up to something, and it was frustrating not to have proof or a clear-cut connection between the two men. Jack's property searches had thus far been fruitless or hampered by rain-swollen waterways. He needed a break in this case.

Absently snacking on some mini pretzels, he pressed the mouse, and the screen shuffled to another image.

A smiling Dani in the framed family picture on her desk caught his eye, instead, as it had done since he'd been burning midnight oil working on her computer the last few evenings. In this photo, she held a young boy in her arms and leaned her head on her father's shoulder, their laughing, hazel eyes a match. A sister—Claire, he recalled—pressed a kiss to Dani's cheek and the loving depiction pressed on his heart and reminded him of his own goofy family pictures.

He and his siblings would have tried the patience of a saint, his mother had always scolded. Whenever she'd attempted to corral her children into a group shot, she'd had her hands full with their so-called tomfoolery. To the six of them, it'd been just flat-out fun to get her riled. Her former lectures came back to him, how she'd chided them to stop messing around, stay still, quit laughing, smile like gentlemen and a lady, not act like the scalawags they all were…

And what kind of boys and girl was she raising, anyway?

He felt his lips twitch up, recalling how Jesse had been the worst, technically the baby of the family since he was born minutes after Justin, his twin. He'd always wanted the spotlight and had hammed it up everywhere, in pictures, at family events, at church…

A memory of Jesse's vocal performances every Sunday widened Jack's smile. He remembered how Jesse had always sung hymns the loudest, often holding a final note until the silent congregation turned to stare and the minister cleared his throat.

He'd never worried about getting the words right and some of his "creative" lyric substitutions had reduced Jack and his brothers to helpless laughter. They'd had to gallop down the aisle as soon as the service was over or risk a swat from their mother, who would follow them, her expression thunderous, Jesse's mischievous.

Jesse's shrill tenor belted in his ear.

That saved a wrench, like me...

Yes. That'd been Jesse. So sincere that you were never quite sure how much of it was him foolin', until you looked into his twinkling eyes.

Jack waited for the inevitable crush to his windpipe that accompanied any memory of his brother, but instead felt, along with the familiar deep sadness and regret, a fondness, too. It was a comfort to think of his family in a way he rarely allowed.

Was this Dani's influence?

Since confessing to Dani, he'd felt a seismic shift, as if the sutures that held him together had begun to part, leaving him more open, light entering the dark corners of him. He was still as intent as ever on bringing down his brother's killer, but now he wanted something else, too.

He cared about Dani. Trusted her. It was undeniable.

The urge to open up to her last night had caught him off guard. Something in her grit, her compassion, her depth had beckoned him, like a beacon across a stormy sea. Giving him comfort and shelter...and much more.

Their kiss.

He traced her smile in the picture and rested the pad of his index finger on her lips.

After hearing the bitter truth about him, she'd touched his scar, kissed it, celebrated what was ugly about him. She'd changed the emotions he associated with it. What had been a reminder of his greatest failure was now also a very personal moment he shared with a woman he had come to care for deeply.

It was no matter that he'd only been here a few days, he was a man who knew his mind and heart, and what they both wanted was Dani, teasing him, challenging him, listening and caring, laughing at and with him to the same degree.

But it wasn't to be. As much as she brought him alive, he'd never be whole or healed until he righted his wrongs and got justice for his brother.

But what if that never happened?

He flipped over the picture. Then a solitary life, chasing shadows, was what he deserved.

End of story.

Not the happily-ever-afters his mother liked reading.

If only he could give one to her…or justice, at least.

He needed a break in his mission. Bad.

An alarm shrilled and he bolted to his feet and raced outside. Flames arced skyward, flickering like a struck match in the night.

Fire!

He thundered down the path, rounded a corner and observed an engulfed structure. Tanya's house. Acrid smoke burned his nose and stung his lungs so that he coughed as he neared, his heartbeat thundering in his ears.

His heart struggled to deliver oxygenated blood, his mind scrambled to unravel the situation, make sense of the smoke billowing from the front windows and door, the scarlet fire flickering inside.

Tanya!

Was she inside?

He reached the porch and squinted through the window, eyeing the best point to enter. Tanya had to have made it out.

And then he saw her. A glimpse of a female figure in the flame-lit kitchen, her arms over her face, caught…trapped…

Adrenaline jittered through him as he pulled his T-shirt over his mouth and pushed himself forward and up the crumbling steps.

Flames rose from the warped floorboards and ash thickened the air, dialing visibility to nearly zero.

"Tanya!" he shouted into the roar of the fire.

"Tanya!" A faint call, a female voice. Why would she call her own name unless...

The horrifying thought nearly knocked him down.

Dani. It had to be.

"Dani!" Shoving through the smoke, his skin so hot it felt like it was peeling right off his bones, he lurched into the kitchen. When he saw the shape of a woman collapsed on the floor, he lunged, snatching her up, his pulse screaming, spots appearing before his eyes.

"Dani," he cried, though he couldn't hear his own voice. Her head lolled, mouth open, eyes shut.

A flaming beam followed by a ceiling section crashed at his feet and he stumbled back, the path back out blocked.

Where to go?

Think.

The flash of a cat's tail caught his eye as it disappeared into the murk.

Mittens. Heading for the back porch. Any chance it still stood?

Only one way to find out.

Relying on his memory, he lurched through the dense gray air, boots grinding on broken glass. All around him the hiss and blat of the inferno beat at his eardrums, louder than the rush of blood.

His foot crashed through floorboards and for one heart-stopping moment, he was trapped. *Stay calm*, he ordered himself, trying to curb the panic. Save Dani. He wiggled his boot right, then left, then right again, each second agony as he held his breath, feeling his head start to spin.

Lungs burning, he yanked his boot loose at last and stumbled several more steps, the back stairs nearly tripping him once more. Mittens streaked away, and then pieces of the night sky appeared through the smoke as he pushed himself outside, tough talking himself to go farther and farther and farther. He was so tired it felt like he was walking through wet concrete.

A fair distance away, he carefully laid Dani on the grass by a fence post, the shrill of sirens growing louder. A fire truck tore up and an ambulance followed. Somewhere behind him, he heard the yelling of a gathering crowd, but no one had spotted him and Dani yet.

"Help!" he hollered, turning and waving, his voice faint and as dry as the ash that rained around him.

A gasping sound snatched back his attention and Dani's eyelids fluttered.

"Tanya," she croaked.

Emotion rushed through him, a powerful, battering wave. "I didn't see her," he murmured against her temple, holding her close.

"Is she okay?" Her lids lifted higher and concerned hazel eyes met his.

"I don't know. I need to get you some oxygen."

She sat up a little more. Looked around. "How am I out here? Did you…? Did I…?"

"You're safe now."

Her trembling hand rose and landed on his cheek. Came away wet. Was he crying? "Thank you."

He clutched her to him. Felt the solid reassurance of Dani in his arms, this woman who hadn't hesitated a moment to race head-on into a fire for a friend, to chase down trespassers and round up escaped horses. Her small size belied her huge heart and spirit, and every moment he spent with her sent him closer to the line he couldn't cross.

He rested his cheek on her head. Maybe

he was fooling himself and he'd crossed that line already. Had fallen hard that first night, when she'd held him at gunpoint without another person for miles to back her up.

He realized, as he held her to him and kissed the top of her head and felt her cling to him, that he would do anything he could to make her happy, to keep her safe. He didn't ask himself how he could know this after four days. It just seemed clearer to him than anything he had worked out in all the years before.

So how, when the time came, would he ever give her up?

TWO HOURS LATER, Jack circled the charred remains of Tanya's house, his thoughts on Dani, who still hadn't returned from the ER with Diane. She'd been more than a little shaky when she'd finally stood and had flat-out refused to go to the hospital without Tanya accounted for...until she'd fainted.

If it hadn't looked strange, he would have brought her there himself, but Diane had stepped in and quietly insisted he stay for the investigation.

Now he could only wait and worry.

One fire marshal squatted inside the gutted house, flashlight in hand, inspecting wires on the now exposed beams while another tramped through the structure, sifting through debris. A third scribbled on a small pad as he questioned the last staff members on site, Jori Lynn and Blake, while a fourth unfurled yellow crime-scene tape as he carefully paced around the structure.

The rest of the firefighters had left an hour ago, the inferno out. The roof had collapsed and burned. One wall had fallen. Breezes stirred thick ash so that it drifted in heaps. The stench of burned wood dirtied the air and his lungs burned as if he'd been chain smoking for hours. A circling blue light on the dash of a sheriff's department SUV caught his attention. The large black vehicle slowed to a halt and Lance stepped out, his uniform so crisp it looked like it could do the walking for him. His polished badge glinted.

"Heard the call come in. Thought I'd stop by."

"Glad you did."

In the distance, the inspector flipped his pad closed, and Jori Lynn and Blake waved before disappearing into the darkness, heading toward staff quarters. With Larry up at the main house reassuring the alarmed guests that everything was fine, he and Lance could speak freely.

He stepped over blown-out window frames and pieces of metal littering the front yard to join his cousin by his vehicle.

"This was Tanya's house. Smiley's girl-friend."

Lance took off his hat and waved it in front of his face slowly, his brow creased. "Any idea what caused it?"

Jack shoved his hands in his pockets. "Waiting on the fire marshal."

Lance propped the heel of his boot on the tire behind him and crossed his arms over his chest. "You okay?"

"Why?"

"You're black, from head to toe, looks like the back of that hand is burned and your knee is cut."

Jack stared down at his pink knuckles and the slash in his jeans, dumbfounded at the red stain. He hadn't felt it, couldn't, not with his mind so full of Dani and how close he'd come to losing her.

"You should get medical attention."

Jack shot him a look. "I'll get a Band-Aid."

Lance pulled out a pack of butterscotch candies and offered the roll to Jack. "Heard

Larry's filing a report on the horses and some missing guest items. We'll have uniforms out here tomorrow."

"Good." Jack waved away the candy. "I need more eyes out for Sam Perkins, too. He didn't show up at the fire."

"Interesting."

"Their stable manager, Dani, was there. She could have been killed."

"How's that?" Lance's cheek bulged and the smell of butterscotch competed with the fumes from the fire.

"She went in after Tanya." One of the fire marshals yelled something and waved the other over.

Lance turned around and they watched the men jabber over a scorched piece of flooring. Lance whistled. "Gutsy gal. Any sign of Tanya?"

One of the investigators began taking pictures while another reopened his pad and jotted down notes. Jack craned his neck, angling for a better look. "No. But her car's gone."

Lance rubbed his jaw. "Smiley."

"Yes. Dani and I spotted him and a partner yesterday up by Spark Canyon. Because of the storm, couldn't get close enough to them to capture him. Thinking he might have been spooked at the close call and came back for Tanya's car."

"She could be an accomplice."

Jack shifted on his feet, his knee starting to throb. "Or a victim. Dani was pretty sure Tanya planned on convincing Smiley to turn himself in."

"Maybe he wasn't persuaded." Lance eyed a dangling gutter swaying in the wind. "If she's not back by morning, we'll file a missing person's report and issue a BOLO for the vehicle."

Jack nodded, his thoughts turning to Dani. If she wasn't back in thirty minutes, he'd head up to the hospital.

"Hey, Gary," he heard Lance say, voice rising, and looked up to see one of the fire marshals approaching.

The pale man neared, shoulders curved inward, as though he recoiled from some unseen blow. Tight curls framed his forehead. He tugged off his gloves one finger at a time. "Sheriff."

"Your preliminary assessment? You can speak freely."

Gary's eyes shifted to Jack. "Inconclusive evidence for arson. We'll be sending in our full team tomorrow."

"Any signs of foul play?"

Gary pulled out a tissue and blew his nose. At Lance's nod, he said, "None so far. I'll be in touch."

Static and garbled voices crackled from Lance's police radio as the marshals left.

"Better get that."

Jack followed Lance to his SUV. Lance pulled out his handset, listened to the dispatcher, then gave rapid-fire instructions on a response to a domestic call. After ending the exchange, he slid behind the wheel and peered up at Jack.

"We located the Phillips' safe-deposit box today."

Jack rested his arm on the top of the SUV and pressed his stinging hand to the cool metal. "What was in it?"

"Three hundred K and passports. Same names as the ones on the Madagascar tickets. Plus some numbers that turned out to be Swiss bank accounts."

Jack chewed on the information for a bit before asking, "Fleeing the country?"

"There's no record of that couple on the manifest."

"They missed their flight." It was more a

statement than question, since they both knew why the would-be travelers were "detained."

"Question is," Lance mused, his expression thoughtful, "what were they running from... or who?"

"Hoping Smiley can answer that. Let me know what you get with the BOLO and I'll check out those caves tomorrow if I can."

Lance's eyebrows rose. "So you'll be finishing up in time for the family reunion. You could bring Dani, though I still make the better date."

A short laugh escaped Jack. "I told you, you're not my type."

"So you'll bring Dani?"

"Let it go, Lance." Jack drummed his fingers on the door panel.

"You know detectives." Lance's shoulders lifted then fell, his smug smile as irritating as it'd ever been. "Once we bite down, we don't let go."

"So that makes you a dog?"

"Wolf." Lance regarded him with grim amusement. "And if you don't show up for your mother, you're an—"

Jack slammed the door shut, cutting off his cousin, and gave Lance a mocking salute as he reversed and drove away, horn beeping.

In the quiet, the mules brayed and bats swooped over roadside ditches, straining insects. Blue spokes of moonlight rotated through the fields.

Dani at Cade Ranch.

For the first time since his brother's death, he could picture himself home again...

...with Dani.

CHAPTER TWENTY

"HEY," DANI CALLED to Jack as she leaned over the corral's fence. All around her, the early morning sky glowed like a pearl as the moon slipped to the horizon, a half-lidded eye. She watched Jack circle a coil of rope overhead then toss it. The rope snapped through the air, and the loop dropped neatly over a fence post.

He and Milly looked up when she called out again and the sight of him, tall and broad-shouldered in the growing light, his feet planted, his jaw firm, briefly eased her anguish over Tanya's disappearance. Since giving her statement to the police at the hospital, Dani had spent the night cuddling the displaced Mittens, unable to sleep, imagining worst case scenarios for her friend.

Finally, she'd given up, gotten dressed and wandered outside, hoping to find Jack. And here he was, faithful to his word about Milly. The horse's ears lay flat, and she stood as far as she could from a saddle mounted on the fence. Maybe it wasn't such a good day for her, either.

"Hey, yourself." After putting the horse back into the pasture, he ambled over and gathered her hands in his. "How's your head?"

She looked up at his face, into his thick-lashed brown eyes, even though she knew it was going to feel like someone was hooking her insides out through her chest.

You love him.

This man had saved her life and stolen her heart. Her hand rose to the small, aching bump on her temple. It didn't bother her as much as her conscience did. "Fine."

You've been falling for him since you met and you haven't told him a thing.

"Glad to hear it."

"I wanted to thank you." Guilt lodged in her throat, making it difficult to breathe. "For last night."

He ducked his head. Examined his boots. He looked good in black, she mused, taking in his dark T-shirt. Like he'd been drawn in charcoal.

"No need."

"You risked your life."

His hands tightened around hers. "And you

could have died." A jagged edge serrated his words.

"I don't remember everything. I mean, I heard the horses and went out to check, saw the fire and ran to get Tanya. The rest is black."

He brought her fingers to his mouth and his words whispered against her knuckles. "You were crazy for going in there." His hand shook slightly.

A shivery feeling began in her stomach, spread. "I know."

"Reckless." He was smiling, but not like usual. There was a vulnerability in it, a hesitancy; it was all over his face, swimming around in those beautiful brown eyes, too.

"Yes."

"And brave." He pressed her hand to his scar and her whole being melted, liquid with joy.

How he must trust her to be so vulnerable. It wasn't so long ago that he'd averted his face around people, hiding his imperfection, which, to her, was what was most perfect about him. He wore what wasn't right about him on the outside, for the world to see, instead of hiding it, like she did. She had to tell him.

How could she tell him?

How could she not?

He might discover it anyway if he found her in his databases.

"Scared is closer," she admitted. With all that he still didn't know about her, she couldn't bear for him to heap false praise on her. "I was afraid Tanya was in there."

"Her car wasn't back when I checked earlier."

She blinked fast, eyes pricking. "Where is she, Jack? Did Smiley take her?"

He released her hand and squinted down the dirt road that led to the front gate. A horse rolled in the grass behind them and a rooster released a throaty crow into the crisp, spring air. "It's possible. A missing person's report will be filed if she doesn't show up in the next few hours. And they'll be looking for her car."

"I blame myself." Her words were a notch above a whisper. She peered at him through her bangs.

He tipped her chin with one finger and searched her eyes. "No. She made her own choices."

A deep tremble shook her. "But I told her to convince Smiley to turn himself in. She said she'd do it herself if she had to."

"And that would have been the right thing to do," Jack said, firmly.

"Even if it means she's…she's…" Dani couldn't say the words she was thinking.

Hurt. Dead.

"We don't know anything yet. Come here." The timbre of his voice deepened and he ducked through the fence and put his arms around her and down the length of her back.

She breathed in his clean scent, the smell of honest, hard work, felt the warmth of his skin and the drum of his heart against hers. All the while her unspoken words fluttered in the back of her throat.

"She's a good person, Jack."

"I know."

The conviction in his voice caught her off guard. She would have expected him to be more suspicious than ever. "You do?"

"She's your friend."

There it was, the quiet confidence, the belief in her that she didn't deserve. She felt tears in her eyes and looked away. "How'd it go with Milly today?"

"She wanted no part of that." He pointed to the saddle and their gazes settled on Milly. She had returned to her distant corner of the pasture and was grazing, her eyes on them.

Concern dropped the bottom out of Dani's stomach. "Do you think she can be broken in again?"

Jack's long breath blew out his cheeks. "Not sure. She's getting better around people...but not enough yet to be pasture sound at a dude ranch. Maybe somewhere else... where she wouldn't have to interact much or be ridden..."

"Then she'll have to be euthanized." Now her eyes full-on stung and she swiped the rush of damp.

"I'm going to do my best to help her avoid that, but I won't have much more time here."

"So, you're leaving?" she asked dully, feeling like the sun had just ducked behind the clouds.

"If Smiley isn't located, I'll still need to check those caves at Spark Canyon. Plus, Sam Perkins is still a question I have to answer for the Mays. But that might be only another day, maybe two."

"The rodeo is at the end of this week. I'd hoped you could ride Milly, since Pokey's gone—show the Mays that she's worth keeping." *Stay with me.*

Stay with me.

"I'd like that, but I can't make any promises if the investigation leads me elsewhere."

What were the chances she'd ever meet someone like him again? Someone she could love forever, someone who would forever love her back the way she knew a man with strong convictions like Jack would love?

A snippet of one of her favorite E. E. Cummings poems came back to her as she stared into his steadfast eyes.

…here is the root of the root and the bud
of the bud
and the sky of the sky of a tree called
life; which grows
higher than soul can hope or mind can
hide.

That was Jack.

"Will you be sorry?" he asked, his quiet words dropping in the air between them, quieting her rambling thoughts.

"You know I will."

He set his forehead against hers and suddenly she didn't know what to do with her hands or her eyes. "I wish…"

"I know…" She sighed, feeling the other day's intimacy return, wanting to say something more, knowing she couldn't, not with his life devoted to capturing his brother's killers and hers devoted to hiding her past.

Denver Sheriff Department SUVs approached on the dirt road, tires crunching on pebbles, chickens squawking and fluttering out of the way, and she stepped out of Jack's arms. The caravan rolled up toward the main house while another vehicle, marked Fire Department, veered left toward Tanya's. What would they find in the ashes? Not Tanya. Dear Lord. Not that.

He rubbed her arms. "You're cold."

"No, I'm not," she said through clenched teeth, fearing they'd chatter.

"You've got goose bumps."

"I'm fine. Really. Listen. The Clarks don't need us today. Mr. Clark hired some 'expert' to come and take him and family fishing. We could search for Tanya and Smiley ourselves."

"I was planning on checking the area where we spotted the men."

"Can I go with you?"

A teasing gleam lightened his brown eyes a couple of shades. Made them glow. Like someone had lit a candle behind them. "Can I stop you, *partner*?"

Jack. When he smiled, Dani couldn't help

smiling. When his face turned sad, something inside her broke a little. She wished she'd met him years ago, before she'd gone left instead of right, taken the wrong turns that kept her from ever traveling beside him.

But she had him for now and she'd make the most of it.

She took his rope and stepped back, twirling the loop until it stretched from her armpit to her toes. Then she twisted it overhead. When she released it, the loop dropped neatly over Jack, tightening when it fell to his waist.

He stared down, then his eyes rose. He whistled. "Nice."

"I *am* a former Stampede Princess…" She tugged a bit to make sure it didn't slide. If only she could rope this cowboy for good. Wouldn't life be simpler that way? "Looks like you can't leave me."

He reeled her in, pulling the rope gently until she stopped a breath away from him, then flipped the hair out of her eyes. "Who says I want to?"

A FLASH OF blue through the trees stopped Jack in his tracks a few hours later. He reached out and stopped Dani, then lifted a finger to his lips.

Her large eyes met his and he was grateful that she didn't ask him what was happening. Knew enough to keep quiet. After spotting a fresh trail behind Tanya's house, they'd been following the same, circuitous trail for the better part of the morning. It was slow, painstaking work as he carefully examined bent branches and shoe impressions until they'd led here, to the same copper mine where he and Dani had waited out the storm.

Where you realized you love her.

He pushed the thought away and pulled her down beside him, ducking behind a group of rocks and waiting. His heartbeat rushed at his eardrums, drowning everything out until he got hold of himself, falling into the familiar patterns and rhythms of his job. Only nothing was the same with Dani along. Keeping her safe was now as much his focus as capturing his target.

Damn.

He should never have agreed to let her come.

The sound of boots, clomping on packed dirt and rocky soil, grew louder and louder. Jack slid his Glock from its holster and cocked it.

Suddenly all was still and he held his breath. Had the man heard him?

Without warning, a hand appeared and grabbed Dani by her shirt collar, yanking her back, hard, so that her boots slid out from under her as she was dragged away.

Jack sprang to his feet, gun drawn, trained on—

"Sam!" he exclaimed, staring hard at the groundskeeper who pressed his 9mm into Dani's temple. Sam's eyes narrowed to slits. "Let her go."

"The hell I will." When Dani jerked, he threw his arm around her, his elbow digging into her windpipe, a chokehold. "Hold still or I'll shoot."

Fury rose inside. Howled through Jack, an unholy anger that washed the world blood red. "What's your business here?"

Sam's eyes flitted to a leather saddlebag. "What's yours?"

"We're looking for whoever's responsible for burning Tanya's house down. And the horse theft. You know anything about that?"

Dani wriggled and Sam pistol whipped her hard enough to make her lashes flutter and her head droop.

Jack's control slipped ever closer to the edge, but he held on, for Dani's sake. A hothead didn't follow logic well. Look what his knee-jerk reaction had cost his brother. "Dani, don't move."

Her lids lifted slightly and then her body sagged in Sam's arms. Alarm rose in him, making his fingers tighten on his gun.

Sam tried to hitch up a slipping Dani, but her knees buckled and she dropped to the ground, the angle catching Sam off-balance.

It was all the opening Jack needed. He prepared to launch at Sam now that the gun wasn't pointed at Dani, but, without warning, her elbow connected with the most vulnerable part of Sam and he doubled over.

"Oof," he moaned, and Dani rolled away just as Jack hurtled for the 9mm and scooped it up, now training both guns on Sam.

"On the ground. Now!"

Sam sank to his knees then flopped onto his stomach.

"Arms out from your sides," ordered Jack.

"Look at this!" he heard Dani exclaim, and he glimpsed her searching through the saddlebag out of the corner of his eye.

"Aren't these the rings Mrs. Clark reported missing?"

Sam lifted his head slightly, then dropped it. Dani squatted just out of Sam's reach. "And look at these cell phones. All guests'. You're the thief."

He recognized the one he'd glimpsed Mr.

Clark talking into the other day. Looked like he could cross that name off his suspect list. The guy was a jerk, but not involved in anything sinister as Lance had suggested.

"Don't think about it, Sam," Jack said quietly, when one of Sam's fingers twitched in Dani's direction. "Is anyone else with you?" They'd been following only one set of human prints, not the two sets of hoof impressions he'd wanted. And they weren't the same size and shape as Smiley's. Still. He had to make sure.

"Nah." Sam turned his head and closed his eyes.

"Smiley?"

"Haven't seen him in days."

"Are you hiding him out here?"

"I'll check the cave," Dani called, and before he could stop her, she'd disappeared inside.

"Why did you murder those people in Denver?"

My brother...

Threads of nausea reached up Jack's windpipe.

"Who?" Sam opened his eyes. Lifted his head and looked confused. An act?

"The Phillipses," Jack growled. "Remy and Cheryl Ann."

"Never heard of them. Look. I may be a thief, but I'm no killer," Sam muttered, sounding indignant. If it was an act, it was a good one.

"So why the gun?"

"Protection."

"From?"

A sly look entered Sam's eyes before he shut them again and gave a fake snore. Did this joker think he was funny? Jack was the one with all the punch lines...the kind that hurt.

And where was Dani?

A moment later she emerged, flushed and breathing fast. Her green-gold eyes sparked. "I followed those tracks a ways and found this." She tilted a box and he glimpsed electronics, cash and jewels.

"Is that why you came up here, Sam?"

He spoke without opening his eyes. "The police are everywhere and the Mays are letting them search our rooms. I had to stash the rest of this week's loot."

"Didn't want to get caught," Dani snarled, resembling an avenging angel with the light setting her strawberry blonde hair ablaze. "Well. Too bad, Sam."

Someone's watched too many Westerns,

Jack thought, his mouth hitching up. He half expected to hear her to say, "The jig's up" next.

"The jig's up, Sam," she said, and this time he did smile, full-on, despite his worry, his anguish, his regrets.

"On your feet, Sam," he ordered.

An hour later, they'd returned to the ranch and turned the man over to Lance. He placed his hand on a cuffed Sam's head, guided him inside the SUV, then slammed the door behind him.

"We found Tanya's car just down the highway," Lance said quietly, keeping his voice low despite their private location behind the May's house and away from prying eyes.

Dani rose a bit on her toes beside him. Her features sharpened. "Did you find Tanya?"

"It was abandoned. Looks like it ran out of gas. We towed it in and we'll know more when we run forensics."

"You don't see any...any..."

"No. No signs of foul play and the fire marshal ruled out arson for the house. Looks like it started from a tipped over candle."

She sighed and Jack slid an arm around her. "What about Sam?"

"We'll run his prints when we book him.

See what comes up that we can connect to the Phillips case. Good work, cousin."

"Dani's the one who brought him down." Pride and admiration coursed through him for her bravado, her heedlessness for her own safety, all things that bugged him, but made him adore her.

Love her.

Lance whistled and Dani shifted beside him, looking a little uncomfortable. "Glad you're on our side, then. So, how do you feel about family reunions?"

"Pardon?" Her wide eyes swerved between Lance and him.

"Cut it, Lance."

His cousin chuckled and swung around to the driver's seat. "Not a chance." He slid behind the wheel and backed out, dust flying behind his wheels as he sped off.

"What'd he mean about a family reunion?"

"He thinks I should bring a date to mine." When she opened her mouth, he hurried on because if she said she'd go with him, he honestly didn't know if he could stay away like he should. "Nice work back there." He nodded toward the mountain.

"It wasn't anything."

"Held at gunpoint?"

"Don't they tell you to play dead if you're attacked in the woods?"

She looked so serious, he couldn't help but chuckle and she joined him, their laughter growing louder until they were holding their sides and she wiped away tears. It felt good to have this moment with her, memories to savor in the lonely nights ahead.

He smoothed her hair off her face. Her skin was as soft as he remembered, smooth as porcelain.

"You're an idiot," he said affectionately, his hands on her cheeks.

"It took you that long to figure out? Guess that makes you an idiot, too."

Before he could respond, Diane May appeared, her hands stirring the air as they lifted and fell. "Larry and I would like a word with you two, if you have a moment."

He and Dani exchanged a quick look and followed her up into the house.

Bella and Beau leaped at the door as it swung open, then trotted behind, hard on their heels, as Diane led them down the hall.

Larry looked up from his computer when they entered the office.

"Here they are," he said to the monitor. "Jack. I know you said not to mention anything, but things have gone too far. Tanya's house burning. Horses stolen. Guests missing things. Smiley… Anyway, I've got Ben on Skype here and he'd like to talk to you."

Jack smothered his disappointment. It was understandable that the Mays would want to tell their son everything, but he needed as few people aware of the situation as possible… especially if it turned out Sam had nothing to do with murdering the Phillipses and he needed to keep searching for Smiley.

"Hello," came a voice from the computer, and Jack squatted beside Larry's chair.

A thin, dark-haired man's smile faded as he squinted at the screen, his eyes as flat and blue as breath mints. He coughed into his hand and pressed a button on his phone.

"Coffee," he said, then he looked back at the recorder. "Sorry about that. Jack, is it?"

"Yes."

Ben's hand flew to his own cheek and Jack fought his old instincts to turn away and spare others from his scar. Dani had taught him to be proud of his marks. He wouldn't feel self-conscious again, not when the person he'd come to respect the most said otherwise.

A breeze ruffled curtains around a large

group of windows behind Ben; a gem-colored ocean rippled in the distance.

"Your parents speak highly of you."

Ben smiled, his earlier unease fading, it seemed. "Exaggerated, I'm sure. Look. Mom and Pop filled me in on what's been going on, and it's alarming."

Jack commiserated. There was nothing worse than feeling far apart from a loved one in danger.

"I agree. I'm keeping an eye out, though."

"It sounds as though the police have apprehended the suspect. Sam Perkins. Who would have thought?"

"He's a friend of Smiley's. It's not hard to imagine. Plus, we don't have a clear link to Sam and the Denver homicide, yet."

"You don't have a clear link between *Smiley* and the double homicide, either," Ben asserted, and Jack remembered Nan saying that he and Smiley had spent summers together as kids, had been close. Understandably, he'd want to defend his friend.

"True. But he's jumped his bond on the drug charge and we're hoping that once I bring him in, he'll confess. Name the other hit man and explain who hired them to kill the Phillipses and why."

"That seems sophisticated for a local boy like Smiley. I know the guy." Ben twirled a pen in his fingers, tip tapping the keyboard.

"People can surprise you."

The pen stilled. "It'd take a lot of proof to convince me. In any case, it sounds as though he's left the area, so no need for you to stay anymore."

Jack stared at Ben. "Actually, I have something to share with your parents." His eyes swung to Diane and Larry, then Dani. She crouched by the file cabinet, scratching the dogs behind their ears, her gaze meeting his.

"Tanya's car was recovered less than a mile away. If we're assuming Smiley left in that, he didn't get far unless he hitchhiked. Also, the fire marshals have ruled out arson."

Ben bent at the waist and his elbows jerked, as if he tied his shoes. "That's good. Look, Jack," he said, straightening. "If you haven't found Smiley by now, you probably won't. Like you said, he could have hitchhiked. If Sam was helping him and now Sam's arrested, that's another reason Smiley won't stick around. Your time is valuable. No reason to stay when I'll be there tomorrow. I've already canceled my last meetings here and booked a flight home. I'll keep an eye out for Smiley in case he shows up."

Jack considered Ben's words. There was logic to them. As a bounty hunter, his time was valuable and it didn't pay to chase after ghosts. Yet for him this had never been about the money, and his gut said he should stay. Smiley was here and possibly his brother's murderer.

Dani snared his eye. Was he being persuaded by other feelings?

"Larry, Diane. What's your opinion?"

Diane knotted the end of her skirt tie. "Well. Ben is cutting his trip short to come home, so I suppose there's no need."

Larry stared out the window. "Your time is valuable. Wouldn't want you to waste it here."

"And those are your only objections? That you don't want to put me out?"

Larry nodded, but Jack noticed the stiffness in his shoulders, the way Diane's mouth trembled before she pressed her lips together.

"Then if it's all the same to you, I'll stick around."

"I wouldn't want the guests to see you searching the area, not when they've already been through a fire, robberies and now an arrest," Ben said. "Many of them are repeat customers. Income my folks rely on."

"I'm very discreet."

"Nevertheless…"

"He's fitting in just fine, Ben," Dani spoke up. She came around the computer to join him. "The staff and guests like him a lot. It'd be more upsetting for him to abruptly leave. Besides, Tanya's also missing and we need Jack to help us look for her."

Dani moved her gaze to his. She'd always told him to loosen up, stop scaring people with his antisocial ways. How far he'd come, for her to think of him this way. And she trusted him to find her friend.

Ben sipped his coffee then lowered it. "Good point. Thanks, Dani. Mom. Dad? It's your business. Your call."

"You mentioned you might have trouble getting a flight last minute," Diane said, joining the group. "If Jack wouldn't mind, it'd put us at ease to know he was around until you're here."

Ben's tense face relaxed and he smiled. "I admit, it'd make me feel better, too, to know someone was there until I get home. Jack, I'm relying on you."

"I'll hold down the fort and hopefully find

Smiley, as well." Although with his leads drying up, he had to admit that Ben had a point about moving on. But he wanted to settle things with Dani before he left. He couldn't make her promises, but he didn't want to go without saying what was in his heart…figure out some path forward.

"Let's hope, and—" Ben said, then the screen froze.

Larry reached forward and tapped on the keyboard. "Shoot. Lost the connection."

Jack met Dani's eyes, knowing there was one connection he had to make soon…before his time ran out.

CHAPTER TWENTY-ONE

THE NEXT EVENING, Jack and Dani parked in front of a honky-tonk. She stared straight at the neon sign that flashed the words Rusty Roof. She was as silent as she'd been the entire ride over to Shawnee…as closed off as she'd looked since he mentioned the anonymous tip he'd received today about a Smiley sighting here. The caller had seen one of his downtown fliers and phoned.

Jack scanned the fields surrounding this ramshackle, one-story bar on Shawnee's outskirts, wondering if his bounty lurked here, knowing it was a long shot. Trees, sky, scrub brush. Darkness falling like velvet. Already a few pale stars. Cars and pickups swerved into the gravel parking lot and couples, dressed to the nines in ten-gallon hats and swinging skirts headed inside for line-dancing night, according to a marquee.

"Why would Smiley come here? Isn't that a risk?" Dani asked, her voice sounding dry.

"Could be any reason." He shrugged. "Maybe he planned to meet someone."

Her fingers shredded a napkin in her lap and she made a choking sound.

"I can drive you back if you're not feeling well," he offered, concern growing. She'd been through a lot these past few days. He'd seen Dani angry, amused, blustering, worried, excited, reckless, headstrong and downright goofy—his favorite side of her, besides the passionate one that tortured him every moment of every day...and night—but never this stone-cold silent.

If this information panned out, he could be wrapping up the case soon, and he didn't intend to leave without figuring things out with Dani. Yet she seemed as distant as the North Star.

"It's okay." She shook back her bangs and the light illuminated her face. Red, then green. Red again. She heaved in a big breath, as if making some decision, slapped her hands on her jeans-clad legs and opened the truck door.

"Hey," he called, and she whirled, her boots already on his running board. "You could stay here. I just need to look around and ask a few questions. It won't take me long. Maybe fifteen minutes, then we can do something fun, like rappel down into Spark Canyon," he said, only half kidding, since he actually needed to do that.

"And miss the line dancing?"

Relieved to see a little of her good humor return, he couldn't help but tease, "Are you any good?"

"Just try to keep up." Her hair looked perfect, every curl shiny and in place, and her lips were a glossy pink. He could tell from here that she'd taste like strawberries. She settled her white hat and hopped out.

Line dancing. Well. He'd been to enough weddings to know a few steps. He hustled after Dani and caught up to her at the door.

She paused, looking so pale he wondered if her head was bothering her. A couple cut around her. A stocky man held open the door and swept his arm wide, ushering him and Dani inside.

A few steps in, Dani turned slowly, her eyes scanning the room. He paid the bouncer the cover charge and joined her.

"Looking for someone?"

"What?" She seemed to jump a little at the question. "Hey. There's Ray." She waved at a mustached man pouring shots of whiskey behind the long, crowded wooden bar that ran the length of the honky-tonk.

Tim McGraw's "Indian Outlaw" pulsed through the steaming room, where lines of dancers decked out in plaid, jeans, rhinestones and spurs stomped forward, sideways and back, twirling, kicking and clapping along to the tune.

He spotted Jori Lynn and Blake on the dance floor, neither seeming to follow any recognizable pattern, more or less making it up as they went, laughing wildly. The fresh smell of ale tickled his nose and a powerful thirst developed for a beer. If he wasn't working, he'd grab one.

Dani took his hand and pulled him through the whooping, hollering partiers and stopped behind an empty bar stool. A patron vacated an adjacent spot and they slid into their seats.

Cupping her hands around her mouth, she yelled, "Ray!" The bartender peered over, his sudden smile lifting his otherwise hangdog face. He slapped a bar towel over one shoulder and hurried to join them.

"Howdy, Dani. Haven't seen you in a while. How've you been?"

"Good." She pushed her hat back and

leaned her elbows on the bar. "Can we talk to you somewhere in private?"

His eyes, magnified by his large-framed glasses, landed on Jack's face. Stayed.

"Ray? Earth to Ray," Dani prompted, and a hint of her old spunk returned to her voice.

"Sure." He tore his gaze off Jack and led them down a short hall, past restrooms and a coin phone, and into an office. "What can I do for you?" Ray asked a moment later. He settled into a chair behind a desk so neat even the paperclips appeared to be sorted in size order. A mounted elk head dominated the small space that smelled of peppermint schnapps and old paper.

"Ray, this is Jack. Jack, Ray, the owner. Jack's a bounty hunter looking for Smiley."

Jack thrust out a hand. "I appreciate your time."

Ray shook it, looking dazed. "Terrill? Is he in trouble?"

"Jumped his bond," Jack said. An overhead fan stirred the muggy air and lifted the hair wisps on the edge of Ray's bald patch. "I got a tip he was seen here yesterday. Can you confirm?"

Ray nodded slowly. "He didn't talk much. Mostly stayed to himself."

"Was he alone?"

"Yeah. He came in just before closing. I would have kicked him out but he had me pouring steady. Plus…he looked like he needed a drink."

"Did he say anything to you?"

"Not me. Someone called him, and he had a good amount to say to whoever it was, but I didn't listen. I respect my customers' privacy," Ray pronounced in a holier-than-everyone voice.

Jack tamped down his frustration. The road to hell was paved with good intentions. "Well. I appreciate your time, sir."

Ray lurched to his feet. "If he stops by again, I'll be sure to call right away."

Jack slid his card across the desk. "Thank you."

Ray walked them back out to the rowdy throng and clapped Jack on the back. "Sorry I couldn't do much for you. Drinks are on the house. Have a good evening."

Tipping his hat, Jack said, "Sure enough," and watched Ray go back to his spot behind the bar and lean over to take more orders.

Jack felt the muscles in his jaw tighten. Another promising lead…another dead end.

"Are you okay?" Dani shouted in his ear,

her hand on his arm. "Ready to get out of here?"

He started to nod, then looked down at her, at her bright face, her lively eyes, and found that he didn't want to go, despite the frustrating night.

He wanted to forget it all, the dead ends, the near misses, and just lose himself in Dani, for once.

"How about a dance?"

"Here?"

"I think it's kind of what they do."

She looked over her shoulder at the door, then back to the dance floor, hesitating.

"You said something about me trying to keep up…" He took her hand and tugged her toward the dance floor's edge. He rubbed her hand against his chest. Just barely. Just enough to make the color flare in her cheeks, to make her eyes turn dewy.

"I don't think—" she protested, but he slung an arm around her waist and twirled her fast for the fun of it. He let himself imagine her lips on his again. He wanted to kiss her. Badly.

"You can outdance me, in linedancing?" he finished for her, lifting one eyebrow. His arms were around her, his face was in her hair and there was no place for the rest of her to go but against him. "That wouldn't be hard to do, seeing I only know two steps. Forward and back."

Dani's hair caught fire beneath the rotating lights. Her eyes were green-gold and shining, and his arms were sure of her. As they lined up with the other dancers, she laughed up at him, slightly breathless. "I might have been exaggerating my own, er, talents."

And she wasn't kidding. Over the next twenty minutes she stepped on his toes enough times to make them lose feeling, maybe permanently, bumped into his side when she forgot to stop or flat-out slammed against him when she went in the completely opposite direction as the crowd.

After another rib-fracturing hit, he threw up his hands and shouted, "You win," when Shania Twain's "Any Man of Mine" squealed to an end.

"What?" She pulled off her hat, and the sight of her squished-down hair plastered against her forehead and her cheeks so red he could barely count her freckles anymore, made something give in him, something that he'd been holding back, something he'd given to her the moment he'd seen her and had been lying to himself about ever since.

His heart.

No more wasting time.

No more hesitating.

Hitting yet another dead end with Ray drove home the realization that the trail he followed was tenuous, lonely and might never end. He wouldn't give up on getting justice for his brother, but maybe he shouldn't give up on himself, either. He didn't want to walk life alone anymore. Looking into Dani's sparkling eyes, he no longer felt like the prime suspect responsible for his brother's death. Maybe he didn't belong on that list at all.

"I said you're terrible."

Her mouth curved in a sassy smile. "I tried to warn you." Her voice was like Big Sky, bright and clear. Her face a field of freckles.

He thought, *I don't want to let you go.*

"Let's get some air."

As they strolled around back, across trampled grass, he found himself breathing deep. Darkness had settled down like a black mantle over the valley.

"Phew." Dani waved her hat in front of her face and scooted up on a picnic table with a tilted umbrella top. "I'm glad we took a break.

The wind feels great." She held her hand up against the steady breeze driving across the overgrown fields that encircled this small, cleared area.

"Thought you said I'd have trouble keeping up."

She arched a brow. "Saw you stumble more than once."

"Yeah. When you creamed me."

She laughed. "So that's how you talk to a lady."

He settled an arm around her back. "How should I talk to you?"

Their gazes clung for a moment, searching, as she seemed to grasp what he intended to say.

"Maybe you shouldn't talk at all."

"Look. I know I've said a lot of dumb stuff, the most idiotic being when I told you I couldn't make any promises."

"What do you mean?" A note of fear entered her voice and she edged away so that he felt the loss of her, as though she'd pulled away some of his skin.

He angled his knees to face her. "I mean that I may never find Smiley. I may never find Jesse's killer, but what I found instead is something I should know better than to lose. You."

"Oh. Jack. No." She put a hand on his chest and leaned back.

Doubt settled inside. He could feel its weight there, as though he had slipped it inside his own mind, a knot. Had he read her wrong? Was he alone in his feelings? "Dani, I—"

"Please stop, Jack."

"Why?"

Her mouth moved silently and then she blurted, "Because I've got a confession to make."

A RISING TIDE of fear rose in Dani's throat, pulling at her words, threatening to wash them away before she could speak.

And she'd stayed quiet too long.

Had Jack been about to say he loved her? He looked ready to make promises. If so, she couldn't let him speak until she told him everything.

Please still want me.

Jack was a man of principles, and he'd put his faith in her, maybe even given her his heart. She knew she could trust a man like that, and he deserved the truth.

So no more delays.

No more excuses.

Dani's stomach muscles tightened in anticipation.

"There's someone else I hoped to see here besides Smiley. Someone I wanted you to meet, though I was afraid."

Jack tilted his head. "What do you mean?"

"Kevin. My ex-boyfriend. He's a bouncer here."

"Why did you want me to meet your old boyfriend?"

She felt the answer right in the back of her throat, like a bomb sitting at the base of her tongue. Keeping it in made her eyes water.

"Because then you would have known who I am."

Doubt slid across his face. "And who are you?"

Her life caught in her throat.

Tell him.

She dragged in a shaky breath and blurted, "I'm wanted as an accessory to a felony robbery in Oklahoma that Kevin committed six years ago. He never gave my correct name as the getaway driver and he did his time. He told me that in return for keeping my name out of it, he'd look me up when he got out. Call in a favor, which he did when he showed up at the ranch a few days ago."

Jack's face seemed to shut down. He rubbed his jaw as if she'd just landed an upper cut. "And you've been in contact with him all these years?"

"No. No. I left the competition world, my home, to come here after the robbery. I thought I'd keep him from finding my family—being a threat to them…"

"I see," he said quietly. She felt her hopes for them dim as the light faded from his eyes, and she struggled to breathe. "I never intended to drive the car."

"Did he force you?"

She hung her head. "No." With that simple question, Jack struck at the heart of the matter. No matter which way she sliced it, she'd participated in a crime she hadn't paid for. "I was caught off guard and didn't think."

He squinted into the night. "Does Ray know his history?"

The wind moved through her thin T-shirt and she wrapped her arms around herself, rubbing goose bumps. "I don't know. Kevin's required to report it on his job application." She rubbed her temples. "He swore he was changed. Had turned over a new leaf. Maybe it was easier to just…"

Jack seemed to stiffen. "Not have to deal with him."

She nearly groaned out loud at Jack's laser-sharp way of seeing straight through to the truth. How he made her see it, too. "Yes."

"Do Larry and Diane know about your outstanding charge?" He slid off his hat and continued, his voice remote, as if he spoke to a stranger.

All of a sudden she wanted to touch him, to run her hand over his where it rested on his thigh just inches from her. To feel it close around hers, strong and reassuring. But the distance could have been a million miles.

"You're the first person I've ever told. The only other person that knows, besides Kevin."

"The timing of all of this—" his nostrils flared with the force of his exhale "—the fact that Smiley came here... Is there any way Kevin could be connected to the robberies at the ranch, the fire...Smiley?"

She pressed her fingers to her mouth. A creeping terror rose from a place beyond thoughts. "No. He said he moved to Colorado to support his sister. His mother died and he's her guardian now."

"And you have proof of this?"

"Just his word, but..." She could hardly

speak over the wet hammer of her heartbeat. Kevin had changed and so had she. Her instincts couldn't be that off anymore. Jack had made her trust them again. Why couldn't he have faith in her?

"So you never thought any of this—your past, Kevin—was worth mentioning?" he asked without looking at her.

A muscle jumped in his clenched jaw. His fingers dented the denim covering his knees. His profile could have been carved from rock, unyielding, giving nothing away. "Not even when I told you about Jesse and why I need to catch his killers? Confided in you. Kissed you." His voice sounded as though it'd been dragged over pebbles. Harsher, somehow, because he wasn't yelling. Because he sounded hurt.

Silence. Heavy for a long moment. Then, she said, "I wanted to tell you but I was afraid." *Still am.*

When she opened her mouth to say more, nothing emerged but her own silent plea for him to understand her, to see that she wasn't perfect, she'd messed up, but that she loved him.

Loved him so much.

He had his eyes intent on the hat he was crushing in his lap. After a moment, he seemed to get himself in hand and he turned, slowly, like he was moving underwater and regarded her with grim despair. "You need to turn yourself in."

Every hair on her body stood on end.

"And if Kevin's in any way linked to what's going on at the ranch, you may become a person of interest in the Denver murder case, as well," he continued.

"You can't think I have anything to do with that?"

"In God we trust. Everyone else is suspect," he muttered. "I'm sorry, but I just don't trust you anymore."

"What?" Her legs went weak as it sank in that his hurt and anger, the disappointment at having been deceived, had already trumped whatever feelings he'd had for her.

"You haven't held yourself accountable. Running away doesn't mean you've left it behind."

"No. It's not that…" she insisted, but it was. It was.

Dani swallowed hard. She wasn't far from tears or fury with herself. "You've been running from your past, too, unable to face a brother you haven't forgiven, unwilling to see your family, hiding from what you think you've done or didn't do."

He resettled his hat on his head and pulled the brim low. "You need to confess to the authorities or I'll have to say something myself. Please don't make me do that."

His words settled around her heart, stinging. Stunned silence had a different quality from any other, she realized at that moment. It stretched, took on greater meaning, then imploded under the weight of unspoken questions. He still saw the world in black-and-white, and it was clear which side he thought she belonged on.

Around a corner, Jori Lynn appeared with Blake, who was laughing so hard he wheezed.

"Hey, we've been looking for you two," Jori Lynn called. "We came in a taxi but thought maybe we could catch a ride home together."

Dani caught Jack's head shake out of the corner of her eye and wobbled to her feet. "Actually, could I split a cab ride back with you?"

Blake's loopy smile faded. "Sure."

"I'll meet you in a minute."

Blake tugged a staring Jori Lynn's arm and they disappeared.

"What are you going to do now?" she

asked, clenching and unclenching her shaking hands.

"Ask Ray for Kevin's address, unless you have it."

She shook her head. Miserable.

His anguished eyes lifted to hers and he pushed to his feet. "You have twenty-four hours to make up your mind."

The words had guillotine force. She staggered backward, cleaved in two, the slice into her heart sharp and sudden.

As he stood there, she watched every recriminating thought she'd had about herself flicker across his face, like clouds scudding across the sky. Without another word he turned and left her.

She crushed her stinging eyes closed and her breath, which had risen like a bubble, stalled in her chest.

She'd finally done the right thing and everything had gone wrong. It was what she deserved. Exactly the outcome she'd imagined. Dreaded. Run from. Only now there was no hiding; life as she knew it—over.

CHAPTER TWENTY-TWO

BACK IN HER ROOM, Dani fell forward onto her bed, holding the hole that seemed to have opened in her chest. Jack. All the love she had for him clobbered her body. Her chest ached. All of her ached. How could she have messed everything up so badly? She should have told him everything the moment she'd seen Kevin. Now he'd never trust her or care for her again.

She groaned into her pillow, then sat up, brushing the dampness on her cheeks at a knock on the door.

"Dani?"

She hurtled off the bed swung the door open.

"Tanya!" They collapsed in each other's arms, Dani's joints loosening with relief to have her friend here, safe. "Where've you been?" she asked when she got hold of herself, pulling Tanya inside.

"Shawnee."

They dropped to the mattress. Tanya shoved

messy hair behind her ears. Dark circles pouched beneath smudged eyes, her makeup looked like she'd slept in it and a cloud of sadness settled across her face. Beneath the artificial light, she looked pale and exhausted.

"Can I get you anything? How about a cola?"

At Tanya's nod, Dani grabbed a couple from her minifridge, handed one over and popped the top on hers. The long, cold swallow soothed her aching throat. Tanya sipped her drink, then lowered the shaking can and cradled it on her lap.

"Smiley and I got in a fight."

"When?"

"He showed up a couple of nights ago. I thought he'd come back because he changed his mind. Had wanted one last romantic evening before he turned himself in, so I lit some candles and…"

Spots of cola dripped onto Tanya's lap and Dani grabbed the tilting can. She set it beside her own and gathered her friend close. Tanya trembled against her.

"Take your time."

Tanya rested her head on Dani's shoulder. "He hit me." She started to cry in a drowning kind of way.

Dani stiffened, rage washing away her initial shock, sadness for her friend following. "That's awful. I'm so sorry," she said, "I'm so, so sorry. He's a snake."

After a couple of minutes, Tanya choked out, "We were fighting. Turned out he wasn't planning to report to the sheriff's department. He just wanted some alcohol. Other supplies. When I told him I was going to turn him in for his own good, he slapped me so hard I fell on that table, you know, the one that tilts when you touch it. Then we really started yelling, so I didn't notice the candle caught the curtains on fire until it was too late. Smiley threatened me. Said he'd kill me if I said anything, and ran off."

"Oh, sweetie." Dani smoothed a hand down Tanya's back, feeling every vertebra through her shirt. "He can't hurt you anymore. I'll make sure he doesn't."

Tanya leaned back and her gaze drifted all around the room. "Took me a while to realize that. First, I panicked. Drove. Then my car ran out of gas. Was so afraid Smiley would find me that I hitchhiked to my sister's friend Amanda's house in Shawnee. Been there since."

"I'm glad you came back. So you think he's still in the area?"

Tanya snuffled and Dani grabbed a tissue box from her nightstand. "Yes. He mentioned something about staying out at Spark Canyon. It's why I didn't want to come back here…in case he found me… But that's not all." She blew her nose noisily. "He did something terrible, Dani."

Her heart squeezed so hard in her chest she could barely breathe. "Okay."

"He said he killed two people in Denver." Tanya lifted red-rimmed eyes. "A married couple. That's why he couldn't turn himself in."

Dani's thoughts hummed desperately. She needed to tell Jack that he'd been right about Smiley…about Spark Canyon… If he was speaking to her again. Her shoulders squared. Well. He'd have to, because this was too important.

"Did he say why he did it?"

"No. That was all he said, because then the fire started."

"That must have been terrifying."

Tanya pressed another tissue to her mouth. "I can't believe it. I just can't. If you could have seen his face. It was like looking at a stranger. I was scared."

"You were brave to stand up to him," Dani insisted.

"But I shouldn't have run off," Tanya said, a hint of an apology in her voice. "Should have told you sooner."

Dani squeezed her friend's hand. Truth time. "I did the same thing once, except I never spoke about it to anyone until today."

Tanya stared at her, mouth agape. "You? What could you have possibly done?"

"It's true." Dani filled Tanya in on her history with Kevin, ending with, "...and now Jack hates me."

"So Jack's a bounty hunter?" Tanya marveled. She smoothed a finger along a stitched seam in Dani's quilt. "And you like him? I've missed a lot."

"You've had a lot of other things on your mind."

"I'm amazed you held it together as long as you did... Much better job than me."

Dani exhaled heavily. "No. I didn't. I've been living a lie, thinking it'd save me when it really cost me a future with Jack."

Tanya brushed Dani's hair back, her eyes gentle. "Maybe he can forgive you."

"No. He's made up his mind and I don't blame him." She sank her chin into her hands, looked out the window, wondering where

Jack was underneath those stars. "He's an honest man and I'm a liar."

"But you're a good person, Dani, and good people make mistakes. If Mr. Do-No-Wrong can't see that, then he's not good enough for you," Tanya declared, and her staunch support made Dani's heart swell.

She dabbed at the wetness on Tanya's cheek and her friend returned the favor, their short laughs mingling. "What would I do without you?"

"I never want to know." A scratch at the door propelled Dani to her feet. "Oh! And I've got a surprise for you."

Tanya bolted ahead and flung it open. "Mittens!" She scooped up her gray kitty and rained kisses on his face, clutching him close. "Thank you for finding him."

"Of course. I couldn't let this cutie get lost." Dani rubbed Mittens behind his ear and earned a rough lick against her palm.

After a few minutes of Tanya cooing, "Who's my good boy?" and cuddling him, she set Mittens on the bed. "Well, I'd better go tell Larry and Diane."

"Hold on, I'll come with you." Dani swept her hat off her bureau. "I need to talk to them, too."

Time to face her past.

Jack's words haunted her. She'd been furious at his ultimatum, but deep down, she knew he was right. Secrets had a way of putting space between people. She'd hidden her crime, hoping to distance herself from ugliness rather than facing it head-on. It was a pattern she'd followed before and it'd kept her from her family. Now, acting the same way had stopped her from being with the man she loved.

She needed to change.

Starting with confessing, alongside Tanya, to the Mays. But first, Jack. It didn't surprise her when her call was forwarded to voice mail. She left three messages about Smiley and Spark Canyon while en route to the main house, hoping Jack's disappointment in her wouldn't mean he ignored this important call entirely.

Hoping he'd hear her unspoken apology.

An hour later, back from talking to the Mays, Dani finished her call to the sheriff's office setting up a meeting the next day. She hung up the phone in her office and stared at the receiver, her mind turning cartwheels. Not only had the bighearted Mays forgiven Tanya and settled her in one of their spare rooms, they'd refused to accept Dani's resignation, even when she warned them she'd most likely be arrested when she turned herself in to the Oklahoma authorities.

They were family, Larry had said. "And family sticks together," Diane had finished.

Now. Only one last, terrifying call to make. She took a deep breath, gathered her courage and dialed home.

Her sister answered the call with a yawn.

"Claire, it's Dani."

"Are you okay?" Her sister's voice rose. "It's after one. Well. Midnight your time… what's going on?"

"Can you ask Dad to pick up the other line?"

"You're scaring me now." At a couple of quick barks, she heard Claire say, "Hush, Roxy."

"Please," she said, weary, dread rising, the horrible feeling of letting down her family nearly choking her.

"Hold on, honey."

"What is it, darlin'?" The warm concern in her father's voice a minute later made her eyes sting. Her throat swell. "Are you in trouble?"

Dani pressed the receiver to her hot ear, her fingers clenched around it. "Yes," she croaked. "But it's my fault."

"Honey, we'll be right out first thing tomorrow," Claire said, fast.

"*No.* I've got to go to Oklahoma."

"What? Why?"

"Dani, what's going on?"

Her blood galloped through her veins. "I have to turn myself in as an accessory to a bank robbery."

Her sister gasped and her father harrumphed. Dani's chest burned. It was as if her lungs were being crushed slowly in a vise, trapping her breath as she waited and waited and waited for someone to speak, the moment excruciating.

What they must think of her.

"That's crazy," Claire said faintly, at last. "You haven't been there in…"

"Six years. I drove a getaway car for Kevin."

"Dani," her father said heavily. "Why would you do such a foolish thing?"

She filled them in on what'd happened.

"So that's why you never moved back home," Claire said, her voice soft and more understanding than Dani deserved.

"I felt guilty. Plus, Kevin knew I came from Texas and I didn't want to take a chance on him finding me there, no matter how small the risk. Didn't want trouble."

"It would have been trouble for him," her

father growled. "Never liked that boy. Where is he now?"

"Dad. Calm down," she insisted, alarmed that her father, who'd been making good progress after his stroke, would get worked up. "He's here in Shawnee. He could be involved in an even bigger crime, something that, if I'd spoken up about him earlier, told Jack…"

"Who's Jack?" her father asked.

"A bounty hunter."

The man I love…

"Hmm." Claire's tone sounded suspicious. Dani could actually feel their sister intuition kicking in.

"Anyway, it's a long story, but Kevin could lead Jack to his bounty and I may have hindered his investigation."

"Okay, enough with the hair shirt." Dani could practically hear her sister's eye roll.

"What do you mean?"

"Look. You messed up. You ran away. Did you kill anyone?"

Dani wandered over to the haphazard state-magnet arrangement on her file cabinet, needing an outlet for the nervous energy firing through her, making her fingers shake. "Not that I know of."

"Sounds like they caught Kevin, so the bank got justice. You drove him, but it's not like he got away."

Was Alabama the first state, alphabetically? She slid it to the left. "Yes, but I shouldn't have stepped on the gas."

"Hindsight is twenty-twenty."

"But I could have said something before." She grabbed Alaska and pressed it into place, followed by Arizona, Arkansas.

"True. But you're coming clean now."

"So you're not disappointed in me?" She dropped back into her seat and all the air seemed to leak out of her.

"What?" her father exclaimed. "Darlin', you and your sister have made me proud every day. I'm the luckiest man in the world to have two daughters like you and I know your mom would feel the same way."

Dani's eyes pricked as she summoned a mental picture: her mom waving to her in that crazy, over-the-top way she had as she'd watched Dani accept her first blue ribbon in a jumping competition. She'd been eight.

"We'll meet you in Oklahoma with Mr. Redmond," Claire said firmly, referring to their family lawyer.

"Text us the info when you start the drive," added her father.

"No. I need to face this on my own."

"We're going to be there whether you like it or not," Claire said.

Dani laughed through her tears, marveling. "I love you."

"Love you, too," her family chorused, and she hung up.

Back at her file cabinet, she turned over the Oklahoma magnet. It'd be her home soon… but for how long?

She supposed wherever she stayed next, her heart would be broken either way, without Jack.

Back in her room, Dani began to pull off her boots, but froze when gunshots cracked through the air, faint but unmistakable.

Smiley? Kevin?

Jack?

She snatched up her cell and her rifle, and dashed out into the black night.

Toward Spark Canyon.

JACK CROUCHED BEHIND thick scrub brush, starlight winking off the barrel of his Glock. Far away, an owl called—a hollow, lonesome song that made him feel the same way. A chill settled in his bones. He stared down at Jesse's belt buckle tattoo, his forearm muscles clenching.

A cave entrance yawned just a few yards away, the dim glow of artificial light spilling out. Luckily the water level had dropped enough since the storm to give him access to the caves.

His heart raced wildly in his chest as he studied the missing horses, Pokey and Cher. They crowded each other, touching noses occasionally, tails beating back nighttime stingers. They were tied to a small tree that grew out of the side of the bluff.

Inside, Smiley and his accomplice were lurking. Had to be.

Jack had spoken to Kevin earlier. Turned out the guy was the anonymous tipster. Ray had taken Kevin on a fishing trip near the Mays' property border, and they'd spotted Smiley there. When Smiley appeared at the Rusty Roof last night, Kevin had recognized him from a wanted poster. The ex-con had even drawn him a map to the spot.

Using the map, Jack had searched in narrowing concentric circles until he'd zeroed in on a trail that'd led him to a descending path down to Spark Canyon.

To Jack's surprise, Kevin had blamed himself completely for what'd happened in Oklahoma. He admitted he'd roped Dani into driving the getaway car and had regretted putting her in that position ever since. Wanting to leave his bad connections behind and have a fresh start for him and his sister, he'd looked Dani up and relocated. It was his hope to someday make it up to her. When he'd seen the poster, he'd become concerned about a wanted man near Dani's place of work and phoned.

Still. It didn't explain why Dani had kept secrets from *him*.

A pair of coyotes howled somewhere close, sending a shiver up his spine. One of the horses nickered. He slipped from his cover and crept along the base of the bluff, his back sliding against the uneven surface, his gun in hand. Step by cautious step, he felt his way in the dark with the toe of his boot, testing for loose rocks that would roll and give him away. At last he reached the cave's mouth, pressed himself against the lip and peeked around the corner.

Inside a wide, rank space, two men argued, the younger one gesticulating while the older man kept shaking his head, his short, salt-and-pepper ponytail whisking across a black leather vest. A burning cigarette dangled from his blunt fingers. All around them, on rectangular folding tables, were bags of white powder and pills.

Oxycodone? Heroin?

Smiley had been caught for drug possession...but this...this wasn't a street-level dealer stash. Clearly they were smuggling drugs. Heat rushed up his body.

He reached for his cell phone, frowned at the blank screen, then shoved it back in his pocket.

Nothing for it. He couldn't risk these guys disappearing.

"Hands up!" he ordered, stepping into the light. "On the ground."

The men fell silent and exchanged a swift look, surprise and dismay on their faces.

"Now," Jack barked, sweat beading at his temples.

"Not so fast," hissed another voice in his ear, followed by the click of a round being chambered and the cold, hard press of a barrel at his temple.

Bile rose in his throat, burning his gut. He'd figured on two...but three?

"Drop your weapon." The voice sounded familiar, but from where?

He rammed his elbow into the stranger's solar plexus and the man's gun discharged, the bullet tearing into the night. The sound spooked the horses, who jumped and pulled against their ties, whinnying, eyes rolling.

The men inside the cave turned on him, weapons drawn. He didn't recognize the older guy at this distance. Shorter pieces of lank hair snaked against a lined face, his small mouth a slash.

"I said, drop your gun," wheezed the man behind him.

Jack swore under his breath and dropped his Glock. Dread seized him, locking up his muscles. He was unarmed. Alone. No one expected him back tonight. Who'd miss him? Come looking?

Dani…

"Inside." The man behind him prodded him with the gun and he lurched forward on stiff legs. "Keep moving."

Inside the cave, shadows lunged across the uneven ceiling. A generator sputtered, powering the lights that hung from hooks drilled into rock. Tables, laden with bags of drugs, occupied both side walls and a hole in the back of the cave loomed dark. He breathed in the dead air, sour on his tongue.

"Who the hell is *this* guy?" Smiley looked like his picture, Jack observed, silently fuming for getting caught so easily.

"Jackson Cade, bounty hunter," announced the man holding him at gunpoint. "I had to cut my trip short to come home because of you."

He started. It took him a moment to register what'd been said. A trip? Coming home...

Who else knew his cover? Larry and...

A thin, dark-haired man walked around him, a smug smile on his face.

Ben.

"We finally meet in person."

Jack swept any trace of expression away, despite the shock.

"Do you always rip off Bond movie lines?" Jack drawled, nonchalant, keeping his face impassive, his voice cocky, despite the clamoring worry ringing in his ears, the rush of blood battering his ear drums.

He had to figure a way out of this...stall.

"I like Bond movies." Ben cocked an eyebrow.

"Then you know what happens to the villains." Each word swaggered off his tongue.

"Now, is that how you talk to people you've just met in person? Some people have no manners," Ben mocked, followed by a *tsking* sound.

"Put down the gun. Let me greet you properly."

The other men echoed Ben's amused laugh, the sound grim and hard, and they advanced closer. "Let me think about it…" Ben tapped his chin. "Um. No. Another time, maybe… Oh, wait…you're out of time. So sorry. Everett—take care of it."

"Everett. Everett Ridland?" As the man neared, understanding washed through Jack with the force of a nuclear blast. Everything around him dissolved. White noise. Static.

One of his brother's killers.

At last.

Every nerve leaped awake.

"How's this idiot know my name?" Everett demanded, gesturing with his pistol. His voice was low, full of pebbles—a sailor's voice or a smoker's. He flicked his Camel Filter into the dirt and a ribbon of smoke rose.

Ben's thin eyebrows crashed together. "Tell us."

"You killed my brother."

"I've killed a lot of people's brothers," Everett said flatly.

"Jesse Cade," Jack bit out, fury mad-dogging

though him. He could feel the words sticking to the insides of his mouth. "Two years ago. Carbondale. Drug deal gone wrong."

"Drug deal? I don't do small-time jobs like that." The guy peered at Jack, stepping close and Jack's hands curled at his side, itching to lash out.

"Wait. You look familiar. Oh, man. I remember now. I would have killed you like your punk brother for what he owed us, if I knew you'd turn up again."

"Us?" Jack echoed, his heart feeling like it'd been kicked into a dark corner of his body. Jesse owed them money? That meant the help he'd asked for was to pay them off, not necessarily to buy more drugs. And Ben? What was his connection?

"Our little opiate outfit. Your brother was in deep and trying to get out." Everett sucked at his teeth for a moment, his expression distant.

Jack's mind whirled. His brother hadn't been looking to get quick-fix money, he'd been in a desperate spot, had tried appealing to his big brother. And what had Jack done? He'd shut him down before he'd had a chance to explain...

"You killed the Phillips couple in Denver," he said, desperate to keep them talking.

All of the air raced out of the room and the men exchanged swift looks. "Now, how do you know that?"

"Because an informant ratted out Smiley."

"What? Who was that?" Ben stormed. He pistol-whipped Jack and searing pain exploded in his jaw. His vision made slow loops, as though something had gone wrong with his balance.

"Answer me or you're dead right now," Ben said, his voice full of menace—not quite as if a shark could talk, but close.

"I don't know." The inside of his cheek burned as blood washed over his tongue.

"Everett, get it out of him."

Everett advanced and Jack's entire body tensed. If he was going down, he'd take this guy with him.

"Sure, boss." Everett nodded at Ben.

"You're in charge?"

Ben preened and waved Everett back, a triumphant smile stretching his lips, clearly enjoying the moment. "Not yet. But after this haul from my latest trip—" he nodded at the packages "—I'll be promoted."

"Plus, you figured out Phillips was skimming from the take and ordered the hit." Smiley grinned. "So I'll get more jobs after this, right, Ben? More than just watching the drugs for you?"

Ben shrugged. "Not now that you've been identified."

Smiley's face flushed, his eyes getting bulgy and wild. "What do you mean? We've been friends... You promised. You said you wanted someone on this job you could trust."

"Hey..." Everett growled. He squared around aggressively. "Who's saying I'm not trustworthy?"

"No one," Ben said quickly, shifting on his feet.

"So you stuck me with this amateur because you didn't trust me? If it wasn't for him, there'd be no connection to that hit and this place. Told you we shouldn't have met up here for the payoff. Rain's kept us out of here until today and I'm not much for roughin' it."

"It was the best place to hide you until I got back."

"Until Smiley got arrested." Everett stabbed a thick finger at his accomplice. "Amateur."

Jack's heart beat icily in a faraway cage. "So this place...these drugs..."

"All of this belongs to our operation," Smiley

pronounced, his chest puffing, looking eager to brag. "Ben got involved ten years ago on a trip south of the border and I've been keeping an eye on things here ever since. He's supposed to be next in charge...and I'll be his right-hand man. Right, Ben?"

Ben barely spared him a glance. "No one can know about this place. Erase this guy." Ben jerked his head toward the cave's entrance.

"Let's go. Time to meet your maker...or your brother." Everett cracked himself up. Smiley joined in, eyes flicking between the men, shoulders jerking up and down so that he resembled a hyena.

"Let's hope your aim is as bad as your lines."

"Shut it, Cade. Out of here."

He marched Jack outside and his thoughts raced each other. Before they reached the horses, he kicked a stone at Pokey's feet and the skittish horse flinched and reared up, just as he hoped, knocking into Everett so that his gun discharged.

Jack bolted for the woods, veering toward the thickest part, and then something slung around his knees, tripping him, and he went down hard. The side of his head cracked against a stone and an ache reached up through the base of his skull. He groaned, scrambling to remove the slingshot rope tangled around his calves.

Spots appeared before his eyes, and for a moment he thought he glimpsed Dani, peering at him from behind a tree, before she dodged out of view.

What the hell was she doing here? He didn't want her help. Didn't want her in danger. He couldn't protect her. Hopefully she had enough sense to get away from these lowlifes, call for help, if she hadn't already, though it'd probably be too late for him.

"On your feet, Jack, or I'll shoot you like a dog, right here," growled Everett, looming over him. "Or do you want to beg, like your brother..."

"I'm not going to beg."

"But you are going to dig." Smiley thrust a shovel into his hand. "Get going."

He prodded Jack, but before he could put the metal in the dirt a shot rang out.

Dani!

Instinctively, Jack lashed out, smacking Everett with the shovel so that his eyes rolled back and he collapsed in a boneless heap.

He lunged for a gaping Smiley, tackling him, snatching the 9mm, then training it on him.

"Freeze, Ben!" Dani stalked out of the trees, her rifle trained on her employer's son. Jack glimpsed the other man out of the corner of his eye. "Or I'll shoot."

"Drop your gun," Jack ordered and Ben's weapon thudded against the rocks. "Now kick it over."

The black metal piece skidded through the grass and Dani scooped it up and tucked it into her belt, her eyes narrow, spitting fire, the ends of her loose hair nearly crackling with static energy.

She'd never looked more beautiful.

"Authorities are…" she began, then stopped when Lance and a couple of other officers emerged behind her.

"Here. We were in the area following up on leads for Tanya when your 911 call came in," Lance said.

Jack filled him in as the deputies cuffed and led the men away.

"Interesting," Lance said when Jack finished. "Explains why the Phillipses were planning on disappearing." He shook his head slowly. "Mountain Sky Dude Ranch, a smuggling operation for the Quintaras."

"Larry and Diane don't know anything about this," Dani vowed, her chin jutting, as she returned leading Pokey and Cher. Her challenging gaze flew between him and Lance.

Lance tipped his hat. "I hope that's true. Thank you, Dani. Jack's lucky to have had you around. Jack, we'll need your statement."

Jack stared at his cousin's disappearing back, every horrible image of what could have happened to Dani shuffling through his mind's eye. How close he'd come to losing her.

"You should never have come here," he growled, all of his emotions, his anguish, incinerating each syllable.

Dani tucked her rifle into Pokey's saddle holder. "And why's that?"

"This was my bounty." He practically fire-breathed, knowing he sounded irrational, but unable to make sense of anything right now, not when she could have died.

He loved her, he thought, fighting the surging desire to hold her, feel her safe in his arms.

Yet she'd lied to him. He wouldn't get involved with someone who kept secrets, not after experiencing firsthand how that ripped apart relationships.

"And you probably don't want a criminal by your side, right?"

"You shouldn't have been anywhere near here," he blurted.

She made a disgusted sound. "I didn't come here for you, anyway. This was for Tanya."

He stared at her, unable to make sense of his thoughts, his feelings, pictures of what could have happened to her, the danger she'd put herself in, exploding in his mind's eye...

Dani scanned the clearing. "So did Kevin have anything to do with this?"

He shook his head, unable to unstick his tongue.

She heaved a long breath, her expression a wrestling match of competing emotions, but it looked like hurt was winning out. "Well, don't worry. You'll never have to see me again. Oh. And you're welcome."

She whirled and melted into the dark forest with the horses, leaving him more alone than he'd ever felt before in his life.

She'd broken his trust; she'd also broken his heart.

CHAPTER TWENTY-THREE

JACK LAY ON his bedroll and listened to the waking calls from birds roosting in the spruce beside him, the spider-webbed light of dawn coming through the conifers. The sky in the east was rosy, slowly lightening. The dew-soaked landscape billowed away, ridged and cut, dark, then gray, then purple-shadowed. Hints of pine and fresh earth blew in on the crisp morning air.

Lacing his fingers behind his head, Jack squinted at the glowing horizon. Would Dani be up? She hadn't answered his knock when he'd returned from the sheriff's office late last night and he couldn't blame her. It'd been dead wrong of him not to thank her properly for saving his hide.

When a signal brought his cell phone to life at last, he'd listened to her messages about Smiley and Spark Canyon, heard the concern in her voice and realized that she hadn't just been looking out for Tanya last night, despite what she'd said.

She'd been worried about him. Despite his harsh words at the Rusty Roof, his vow to turn her in, she'd put her life in danger on his behalf.

How did he reconcile that with the woman who'd been hiding from her past, who'd kept secrets from him, just like Jesse?

Who still held his heart?

He sat up and leaned his elbows on bent knees, dropped his chin to his knuckles.

Time to leave and stop the second-guessing that'd plagued these sleepless hours.

He'd thank her, then head out.

But where?

A longing for home seized him. With Everett behind bars and Smiley cutting a deal that'd take down the rest of their operation, he could draw his first, unimpeded breath. His brother was avenged.

But did that absolve his part in what'd happened to Jesse?

Jack pushed to his feet and rolled up his bedding. If he hadn't rushed to judge his brother, had paid the twenty thousand Jesse owed or, better still, had stayed with his brother and defended him, his sibling might still be alive. Might be living a sober, safe life. He glanced down at his tattoo: *aJc*.

Then again, the painful realization came—Jesse might have relapsed, too.

There were no guarantees.

Did that mean he didn't love his brother? Wish every day that he was still part of Jack's life?

He thrust the sleeping bag under his arm and trekked back to the dude ranch, his boots clipping the stone patches that broke up the grassy knoll.

Of course not. Lies and addiction made up only a part of Jesse—not the sum total, not even close. His brother had his heart and his loyalty, no matter what.

So, what about Dani?

The shapes of horses grew more distinct when he reached the bottom of the hill and neared the pasture. On the horizon, the sun swelled, chasing away the last, lingering stars.

He needed to talk to Dani, though what he would say after "Thank you" wasn't exactly clear.

She'd lied to him. Betrayed him.

Yet she hadn't hesitated to jump into danger to help him. Her impulsive nature had put her at risk, just as it had when she'd driven her boyfriend from a bank heist.

She'd done wrong, especially in keeping it hidden, but everyone made mistakes.

Jesse had.

He had.

When his boots crunched on the gravel path, he slowed his gait until he stopped and leaned on the pasture's fence. His gaze swept over the dozing horses and settled on Milly, who lurked in her usual spot in the back corner.

His leaving would doom her to euthanasia. Regret gripped him. Despite his hard work, she wouldn't take a saddle. Wanted no part of riding or much human contact, unable to overcome her past.

Was he any different?

Slowly, cautiously, she edged closer when she saw him, stopping and grazing every few steps, lifting her head as if to check if he still stood nearby, until, to his surprise, her head dropped over the side of the fence and butted his hand.

He stroked her velvet nose. Felt the warm blow of her breath against his palm.

"Hey, girl."

She bobbed her head and nickered when he patted her neck.

Second chances. Milly deserved one. Just because she wasn't rideable or sociable didn't mean she didn't have a right to a happy life.

His brother had been damaged, too. Yet Jack had refused to see past those flaws, had stopped supporting his sibling, decided when enough was enough.

He'd set a limit on his capacity to forgive, never realizing, until it was too late, that his heart would never quit his brother, no matter what his brain decided.

"Jack!"

He turned and spied Nan huffing his way, a walking stick in one hand, wildflowers clutched in the other. "Morning, Nan." He lifted his hat and felt a smile come on, despite the twist of pain in his chest.

Her sharp blue eyes studied him when she halted. "Quite a night."

"Yes."

"Poor Larry and Diane. They're devastated."

He recalled the couple's pale faces when he'd spoken to them at the sheriff's office. "I'm sorry this happened. It must be a shock."

Her bouquet waved through the air as she gestured. "Ben's always given them a hard time. Asking Smiley up here in the summers wasn't just to help a troubled kid. They wanted Ben to have a friend, too. He never made them easily. Always acted a bit off."

A sheriff's department SUV passed them, kicking up dust, part of the steady caravan that'd been carting off evidence all night.

When the purr of the engine faded, he said, "The Mays are decent folks."

"Oh, they are." Nan stroked Milly's forelock and to his surprise the mare didn't shy away. "Not perfect, of course. But who gets through a life without making any errors, right?"

He blinked at her. Who, indeed? Not Dani, not his brother and not him. Did that make them unlovable? Not worthy?

No, came the swift, certain answer. Something heavy and winged took off from his chest.

He hadn't faced his regret, his anger with himself, and had become a wanderer because of it, hunting for the vengeance he thought could absolve him.

He'd judged himself as harshly as he'd assessed everyone in his life, his unwillingness to accept his mistakes, to learn from them, keeping him apart from others—not just his family, but Dani, too.

Supporting someone, caring about them,

even if they had the capacity to hurt you, wasn't weakness. It took strength and conviction to stand by those who'd let you down. To believe that, together, you could make things right, and if not this time, the next…and the next after that…because that was what unconditional love meant.

And he loved Dani.

Unconditionally.

She'd stuck by his side last night, despite everything, and he wanted to do the same for her…and Milly, he realized, an idea firing through him.

He filled Nan in on his impromptu plan, and when he finished, she cocked her head and studied him.

"You're sure about this?"

"Yup."

"All right. So I suppose you'll be leaving us, then." Nan gave Milly a final pat and turned. "Now that you've got your man."

He stared at her, dumbfounded.

"Oh. You thought I didn't know about your cover?" She made a clucking sound. "Like I said, no one notices the old lady reading in the corner. I overheard you and Dani talking a couple of times, as well as Larry and Diane, and began putting two and two together."

"You are a wonder, Nan."

She smiled back at him, humor peeking out of her queenly face. "No need to wonder. I'm just fabulous, is all… Least, that's what my mother always told me. Not that her family felt the same way. They called me a mistake. Said I wasn't good enough for them. Wanted Ma to give me up, but she wouldn't. They were the ones that missed out, she said."

Jack wrapped an arm around her narrow shoulders. "Yes they did. You *are* fabulous."

Nan laid her head against his arm. "Well. Not always, I'll admit. But life's a hard enough journey without carrying around regrets."

He felt her nod and found himself agreeing. Your past, your background, couldn't be carried like a yoke on your shoulders forever. At some point you needed to let it go. Start new.

He had to make things right with Dani and not waste another minute. She had to know how much he cared. And how wrong he'd been.

A few guests appeared on the road, heading for breakfast, the rise and fall of their conversations carrying in the morning air. Bella and Beau appeared, joyously barking.

"Well, I'd better go." Nan touched his arm, then stepped back. The dogs wagged their way to her, circling, sniffing, pushing their heads against her hands. "I'm in charge while the Mays and Dani are gone."

It took him a moment to register what she'd said. "Dani's not here?" he asked, his pulse slamming through his veins.

"She went to Oklahoma to turn herself in."

"What?"

The corners of Nan's mouth drooped. "She woke me around three this morning. Said she was headed to Oklahoma City because of some wild oats she'd sowed years ago. Sounded like a bunch of nonsense to me, but she was serious about it. Said she'd made up her mind and didn't want to wait around till sunup in case she changed her mind. Anyway, she was worried Larry and Diane might not be back in time to run things this morning—which I'd better get to doing. Goodbye, Jack."

With a wave, she strolled away, the dogs hard on her heels, leaving him reeling, her information a chop to his windpipe, knocking the breath out of him, making his chest burn.

Dani. He'd sent her from him just as he'd pushed his brother away.

His jaw tightened as he strode to his truck and yanked open the door, tossing his hat on the passenger seat.

But he'd be darned if he'd lose her, too.

Her iridescent eyes glowed in his mind. He'd looked into them this week and seen her soul. Had glimpsed his, too, in their reflection, and what he'd saw was the man he wanted to be. Strong and certain, someone who could protect her, cherish her, bring her joy through sheer force of will.

The engine revved and his tires crunched on gravel as he sped toward the front gate and the open road that'd lead him to Oklahoma City.

To Dani.

Could he reach her in time to stop her?

DANI RETURNED HER sister's and Mr. Redmond's waves, smiling through tears as their father's pickup sped away, carrying her family back to Coltrane. They wanted to catch the tail end of Claire's son Jonathan's school band performance.

She lowered her arm and blinked at the slanting, late afternoon sunlight.

Free.

Free to leave this state.

Free to live her life.

Free not just of the robbery charges, but of her guilt and the secret she'd hidden all this time. She should have done it years ago, but she'd caged herself with guilt and shame about her past, as surely as Kevin had been imprisoned for his own role. She'd carried the guilt over letting her family down, and she'd let herself down, too. Maybe she'd needed that time to repent her mistakes and bad decisions.

She walked along a small path bordered with purple-headed rhododendrons and reached for her phone, eager to tell Jack. Then she remembered—she wasn't free, after all.

Not when Jack had shut her out of his heart.

She pictured his betrayed expression when she'd confessed to him, how he hadn't relented, even after she'd ridden to his aid in Spark Canyon. Clearly, unlike the Oklahoma legal system that'd dismissed charges after hearing Mr. Redmond's arguments, her story and a corroborating statement from Kevin, he couldn't forgive her past sins.

Her legs wobbled from the exhaustion of the last twenty-four hours. She ducked beneath a massive weeping willow tree and dropped down to the pretty white bench beneath it, jittery and light-headed. Yellow-green strands lifted and swung in the breeze as she sat beneath an umbrella of trembling, sunlit leaves.

She stared at the glimpses of spectacular blue sky that appeared between the thick drapes of leaves. Hopefully Jack was gazing up at it, too, finally finding peace over what'd happened to his brother.

Despite everything, she only wanted his happiness.

No matter where she looked inside herself, she came across more love for him, for everything about him, his anger as well as his tenderness. He'd been hurt and let down because he'd cared—because she'd mattered to him.

And she'd ruined everything.

A groan rose in her throat and she covered her face with her hands. She had a second chance at a future, but without Jack, it stretched ahead as bleak and lonely as her past.

"Dani!"

Her shoulders shook at the remembered sound of his voice, so clear she almost believed she hadn't conjured it.

"Dani," she heard again, and then strong hands gripped hers and lowered them.

Jack.

He was down on one knee in front of her,

his thick-lashed brown eyes searching hers, and she thought she might fall like a tree at his tender, concerned expression.

This had to be a dream.

She met his gaze head-on. It was impossible to look away and he couldn't seem to, either. Time slowed and she could hear the blood rumbling through her body, drumming in her ears.

"Jack?" She touched his face, his scar, needing to know he was real. "What are you doing here?"

He pressed her hand to his cheek, his eyes intent, full of the same ache she felt. "I came to stop you. The clerk told me you'd just left, and when I spotted a car with a Mountain Sky bumper sticker, I scouted the park."

"Why?" Confusion and surprise pounded in her heart.

"Because I'm sorry."

A skyful of hope knocked into her. "I—" she started, but he shook his head and sat beside her, his thumb now skimming her knuckles, releasing a flock of butterflies in her belly.

"Please. Let me say this first," he said, his voice thick with emotion.

At her nod, he breathed deep, exhaled and

began. "Judging you was wrong. Hypocritical. Shortsighted and insensitive. And then, when you put your life at risk to help me, I didn't even thank you. Nan told me no one lives a life without errors, and I realized that the biggest one I could make was letting you go."

He tucked her hair behind one ear before continuing, his direct gaze seeming to reach down deep. "Thank you. Not just for last night, but for every minute of every day of this past week when you brought this broken man the real redemption he needed, though he was too pigheaded to see it."

The rich, low timbre of his voice moved right through her, settled in her heart, broke it open and healed it a split second later.

"You gave me that, too," she said, her voice cracking. "Even if you'd caught me in time, I still would have turned myself in. You were right to make me see that I needed to face my mistakes and take responsibility. I never would have been free of them until I had, and if not for you, I wouldn't have done it."

He gathered her close, his large arms engulfing her. "Will you forgive me?"

"If you forgive me."

He pulled back slightly, placed a finger beneath her chin and tipped it so that their mouths were a breath apart. This close, she could make out the beginning of stubble on his cheeks, see the shadows under his eyes, and understood, more than words could say, how much she meant to him. Knew, down deep in her bones, how much she loved him.

"No one's like you for me." He peered into her eyes in a way that made her tremble. "I'm in love with you."

"I love you, too," she breathed as their lips met.

He kissed her, and at last everything was as it should be. Her body melted against his with exquisite relief. It was like sinking into a hot bath after being caught in the rain, like sliding under crisp cotton sheets after an exhausting day.

He kissed her, slowly, tenderly, his mouth slanting against hers, his fingers tunneling through her hair then stroking her back, until her insides turned molten, her body languid in his arms. She traced his face, resting her fingers briefly on its marks, then wound them through his soft, dark hair. Her body caught fire at his hungry growl and she fitted herself into the contours of his body, wishing she could fall all the way into him. She wanted to be that close, to share his heartbeat, his breath.

And then he kissed her with a ferocity that

incapacitated her. He was electric, pulsing with energy, greedy for her and alive. His body moving restlessly, jumbling her thoughts, quickening her breath.

"I love you," he murmured after a moment into her ears, her neck, her hair, and each time he did she said, "Me, too," and then they were kissing again and she couldn't believe there was anything in this world that could feel this right and real and true.

Later, when his lips whispered off hers, he cradled her close and it seemed as though a growing circle of light surrounded them. She traced his arm tattoo, proof of his dedication, his courage, the loyalty that'd compelled him to avenge his brother...that'd driven him straight to her.

She sent a silent prayer of thanks to Jesse, to her mother, to Jack's father, the silent witnesses to this incredible moment.

"Now that you have your freedom, will you consider spending some of it with me?" he asked, holding her gaze. It was entirely possible she was going to faint, she thought. Or burst into flames.

"Of course, starting with your family reunion..." Now that she'd faced her painful past, she wanted to help him do the same.

He lazily brushed his hand across her neck and down her back. She felt like a tuning fork, her whole body humming. "Good. I thought Milly would have to be my plus one."

She blinked at him. "What do you mean?"

"I spoke to Larry on the way out here. When I offered to buy her, he gifted her to me, instead. As thanks. She's going to live her life at my ranch where she can graze all day and only be ridden if she wants to."

She melted at the generosity of this hard-bitten man with the soft core she adored. "Jack. That's exactly what she needed."

"And you're what I need. So, first my family reunion and then your sister's wedding…"

She laughed, amazed. "I can't believe you remember that."

"Everything about you is branded." He tapped his chest. "Right here." His lips fell on her cheeks. "Your freckles." He kissed her there. "Your eyes." He pressed his mouth to each lid. "This mouth…" And then they were lost in each other until he pulled back, angled his head and gazed down at her. "I could never forget a thing about you," he finished, the sincerity in his voice, his gaze, knocking the breath out of her.

"I never want you to."

"So, then…a life sentence?" At the warm humor in his voice, she smiled. She'd see his corny and raise it with cheesy.

"Oh…so you want me to be your ball and chain?"

He placed a hand over his heart and a giggle bubbled out of her at his exaggerated expression. "You know me. Always a hopeless romantic."

"Ha. Good one." She biffed his arm. "Guess you'll have a lifetime to prove it."

His eyes twinkled down at her, his quirked mouth full of mischief. "So you'll surrender yourself to me?"

"Don't get ahead of yourself, bounty hunter. Let's just say, as long as we're doing time with each other, let's give ourselves the maximum sentence. Forever."

"Good, because I'm never letting you go," he murmured, then he cupped her face and captured her lips with his, kissing her like it was the end of the world.

Or the start of their new one.

* * * * *

LARGER-PRINT BOOKS!

**GET 2 FREE
LARGER-PRINT NOVELS
PLUS 2 FREE
MYSTERY GIFTS**

Love Inspired
SUSPENSE
RIVETING INSPIRATIONAL ROMANCE

Larger-print novels are now available...

WESTERN WP PROMISES

YES! Please send me **The Western Promises Collection** in Larger Print. This collection begins with 3 FREE books and 2 FREE gifts (gifts valued at approx. $14.00 retail) in the first shipment, along with the other first 4 books from the collection! If I do not cancel, I will receive 8 monthly shipments until I have the entire 51-book Western Promises collection. I will receive 2 or 3 FREE books in each shipment and I will pay just $4.99 US/ $5.89 CDN for each of the other four books in each shipment, plus $2.99 for shipping and handling per shipment. *If I decide to keep the entire collection, I'll have paid for only 32 books, because 19 books are FREE! I understand that accepting the 3 free books and gifts places me under no obligation to buy anything. I can always return a shipment and cancel at any time. My free books and gifts are mine to keep no matter what I decide.

272 HCN 3070 472 HCN 3070

Name	(PLEASE PRINT)

Address	Apt. #

City	State/Prov.	Zip/Postal Code

Signature (if under 18, a parent or guardian must sign)

Mail to the **Reader Service:**

IN U.S.A.: P.O. Box 1867, Buffalo, NY 14240-1867
IN CANADA: P.O. Box 609, Fort Erie, Ontario L2A 5X3

LARGER-PRINT BOOKS!
GET 2 FREE LARGER-PRINT NOVELS PLUS
2 FREE GIFTS!

HARLEQUIN®

super romance®

More Story...More Romance